A Book And A Family You Will Never Forget!

"Pulses with kinetic energy... Seizes the reader on its opening page with a rhythm, a language, a knockabout country humor unmistakably its own."

—*Newsweek*

"Chute does not gloss over any of it... the Beans are not what we would call good-looking... Chute takes care to give them a wonderful, low, brutish appeal. There is a kind of thrilling strength in their shoulders and arms and big hands. And, when their logging trucks rumble down the road, the whole earth seems to shake... Carolyn Chute may well have lived in poverty, but what we learn here is that she has a wealth of knowledge about the human spirit."

—*Washington Post Book World*

more...

"Unsparing, unsentimental... tough, passionate ... emphasize[s] the Beans' strength and profound connection with the physical world without trying to minimize their often brutal behavior."

—*Philadelphia Inquirer*

"Dazzles... She tempers her harsh depiction of perpetual hard times with flashes of humor and hints of heart-felt tenderness. She gently nudges us into empathy with her memorable, sublimely drawn characters without ever turning preachy, shrill or maudlin."

—*Cleveland Plain Dealer*

"An impressive first performance... the poverty of these people is evident everywhere... Mrs. Chute's sensuous language makes one aware of it also in the way the characters are perceived—noisy, crude of feature and reeking."

—*New York Times*

"A novel full of both violence and love... Chute writes with tremendous vigor and precision, rendering Egypt and its inhabitants with a stark but lyrical poetry."

—*Village Voice*, **New York City**

"With humor and a huge supply of good will, she simply shows us the faces of those who cannot pull themselves up by their own bootstraps because their boots are rotting on their feet. If you care about fine writing you owe it to yourself to read this book... we are present at the birth of a great American artist."

—*Boston Globe*

"One puts this short, fast-moving novel down reluctantly, for Chute has created a fictional world so vivid and compelling that one feels at a loss when it ends."

—*San Jose Mercury News*

"A literary Arbus... *The Beans of Egypt, Maine* has its own voice and vision."

—*Vogue*

"Like the Snopes clan of Faulkner's Yoknapatawpha, the Beans of Egypt, Maine, know a stark poverty that discolors every part of their lives... Chute is startlingly original... fiction at its most involving, resonant and clear."

—*Publishers Weekly*

THE BEANS OF EGYPT, MAINE

CAROLYN CHUTE

WARNER BOOKS

A Time Warner Company

Thank you, Ken Rosen, poet, teacher, and friend.

WARNER BOOKS EDITION

Copyright © 1985 by Carolyn Chute
All rights reserved. No part of this work may be reproduced or transmitted in any form or by any means, electronic or mechanical, including photocopying and recording, or by any information storage or retrieval system, except as may be expressly permitted by the 1976 Copyright Act or in writing from the publisher. Requests for permission should be addressed in writing to Ticknor & Fields, 52 Vanderbilt Avenue, New York, New York 10017.

This Warner Books Edition is published by arrangement with Ticknor & Fields, 52 Vanderbilt Avenue, New York, New York 10017

The chapter entitled "Tall Woman Love" originally appeared in the Winter 1984 issue of *Ploughshares*.

Cover art by David Tamura

Warner Books, Inc.
1271 Avenue of the Americas
New York, N.Y. 10020

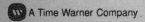 A Time Warner Company.

Printed in the United States of America

First Warner Books Printing: July, 1986

10

In memory of real Reuben.
Who spared him this occasion?
Who spared him rage?

story."

The stranger squints for a long time on Beal.

"Can't you see good?" Annie asks.

CONTENTS

EARLENE

ONE

Lizzie, Annie, and Rosie's Rescue of Me with Blue Cake

We've got a ranch house. Daddy built it. Daddy says it's called RANCH 'cause it's like houses out West which cowboys sleep in. There's a picture window in all ranch houses and if you're in one of 'em out West, you can look out and see the cattle eatin' grass on the plains and the cowboys ridin' around with lassos and tall hats. But we ain't got nuthin' like that here in Egypt, Maine. All Daddy and I got to look out at is the Beans. Daddy says the Beans are uncivilized animals. PREDATORS, he calls 'em.

"If it runs, a Bean will shoot it! If it falls, a Bean will eat it," Daddy says, and his lip curls. A million times Daddy says, "Earlene, don't go over on the Beans' side of the right-of-way. Not ever!"

Daddy's bedroom is pine-paneled . . . the real kind. Daddy done it all. He filled the nail holes with MIRA-CLE WOOD. One weekend after we was all settled in, Daddy gets up on a chair and opens a can of MIRACLE

WOOD. He works it into the nail holes with a putty knife. He needs the chair 'cause he's probably the littlest man in Egypt, Maine.

Daddy gets a pain in his back after dinnah so we take a nap. We get under the covers and I scratch his back. Daddy says to take off my socks and shoes and overalls to keep the bed from gettin' full of dirt.

After I'm asleep the bed starts to tremble. I clutch the side of the bed and look around. Then I realize it's only Rubie Bean comin' in his loggin' truck to eat his dinnah with other Beans. Daddy's bare back is khaki-color like his carpenter's shirts. I give his shoulder blades a couple more rakes, then dribble off to sleep once more.

2

Gram pushes open the bedroom door. "What's goin' on?" Her voice is a bellow, low as a man's.

Daddy sits up quick. He rubs his face and the back of his neck. Beside the bed is a chair Daddy made. It is khaki-color like the walls and khaki-color like Daddy. And over this chair is them khaki-color carpenter's clothes, the shirt and pants, laid flat like they just been ironed. Gram's eyes look at the pants.

Gram plays the organ at church. Her fingers in her pocketbook now are able to move in many directions at once, over the readin' glasses, tappin' the comb, pressin' the change purse and plastic rain hat, as if from these objects musical refrains of WE ABIDE will come. One finger jabs at a violet hankie. Then she draws the hankie out and holds it over her nose.

I sniff at the room. I don't smell nuthin'.

"LEE!!!" Gram gasps through her hankie. "What is going on here? Can't you *tell* me?" It is warm. But Gram always wears her sweater. You never see her arms.

Gramp comes into the bedroom doorway and holds a match over his pipe. Whenever Gramp visits, he wears a white shirt. He also wears his dress-up hat. Even in church. He never takes it off in front of people . . . 'cause underneath he's PURE BALD. Daddy says he's seen it years ago . . . the head. He says it's got freckles.

Gram puts her hankie back in her purse, straightens her posture.

On Daddy's cheeks have come brick-color dots and he gives hisself a sideways look in the vanity mirror.

"LEE! I'm talkin' to you!" Gram's deep voice rises.

Daddy says, "I'm sorry, Mumma."

Gram sniffles, wrings her hands.

I says, "Hi Gram!"

She ignores me.

"HI GRAM!!!" I say it louder.

Through the open window I hear the door of the Beans' mobile home peel open like it's a can of tuna fish. I see a BIG BEAN WOMAN come out and set a BIG BEAN BABY down to play among boxes of truck parts and a skidder wheel. The woman Bean wears black stretch pants and a long white blouse with no sleeves. Her arms are bare. The baby Bean pulls off one of its rubber boots.

Somethin' else catches my eye. It's the sun on the fender of Daddy's little khaki-color car. Inside the trunk is some of Daddy's carpenter tools and some of the birdhouses and colonial bread boxes he made for the church fair. On the bumper is Daddy's bumper sticker. It says JESUS SAVES. The sun shifts on the fender, almost blinds me, like it's God sayin' in his secret way that he approves.

But in here in Daddy's bedroom it's different. The light is queer, slantin' through Gramp's smoke. Gram covers her face with her hands now, so all I can see is her smoky blue hair wagglin'. She says through her fingers in her deep voice, "Earlene, you don't sleep here at *night*, do you?"

I says, "Yep."

The dots on Daddy's cheeks get bigger. Gramp looks across the hall at the thermostat to the oil furnace which all ranch houses got.

Daddy swings his legs out from the covers, hangs on the edge of the high bed in his underwear, with his little legs hangin' down. He says, "Mumma . . . I'm sorry. I didn't think."

Gram moans.

Daddy has said a million times that this house is a real peach . . . good leach bed . . . artesian well . . . dry cellar . . . the foundation was poured . . . lots of closet space. He went by blueprints. He says all carpenters can't read blueprints.

"Praise the Lord!" shouts Gram. She holds her clasped hands to her heart, a half-smile, a look of love. "Praise God!!" Her pocketbook is hooked over her elbow. Her arms go up and she waves them and the fingers march, stirrin' up the queer smoke overhead.

Daddy's eyes go wild. "But Mumma! It don't mean nuthin'. She's just a baby!"

"I ain't a BABY!" I scream. I drop to the floor from this high bed Daddy made, made with his lathe, hand-carved acorns on the posts, stained khaki like everything else. I don't remember him makin' the bed. Daddy says he made it before my mother went to the hospital to live. He says he and my mother used to sleep in it and she had the side he's got now.

I like my side of the bed best. I can, without takin' my head up off the pillow, look out across at the Beans' if I want. As I look out now I see a pickup truck backin' up to the Beans' barn. A BIG BEAN MAN gets out and lifts a spotted tarpaulin. It's two dead bears. I look back at Gram.

I pull Gram's sleeve. "Oh Gram...What's the matter?"

"Where's your *jeans*!!?" she says. "Your *jeans*!!?"

"Under the bed," I says.

"Well, *get* 'em," she says.

Daddy's cryin', workin' his shoulders. The shoulder blades open and close.

I pick up a sock.

Gram's cool bony fingers close up around my wrist. She yanks me off my feet.

Daddy stands up in his underwear and folds his arms across his chest like he's cold. But it ain't cold. He looks the littlest I've ever seen him look. Gram pushes past Gramp and hauls me to my room. My bed is covered with cardboard boxes and coat hangers. She says deeply, "Start pickin' this stuff up!"

I says, "But Gram. Our nap is over. It's time to get up. Ask Daddy!"

"I ain't askin' that sick man nuthin'!" She hurls a pile of dresses I've outgrown upon the wall. I watch 'em slide down. Gram roars, "You stay in this bed for the rest of the day, maybe *two* days. And *no suppah!*"

"Gram!"

She is panting.

"GRAM...I'll be HUNGRY!"

"Don't sass!" She narrows her eyes. "The Lord's good meat and tatahs ain't for no dirty little girls." As

she hauls the covers back, she's whimperin'. And I hear
Daddy out there in the hall cryin'. He's pullin' on his
pants out there . . . right in the hall. Gramp just stands
there, lookin' lost under the brim of his little brown hat.

Gram takes up both my wrists and shakes them in my
face. She says into my eyes, "Of course nuthin's happened!!
Of course. I ain't sayin' somethin's *happened*!"

Daddy's in the kitchen slammin' chairs around. He
made all them chairs hisself. With his lathe in the cellar.

Gram fits me into my bed, then kisses my cheek. She
smells like rubber. Like rubber when it's hot. I see the
lions and tigers of my bedspread reflectin' in her eyes.
She says, "Are you Gram's little pixie?"

I says, "Yes."

She pulls the door shut.

3

Daddy stays out there in the kitchen a long time cryin' . . . a
way long time after Gram and Gramp are gone. The
water runs in the kitchen. Prob'ly Daddy's got his favorite jelly glass out of the dirty dishes and is rinsing it out.
Our well, Daddy says, will never go dry. "It's a thousand feet!" he always says. Then Daddy likes to say how
the Beans got the worse side of the right-of-way for
water. "All ledge and clay!" In summertime you see 'em
back one of them old grunty trucks to the door and they
go in and out with plastic milk jugs by the dozens.

As I lay here I can still smell Gramp's pipe tobacco.
It's the sweetest kind. Where Gram and Gramp live up in
the village, Gram's doilies have gotten yellow from
Gramp. So Gramp stopped smokin' in the house. He gets

in his car with the plaid blanket on the seat and has a smoke out in the dooryard. Or he scuffs over to Beans' Variety to sit with his friends near the radiator. Gramp's got a trillion friends . . . even Beans. When he goes over to the store, he puts on his white dress-up shirt and, of course, his hat.

In the middle of the night Daddy finally comes in my room. When he puts the hall light on, my heart hits the sheet. He stands in the doorway with the hall light on his back, his hands in the pockets of his khaki pants. He stretches across my bed. He is so little his body across my ankles and feet is not much heavier than one of Gram's cotton comforters.

We sleep.

---------------------- **4** ----------------------

It's Saturday morning. All clouds. Very cold.

When Daddy's downcellah busy with his lathe, I go to the edge of our grass to get a look at the Beans. The Beans' mobile home is one of them old ones, looks like a turquoise-blue submarine. It's got blackberry bushes growin' over the windows.

I scream, "HELLO BEANS!"

About four huge heads come out of the hole. It's a hole the Bean kids and Bean babies have been workin' on for almost a year. Every day they go down the hole and they use coffee cans and a spade to make the hole bigger. The babies use spoons. Beside the hole is a pile of gingerbread-color dirt as tall as a house.

I say, "Need any help with the hole!!?"

They don't answer. One of 'em wipes its nose on its sleeve. They blink their fox-color eyes.

I mutter, "Must be the STUPIDEST hole."

The heads draw back into the hole.

A white car with one Bondo-color fender is turnin' off the paved road onto the right-of-way. It musta lost its muffler. It rumbles along, and the exhaust exploding from all sides is doughy and enormous from the cold.

The blackberry bushes quiver, scrape at the tin walls of the mobile home like claws.

The white car slowly backs into Daddy's crushed-rock driveway and a guy with yellow hair and a short cigarette looks out at me and winks. His window's rolled down and he's got his arm hangin' out in the cold air.

I scream, "NO TURNIN' IN DADDY'S DRIVEWAY!"

There's another guy in there with him. He has a sweatshirt with a pointed hood so all that shows is his huge pink cheeks and a smile. The car pulls ahead onto the right-of-way and the two guys get out.

I scream, "Daddy says KEEP OUT! You ain't ALLOWED!"

The men look at each other and chuckle. The yellow-hair guy is still smokin' his cigarette even though it's only a tiny stump.

My eyes water from the cold. My hair, very white, blows into my mouth.

The sweatshirt guy opens the back door and I see there's feet in there on the seat. The sweatshirt guy pulls on the feet.

The other guy helps. They both tug on the feet.

Out comes a big Bean, loose, very loose, like a dead cat. His arms and legs just go all over the ground. His green felt hat plops out in the dirt. About five beer bottles skid out, too, roll and clink together. The guy with the yellow hair snatches a whiskey bottle off the seat and puts it in the Bean's hand, curls his fingers around it. Both the guys laugh. "There's your baby!" one says.

They get in the car and drive away.

My heart feels like runnin'-hard shoes. I look around. No Beans come out of the mobile home. No Beans come out of the hole.

I take a step. I'm wicked glad Daddy's in the cellah with his lathe. I can picture him down there in the bluish light in his little boy-sized clothes, pickin' over his big tools with his boy-sized hand.

I take another step.

Now I'm standin' right over the Bean. He looks to me like prob'ly the biggest Bean of all. He's got one puckered-up eye, bright purple . . . a mustache big as a black hen. I cover my nose. I think he musta messed hisself. His green workshirt has yellow stitching on one pocket. I read out loud, "R-E-U-B-E-N." I squint, trying to sound out the letters.

The whiskey bottle rolls off his hand.

I says, "Wake up, Bean!"

Then some heads come out of the hole.

A noise comes from the big Bean on the ground: GLOINK! And I say, "Wowzer!" It's blood spreadin' big as a hand in the dirt.

The kid Beans are comin' fast as they can. They bring their spade and spoons, cans and a pail.

I look into the Bean man's face. I say, "YOU! Hey you! Wake up!" I scooch down and inspect the pores of his skin. His wide-open mouth. Big Bean nose. My quick hand goes out . . . touches the nose. I say, "Stop bleedin', Bean."

His good eye opens.

I jump away.

Fox-color eye.

Out of the open mouth comes a hiss. The chest heaves

up. Somethin' horrible leaks out the corner of his mouth, catches in the hairs of the big mustache.

The kid Beans stand around starin' down at the green workshirt with the blood movin' out around their shoes.

I says, "Some guys brought him." I point up the road. I look among their faces for signs of panic. I say, "R-E-U-B-E-N. What's that spell?"

They look at me, breathin' through their mouths. One of 'em giggles and says, "That spells coo coo."

Another one pokes at the big Bean's shoulder with its green rubber boot. The big Bean goes "AAAARRRRR!" And his lips peel back over clenched yellow teeth.

A kid Bean with a spade says to a kid Bean with a pail, "Go get Ma off the bed. Rubie's been stabbed again."

"Go tell 'er yourself," says the kid Bean with the pail.

"No . . . you!" says the one with the spade.

"No-suh. I ain't gonna miss gettin' to see Rubie die."

I look down at the big Bean and his hand slowly drags across the dirt to his side to the torn fabric, a black place in the body, like an open mouth. And blood fills the cup of his hand.

Daddy opens the front door and hollers, "EARLENE!"

The big Bean's eyes is lookin' right at me.

I says to the eye, "In heaven they got streets of gold."

Daddy screams my name again.

The big fox-color eye closed.

I say, "Oh no! He's dead!"

The kid with the spade says, "Nah! He's still breathin'."

Daddy comes off the step. "Earlene! Get away! NOW!!"

I says, "Bean wake up! Don't die!"

Rubie Bean don't move. His mouth is wide open like he's died right in the middle of a big laugh. I see the blood has surrounded my left sneaker, has splashed on my white sock. I can hear the Bean kids shift in their rubber boots.

I drop down on all fours and put my ear right there on the shirt pocket where it says R-E-U-B-E-N.

"Get away from there!" Daddy almost whimpers. He's comin' fast across the grass.

The heart. A huge BOOM-BANG! almost punches at my temple through the Bean's shirt.

"Hear anything?" a Bean with a coffee can asks.

The fox-color big Bean eye opens, the teeth come together, make a deep rude raspy grunt. He says, "You kids...get the hell away from me, you goddam cocksuckin' little sons-a-whores!!"

'Bout then Daddy's boy-sized hands close around me.

5

I stand by the stove and Daddy gets out a new bar of LAVA soap, unwraps it. I says, "Daddy! I didn't say no swear words."

He gets one of the chairs from the suppah table and faces it in the corner where he keeps his boots. "Okay, Earlene," he says. "We're all set."

I says, "But, Daddy, soap's for swear words!" I fidget with the hem of my sweater.

His face is red. He pats the chair. I get on the chair facing the corner. I open my mouth. He sticks in the soap—hard, gritty. My mouth is almost not big enough.

He says at my back, "How many times have I told you to stay on your side of the right-of-way?"

I take the soap out. "Daddy! I was in the middle!" I wipe my mouth with my sleeve. I sputter.

"What those Beans would do to a small girl like you would make a grown man cry," he says.

I sputter some more.

Daddy says, "Earlene, put the soap back in."

"But Daddy!"

"When I used to do what Gram told me not to do, I got the *strap*," Daddy says.

I narrow my eyes. I says, "But those was the olden days, Daddy."

"Spare the rod, spoil the child," Daddy says.

We hear the siren. I start to get off the chair. Daddy puts his hand on my shoulder. "Earlene, I'm serious. Listen to me."

Them rescue guys outdoor are makin' a racket, radios and everything, havin' a time gettin' Rubie Bean off the ground. He makes the wickedest snarlin' noises. But Daddy don't seem to notice. He puts his face close to mine. "If I *ever . . .*" he says slowly, "ever . . . *ever . . .* see you near them Beans again, you are gettin' the horrible-est lickin' the Lord has ever witnessed."

I says, smiling, "Daddy . . . you wouldn't really do that."

He folds his arms over his chest. "Then I'll get Gram to do it."

--------------------------------- 6 ---------------------------------

It's Thanksgiving and I help Gram set out the matchin' dishes. Every Thanksgiving is the same. Auntie Paula comes with her kids and Uncle Loren comes in his pig truck alone. You can see snow between the tree trunks goin' up the mountain overway and the gray air cracks with guns.

I says, "Gram, did you used to hit Daddy with a strap?"

Gram's sharp little fingers move over the potatoes,

feelin' for bad spots. She says, "Spare the rod, spoil the child. Praise God!"

Loren keeps going out on the back steps to get some air.

Grams says, "Darn fool dresses too warm. He's got at least ten shirts on, you know."

I look out through the kitchen glass. It's raining on Uncle Loren. His arms dangle down through his legs. He smokes hard and slow.

I hum one of the songs Gram plays on the organ at church . . . the one to give thanks after they pass the plate. Uncle Loren don't go to church. Gram says Uncle Loren ain't accepted Jesus Christ as his Savior. Uncle Loren lives alone. We never visit him. We've seen the *outside* of his place about a million times. When we drive by, only his kitchen light is on. Daddy says Loren sleeps in the kitchen. Daddy says Loren's big house is cold as a barn. Uncle Loren comes back indoor and trudges into the living room where Jerry and Dennis and I are playin' the Cootie Game which Gram keeps for us kids. Uncle Loren sits on Gram's flower-print divan and he looks me in the eye.

Gram hollers from the kitchen, "Loren . . . don't go layin' your head on that lace scarf!"

Uncle Loren wears striped overalls. When I look in his eyes, I get a shiver.

Gram comes to the living room door and says that Auntie Paula made that divan scarf and that the oils off Loren's head would make it black . . . eventually.

Uncle Loren says, "Earlene . . . did you know I got ghosts in my house?"

Gram says, "He's just tryin' to scare you, Earlene. Don't listen to him."

He looks big and solid and square settin' there on the divan . . . but he's really as short as Daddy. He says,

"Ghosts bust up my house all the time. They don't hurt me . . . but they keep me awake rollin' them big Blue Hubbards around and smashin' up glass. They get right under the sheets with me and run around in there under the sheets."

Jerry and Dennis watch Uncle Loren with open mouths.

Gram snorts. "He just says stuff like that so no one will visit him and discover his squalor. He *hates* people visitin' him. People, good Christian ones, upset him. He don't know Christ as his *Savior*."

Then he moves his deep pale scary eyes on me.

I look away fast.

_____ **7** _____

After dinner, I go out to where Uncle Loren is settin' on the back step and watch him strike a match on the buckle of his overalls. It's almost dark, but there's still some shots up on the mountain.

Uncle Loren don't say nuthin', just squints his eyes as the smoke sifts up over his face.

I twirl a piece of my white hair and put it in the corner of my mouth.

Loren shifts his boots on the step.

"How's the hogs?" I ask.

"Good," he says.

He smokes.

I twirl my hair.

"Uncle Loren," I says, almost in a whisper, "you ever heard this word? . . . Goddamcocksuckinlittlesonsa-hoowahs?"

Uncle Loren chuckles, sends his cigarette butt spinning

through the rain. It hisses in the grass. "Why don't you ask your daddy, Earlene?"

I trace one of my dress-up shoes with my pointing finger. I narrow my eyes. " 'Cause . . . I got a *feelin'*."

Uncle Loren puts them pale scary eyes on me. And I shiver.

3

Across the right-of-way the Beans' black dog stands by an old rug, looking at me. "Yoo hoo!" I call through cupped hands.

Daddy's gone to Oxford to work on a bank . . . He's late gettin' home. They say the roads are greasy.

I take a step onto the Beans' side of the right-of-way. The black dog watches me, the hair on its back raised. But it don't bark.

I step over a spinach can with water froze in it, a clothespin, an Easter basket, the steerin' wheel of a car.

Out of the dog's nose its frozen breath pumps. I draw nearer to the hole with the spoons and coffee cans ringed around it. The dog charges. It gallops sideways with stiff rocking-horse legs.

I says, "You bite me and you'll regret it!!"

I look up at the closed metal door. No Beans.

The dog's eyes glow a bluish white. Its bluish tongue flutters. I say, "Beat it!" and kick a beer bottle at it.

It noses the beer bottle, picks it up in its teeth, and drops it at my feet.

"Go away! I ain't playin'." I look at the Bean windows. No faces. The dog smells my small moving feet. "You ugly grimy Bean dog. You're gointa BURN IN HELL!"

There's a scalloped serving spoon at the edge of the hole. "So this is the hole," I says to myself. The dog watches me pick up a trowel. I point it at the dog. "ZEEP!" I scream. "You are instantly DEAD!" The dog blinks.

The corridor of the hole is curved. I slide down on my bottom, workin' my legs, the entrance behind me dwindling to a woolly little far-off cloud in the distance. I feel soda bottles along the way. A measuring cup. A rock drops from the ceiling and thwonks my shoulder. A spray of dirt lets go and fills my hair. I enter a big warm room. In apple crates are what feels like Barbie clothes and Barbie accessories. There's a full-sized easy chair.

"Jeezum!" I gasp. I sit in the chair. "This is real cozy."

I lean forward and feel of the dirt walls, dirt floor. My hand closes around a naked Barbie.

All of a sudden there's a thunder up there.

The warm earth lets go, feels like hundreds of butterflies on my face.

"It's GOD," I says in a choking whisper. My heart flutters.

It's Rubie Bean. The tires of his old logging rig hiss over Daddy's crushed-rock driveway. There's the ernk! of the gears.

"Uh oh!" I says to myself. "I'm trapped in this hole. I can't go up there now."

A rock from the ceiling punches my outstretched legs.

More Beans come. Three or four carloads. The mobile home door opens, closes, opens, closes. Out in their yard Bean kids big as men run over the earth's crust above me. THUMP THUMP THUMP THUMP. The soft slap of sand is on my neck. The Bean kids throw something for the black dog to catch. It sounds like a piece of tail pipe.

I hear Daddy's car.

After a while there's Daddy's voice: "Earlene! Supper!"

It's very very dark. The Beans have gone indoor.

The dog is up there at the top of the hole, sniffin' for me.

Hours and hours and hours pass. Hours of pitch black.

I says to myself in a squeak, "I am goin' ta get the strap." I turn naked Barbie over and over in my nervous fingers. I mutter, "Well . . . I just ain't ever gonna leave THIS HOLE."

9

There is light again at the top. The light flutters. Boots tromp. They come down waving a flashlight—Annie Bean, Lizzie Bean, Rosie Bean. They put the light in my face. "What're *you* doin' in here?" one of 'em asks.

"Nuthin'," I says. My stomach growls.

They make wet thick sniffin' sounds. Their open mouths are echoey. They fill this dirt room with their broad shoulders, broad heads. Dirt sifts down from the ceiling through the enormous light.

"You runnin' from the law?" one of 'em asks.

"NO WAY!" I scream. My scream makes more of the ceiling fall. I think I'm gonna gag from this light in my face. Now and then I can make out a Bean nose, a sharp tooth. Then it fades into the glare.

"You're runnin' away from home?" asks one of them.

I bristle. "No! I ain't!"

"Well, how come your father's up there cryin'?"

One of 'em pushes a saucer with cake on it into the light. There is only the cake, the saucer, the hand. The cake is sky-blue. "Here!" a voice says.

Their clothes rustle.

"What's *that*?" I scrunch up my nose.

"We was goin' ta eat it, but you can have it. Ain't you starved?"

I look at the cake, squinting up one eye.

"I didn't run away," I says softly.

"You prob'ly fell in here," one says.

"No-suh!" I holler.

I make out a fox-color eye which is round and hard and caked with sleepin' sand.

I take the saucer and arrange it on my knee next to Barbie. I says, "I ain't never leavin' this hole. I'm stayin' here forever . . . as long as I live."

"You like it here pretty well, huh?" one of 'em says.

I am alone. Between me and them is this wall of light. I hold the saucer with both hands, careful not to touch the cake. A bit of sand spills from the ceiling onto the cake.

The three of them giggle.

The cake is the blue of a birdless airplaneless sunless cloudless leafless sky . . . warm steaming blue. "Prob'ly POISON!" I gasp.

"No way!" one of 'em says. "It ain't. It's Betty Crocker."

THE BEANS

TWO
Merry Merry

Beal Bean comes into the low-ceilinged room where his Auntie Roberta lies on a mattress with her new baby and her old baby. Beal's black dog, Jet, stands back out of the light, her bluish tongue fluttering. Jet is pregnant again.

Roberta says, "The TV, she's rollin'. Beal, can ya fiddle with that thing in back?"

Beal yanks off his new nylon mittens and tosses them on the mattress. He fiddles with the TV and he says, "Auntie, it's wicked bad back home . . . Can I stay here tonight?"

She shifts her feet around. The old baby watches Beal hard.

Roberta murmurs, "Rubie cranky?"

"Ain't Rubie . . . It's everyone else."

"There! That's good. She's stopped rollin'. Come-sit here." A veiny, almost fleshless arm reaches for the nylon mittens on the covers. "Holy cats!" Roberta exclaims in her long-neck reedy voice. "Ain't that funny-feelin' stuff!"

The only light is the queer grayish haze of the TV, and through this haze Beal sees she has her hair in a messy bun tonight. The whole room smells like Bag Balm, but Beal can tell Roberta is the source. It roils out from her each time she shifts the covers.

"Can I, Auntie?" He scooches down on the mattress next to the peaks in the quilt which are her feet. He looks straight ahead at the TV.

"Ayuh . . . but Auntie Hoover's gonna charge over here in the mornin' rantin' and ravin'.''

The TV picture rolls three times.

"I doubt it. Ah-ah-ah-auntie Hoover's back at the mill," says Beal.

"Third shift?"

"Yeh," says Beal. The black dog watches Beal. She's not used to the inside of a house. Her sides heave in and out. She moans.

"Bet she hates it goin' back," says Roberta. "I ain't never goin' back."

"She hates it," says Beal.

"You gotta toe the mark in that ol' hole," says Roberta.

Beal says softly, "Pa says she ain't gonna last."

"What's Pa know?" Roberta asks.

The new baby stirs and punches its fist into its mouth. Roberta rearranges her pillows and wipes her hair out of her eyes. Her head is queerly small and her eyes are ringed in black like the way football players darken their eyes against the sun.

Beal sighs.

"Take off your coat, Beal," Roberta says.

He doesn't move. He stares at the TV, which now and then rolls. "Auntie . . . Are *you* my mother?"

She shifts her feet. "Beal! I'm just a child myself!"

He turns and looks her up and down. "Maybe I ain't got one."

She smiles. Her tall teeth open up. "Beal, you're a lucky boy. You got a buncha mothers."

The old baby gets under the covers and looks from the TV to Beal and back to the TV.

Beal scowls. "Yeh... but which one did I come out of? Which one let me lie on her like *that*?" He points at the new baby sprawled on Roberta's narrow chest.

"Well... it ain't no secret... I guess they just figured you knew. I mean... they prob'ly told you when you was little."

"I forgot."

She takes his arm in her scarred, hard fingers and kneads it. "I wish you *was* mine. You're steady as a brain surgeon... Some day you're gonna be quite the prize. I got eyes for that kinda thing, you know..." She flutters both eyelids.

He looks at her with his steady fox-color eyes.

She says reedily, "But you ain't mine. You're Merry Merry's."

Beal's broad-shouldered at thirteen, big as a man, looks so much like Ernest Bean and Chris Bean, you can't tell one from the other. He flattens his hands on his thighs.

"You ain't surprised?" says Roberta. Her fingers travel down his forearm. She takes his hands and plays with his fingers.

"No, I ain't surprised," he murmurs. He looks at the TV. The TV makes such eerie light on his face. Jet moans and drops to the floor, head on the corner of the mattress, panting more softly now, eyes on Beal.

Roberta says at Beal's back, "And, of course, you ain't got no dad. You know how *that* goes. Like these

babies here . . . You see . . . they ain't got one. It happens
now and then.''

He closes his eyes. "I wish you wa-a-ah-was my
mother, Auntie.''

She keeps playing with his fingers. She says, "Shit! I
ain't nuthin'.''

———————————— **2** ————————————

Merry Merry is prisoner again. When she paces up there,
the whole tree house shakes. She pokes her broad Bean
nose through the bars and calls, "Beeeeee!''

Beal stands with his shotgun across his thighs, looking
up, while Lizzie, Annie, and Rosie balance like cats on
the outside platform of the tree house. "She's prizna!''
Rosie shouts.

"Beeeee!'' Merry Merry calls. He sees her hands, a
bloodless white, take the bars and shake them.

"Let her down!'' Beal commands.

"There's Beal Pimplehead who stutters!'' one of them
sings out. They use rusty saws and hammers to put up
more bars on the jail.

"You guys ain't supposed to take her up there . . . I'm
teh-teh-teaaaah-tellin'!'' Beal yells up the tree. He prowls
slowly around the tree. Although he is thirteen, he has
the hesitation of an old man. Jet circles the tree with him.

Annie squeals with laughter, "She's prizna! She broke
the law!'' All three of them giggle.

Jet stands, puts her paws on the tree.

Beal says, "You c-ah-aaah-creeps! If I get you, I'm
gonna bah-aaaah-ust your heads!''

He clasps a rung of the ladder and pulls himself up, his

shotgun under his arm. Jet barks. She races around the tree.

"He's gonna get us," one of them says to the other. They giggle wildly. "Pimpled Stutterhead is goin' to get us!"

"Beeeee!" Merry Merry calls through the bars.

"Here he comes," whispers one of them. Their fox-color eyes water from the cold.

Beal keeps the shotgun against his ribs.

A nail drops on his neck. Another on his shoulder. Nails rain down. He keeps his face down.

"Beeee!" Merry Merry calls. Her feet march and the tree-house floor groans.

Lizzie, Annie, and Rosie hold their hammers over Beal's fingers on the top rung. "Wanna see Pimpled Stutterhead let go?" says one of them.

The other two shriek, "Yessss!"

Jet circles beneath . . . whining.

Above, Merry Merry is whining. Her dark braids swing against the jail bars. Beal can see the colored elastics the aunties used to fix her hair.

With watering eyes, broad heads, broad bodies, mittens dangling on safety pins, the cousins shake their hammers.

Beal looks down. Jet's tongue flutters like it was a hot day.

The tree house creaks, the broad gray beech riddled with nails . . . Eeeck . . . eeeck! Merry Merry shakes the bars.

Annie exclaims, "Anybody who pees theirself right in the road goes ta *jail* . . . From now on *this* is where they go, right?"

"Right," Rosie says.

"Right!" Lizzie says.

"And anybody who is the stupidest one around . . . *big* and stupid . . . goes in this here fancy jail!" Rosie says.

"Right!"

"Right!"

"She can't help it," Beal says softly.

"Sentenced to bread 'n' watah!" Rosie screams.

All three hammers tap Beal's fingers lightly.

"That's for now," says Rosie. "Next gets harder!"

"I'll kill you," Beal murmurs, "wuh-wuh-with this gun."

"No-suh! Aunties don't let you have bullets!"

"You fuckers," Beal says softly.

The hammers drop on the fingers . . . with the pressure it takes to drive a thumbtack . . . perhaps to hang a calendar.

Beal's chin puckers.

"He's cryin'!" rejoices Lizzie.

"I'm tellin'," says Beal.

Rosie leans forward and gurgles happily, "What you gonna tell 'em, Pimplehead? You gonna tell you was *cryin'*?"

He starts back down the tree.

Lizzie, Annie, and Rosie wave their hammers over their heads. "Yay! Yay!"

Beal's foot touches the leaves. He sobs. He turns his face away so they won't see the rivers on his pimpled cheeks. A few yards down the path, he kicks a rotted stump to pieces. The voices behind him cry out very faintly, "Ain't loaded! Ain't loaded! Ain't loaded!"

----------------- 3 -----------------

Beal sees the stranger coming down the road through the dark trunks of spruce. Beal squares his shoulders.

The stranger turns down the right-of-way.

Lizzie, Annie, and Rosie are perched on the hood of Rubie Bean's purply-red logging truck, making snowballs from the brand-new snow. "Who's *that*?" says Annie.

Jet bristles, watches hard with her blue eyes.

Beal lays the bucksaw down.

Rosie shapes her snowball round and hard, pitches it into Beal's back. He ignores it.

The stranger wears a long coat, unbuttoned. No hat. He is balding. He moves with rhythm, like his long legs and swinging long arms are accustomed to miles uncountable. There is a black beard with gray rivulets through it all the way to his belt. The stomach is rounded.

Another snowball thuds into Beal's back. The three cousins giggle. "Pimples! Hey, Pimples!" screams one of them. "Turn around. Let's see some pimples!"

Sometimes Beal wishes he had no face at all, just a soft white empty place like the sky. But if he could really wish—and make the wish come true—he'd wish for his cousin Rubie's face, the eyes always steady on you and, around the haggard mouth, a black mustache like the lowered wings of a crow.

Another snowball. Another. Another. One breaks apart on his neck.

Beal thinks he's seen the stranger before, but realizes it's just because the stranger looks like Santa Claus, a big, young Santa Claus.

"Looks like Santa Claus!" exclaims Rosie.

"Not Santa Claus," Lizzie hisses. "The Boogie Man... Ernck!"

Lizzie, Annie, and Rosie are whispering.

The stranger doesn't raise his hand in greeting. The face is gray and grained as barn boards. There are no white hairs in the mustache, only in three distinct streaks, one spewing from the chin, two from the temples.

Jet growls.

"Be good girl," says Beal.

Jet's tail thumps.

Annie, Lizzie, and Rosie slide off the hood of the truck. Lizzie sucks snow from her mitten. Lizzie and Annie and Rosie look the stranger up and down. Hanging from his belt is a homemade sheath of dark leather and shoelace, the handle of a huge hunting knife sticking out.

"That your knife, mistah?" Rosie asks.

The stranger squints at them all as if he can't quite make them out. Beal is just opening his mouth to speak when the metal door of the mobile home peels open. Auntie Hoover and Auntie K. run out into the snow in their sneakers, screaming, "Merry Merry!"

They gallop toward the barn with their eyes on the stranger, his eyes squinting after them . . . trying to focus on their zigzagging path. Beal glances at the stranger, the steady hands with no gloves. The stranger puts him to mind of a workhorse, a great docile Belgian, tired of the plow, but with smooth-striding shoulders and large sniffing nostrils, gentle mouth.

"Ain't you got mittens, mistah?" Lizzie asks.

Beal says, "Get lost, Lizzie."

Lizzie sneers, "Get lost yourself! Crybaby!"

The stranger settles his green almost milky eyes on Beal and squints. "Well, I know you. Ain't you Rubie?"

Beal squares his shoulders. "I'm Beal."

"Beal? What an awful name . . . Well, no worse'n Granville." He moves closer to Beal, trying to make out the face. "Ain't hearda you, Beal. But I imagine there's a story."

The stranger squints for a long time on Beal.

"Can't you see good?" Annie asks.

"Good as a bat," the stranger says.

Lizzie, Annie, and Rosie giggle ferociously.

In the barn there's the sound of a cage slapping shut.

The man looks long and hard that way. "Them women gettin' ready ta fix me a cage?"

"That's Merry Merry's bunny they're puttin' back. Name's Whitey," Lizzie says.

Annie says, "Jeez . . . Ain't you ever shaved, mistah?"

The aunties lead Merry Merry out of the barn. Merry Merry walks between them like a captive Indian princess, her thick braids swaying. She has a small smile and hundreds of acne scars. When she sees the stranger, her smile does not increase or decrease.

"Why you actin' so crazy, Aunties?" Lizzie asks as they pass by.

"You girls go play!" Auntie Hoover commands.

"Cripes," says Annie, "there's weirdness today."

Auntie Hoover's getting ready to close the tin door behind her . . . She stops, and says out of the corner of her mouth, "Well, you got the barn to yourself, Granville! Get in it and we'll bring you some dinnah! Beal Bean, you look after them girls . . . Don't take your eyes off 'em!"

"Cripes!" says Annie.

The stranger smiles. A kindly Santa Claus–pink tinge comes to his face. "Well, I know a good barn when I see one," he says, and moves toward it. He moves like a workhorse, happy to see the barn, happy to enter it, the huge back and shoulders passing out of the white light of outdoors into the cavity of darkness, swinging his arms.

"What a weirdo," says Rosie.

"One of Pa's friends prob'ly," says Annie.
Lizzie sucks her mitten.

———————— 4 ————————

Pa comes down the right-of-way with his plow down and
his cemetery shovels in the back of the truck. Pa's gray
hair stands straight up as usual. He takes his Thermos off
the seat. Pa looks at the ground, the huge footprints
leading to the barn. "Granville Pollard's here, ain't he?"

Beal is cutting cordwood with the bucksaw. The aunties never let him use the chain saw. He says, "Yup."

Lizzie, Annie, and Rosie, building what looks like an
upright grizzly bear out of snow, squinch up their noses.
"What a weirdo!" they exclaim.

Pa grins. "I seen him comin' up through, but I was
down back. Called ta him, but he don't see 'n' hear when
he don't want . . . Goddam wild turkey."

"He your friend?" Annie asks.

Pa laughs.

Jet follows Pa to the barn. Rosie takes Beal's hand and
hangs there a moment, all of them watching the silent
barn with unblinking eyes.

———————— 5 ————————

"Pass the tatahs," says Pa.

Pa has a chair. Not everybody has a chair.

Pa doesn't take off his coat.

Merry Merry is at the table next to Pa. She has a seat with
arms and a cushion. She thumps her foot while she eats.

Rubie Bean is at the table, one elbow on each side of his plate. "Gimme the buttah, Ma."

Auntie K. and Auntie Hoover just stand around and watch the rest. They've already filled up while they were cooking, tasting this and that from the big kettles.

Lizzie dumps gravy on Merry Merry's potatoes. "An' here's your bread, stupid," she says.

Rosie rips up Merry Merry's turkey meat with her fingers.

"Don't do it with your fingers," says Auntie K.

Uncle Wayne eats standing, holding his plate. He laps gravy off the edge.

There's a car coming in the yard. Auntie Jeannie and her kids.

Auntie Hoover gets out more plates.

Auntie Hoover and Auntie K. both look like they're waiting for a ride to an American Legion dance . . . always dressed like any minute someone might show up and say, "Let's go!"

Beal stands against the wall with his plate. Auntie Jeannie comes in and one of her big babies hugs Beal's legs.

"Hurry with the door!" Auntie Hoover tells Auntie Jeannie. "Where's Walt?"

"Ain't comin'."

Another thing Auntie Hoover and Auntie K. both do is pluck their eyebrows off and draw new ones on from scratch. And both are bottle blonds. They are both big with big hands . . . but actually only Auntie K.'s a Bean by blood. Auntie Hoover's Bean by marriage.

Ernest is just coming in. He stomps his boots at the door.

"Hurry with the door," says Auntie Hoover.

Ernest fills his plate, then stands next to Beal, and he and Beal both eat without talking.

Rubie Bean makes snorting noises while he eats.

Auntie K. washes pots in the sink.

Auntie Hoover says, "Reuben, get that squash off your whiskahs!"

Rubie wipes his mouth on his sleeve.

"Ain't he ever goin' back to his wifey?" Annie says.

"Shut up!" says Rubie. He belches.

"You quit bashin' her, maybe she'll like you," Annie says. She pours herself some milk.

Beal drops one of Auntie Jeannie's babies a piece of turkey skin.

The babies circulate. One climbs over Pa's knees.

Merry Merry pats her turkey meat with the palm of her hand. "Keeee!" she says. She fingers all the things on her plate. Her hands meet each warm, wet surface with tenderness and playfulness like when she holds her bunny, Whitey.

Annie says, "I like the part best where she calls the cops on you and they come out and got you and kept you in the jail for *this* many days . . ." She holds up both her hands.

Rubie wipes his mouth again. He glares at Annie with his fox-color eyes. Some of his fingers are missing. One nail is shaped like a claw, and with this one he picks something from his back teeth.

Pa butters a piece of bread. "Ain't this Wonder Bread?" he asks.

"No, Pa, it's the store bread," says Auntie Hoover.

"Goddam shit," says Pa.

Auntie Jeannie, big and square like all Bean women, sits cross-legged on the floor and unbuttons her white shirt. With her left hand she pushes a baby to the almost black nipple; with the right hand she eats turkey stuffing from a plate on her knee.

"We got them lights on for you, Pa," Auntie Hoover says.

"Hoover, dear . . . I ain't in the Christmassy mood today!"

"Well . . . there they are! . . . in the hall . . . Till they go up . . . we'll be steppin' on 'em."

"Put 'em away, then."

"Pa! You know the trouble we went through draggin' all that stuff out!"

Pa laughs. Chewed-up bread drops from his mouth to his plate.

Uncle Wayne eats silently. His mouth, like a feeding fish, opens and closes around the edge of his plate. He paces in front of the TV. A pair of orange work gloves sticks out of his back pocket like feathers stick out of a rooster's rear.

"Who is Granville Pollard?" Beal asks.

Rubie and Pa and the three aunties look at each other. Rubie's eating noises stop. The air is quiet, almost snowy.

Lizzie pipes up, "A horrible sight if you ask me!"

Auntie K. sighs. "He'd be a handsome man if he got ridda them Christly whiskahs."

"Yes-suh," Auntie Hoover groans. "Every time he breezes in, them whiskahs is hangin' another inch below his belt. Looks like hell."

Pa is watching Beal. Pa's mouth is open with the chewed bread at rest in there in full view.

Auntie Hoover says, "Looks ain't nuthin' . . . It's his morals . . . He's got the morals of an old cat."

Rubie laughs. Wipes his mouth.

Auntie Hoover glares at Rubie. "There's nuthin' atall funny, Reuben."

Merry Merry laughs.

Auntie Hoover pulls some dishes off the table, jams

them in the sink. "Ain't no time to be discussin' Granville
Pollard's habits with all these kids in the room."

Rubie snickers. "You're always crankin' on *my* morals. Let's give ol' Granville's morals a whirl."

Annie leans forward. "Does this have anything to do
with sex?"

"Yes," says Rubie.

Lizzie claps her hands. "Oh, boy! This is like Twenty
Questions. Ain't it like Twenty Questions?" She looks at
Rosie.

"Yip," says Rosie.

Auntie K. says, "Reuben, let's not start now. I don't
think when you got one of your hangovers you're fit to
talk at the dinnah table."

Annie makes a face at Rubie with her thumbs in her
ears.

Rubie lunges forward, scooping hot squash from a
bowl . . . His chair falls over. Annie's face gets the squash.
Annie screams through Rubie's long and short fingers.

"Reuben, simmer down," says Auntie K. softly. She
puts her hand between his shoulder blades, pats him.

Auntie Hoover waggles her penciled-on eyebrows.
"Reuben's always gotta make some scene."

Rubie laughs deeply, stoops to pick up his chair.

Annie is crying, getting up from her chair.

Pa says, "Reuben, take an aspirin."

"Let's talk about sex!" Lizzie squeals.

Pa looks sideways at Lizzie. "Eat!"

Rubie says, "Ain't it a pisser how Granville can't keep
his hands off Merry Merry—I mean, Jesus fuckin' Christ!
—Merry Merry ain't no Marilyn Monroe, you know!"

Lizzie looks at Merry Merry. "Her?"

Beal looks at Merry Merry.

Merry Merry chirps, "Keee!" and stretches forward to
pat the turkey carcass in the middle of the table.

Beal can't take his eyes off Merry Merry.

Now everyone is looking at Merry Merry's hands. Her right thumb pivots on the turkey's spine. The wrist kicks back. They watch in foolish silence this reflex none of them can make heads nor tails of.

6

They're hunkered around the radiator at Beans' Variety ... a half-dozen or so ... You can just make them out in the loam-color light. Merry Merry shuffles behind Beal in her green rubber boots. Beal commands, "Go set over there with them!"

The men around the radiator look at Merry Merry, then look at each other. Nobody talks.

Outside, Pete Bean's loaded logging truck idles. Pete is closest to the radiator, opening an Italian sandwich with triple black olives. The oil runs off the paper. He picks the black olives out first, one at a time, and eats them. Without teeth.

Merry Merry flops down into the folding metal chair next to Pete. Her hands in her lap do something that looks like two furious white gamecocks.

Pete is the fattest of all Beans ... And you wouldn't call what he's got a beard ... it's just a poor shave. He murmurs, "Black olives make you passionate, you know."

Marty Gallant is the school bus driver, has a cold pair of gray eyes, enormous gray hands. He looks through the loam-color light at the Budweiser clock. "Don't eat 'em, then."

Merry Merry watches Beal wipe a can of tuna fish on his pant leg.

Pete Bean's union suit has no buttons, is done up tautly

across his belly and breasts with safety pins. He says, "I hear Granville Pollard's up your place, Beal."

Beal looks among the faces. "Yip," he says.

Pete chuckles. "He 'n' your gramp always been thick."

All the men smile.

Merry Merry rocks her body to and fro . . . but there's no rocking chair. The bus driver narrows his pale eyes on her.

"Pa 'n' him's been keepin' the cemetery open . . . plowin' an' stuff," says Beal. "Pa pays him ta help."

The men look at each other. The radiator clangs.

"Now there's quite a ticket, that Granville feller," Pete says. He picks a cigar off the mopboard and takes three loud, juicy draws. "Down Four Corners we always call him Rip . . . you know . . . Van Winkle . . . Well, you call him Rip and see what he does, Beal." Pete looks like he's chewing a good piece off his cigar. He sets it back on the mopboard.

"Woi!!!" shouts Merry Merry, pointing at Pete's plaid wool pants.

"Don't get excited . . . It's just an olive, woman!" Pete picks the olive from his pant leg, eats it.

At the counter, Beal picks out a handful of Dubble Bubbles.

Howe Letourneau looks outdoors. He has one empty sleeve, pinned up to the shoulder, and a face of silver scars. He says, "When's your Lab going ta drop dem pups, Beal?"

"Pups?" says Beal.

Pete leans over the radiator and looks, too. "Ayup," he says. Pete's suspenders are also safety-pinned here and there. The union suit is orange under the arms . . . and the elbows look like they've been dynamited away.

"Ain't been no males around," Beal says. He pays for

the gum and tuna. The Bean behind the counter squints to count out change. There's not much light.

Merry Merry sees Beal turn around with the gum. "Reeeeium!" she rejoices, starting to get up.

"Stay put," murmurs the bus driver. He looks at Beal. "Hurry with them gums, Beal."

Pete uncrosses his legs and runs a finger around in the Italian sandwich. "Don't always need the male," says Pete. Pete winks at Howe Letourneau. Howe winks back. Pete says, "After all, babies is always comin' ta single women, ain't they, Howe?"

Howe says, "Aye."

Pete looks Beal in the eye. "Why, look at the Virgin Mary. You know what *virgin* means, dontcha?"

Pete's still looking Beal in the eye.

"Yes," says Beal.

Pete digs out a quivering slice of cheese, lowers it into his mouth. He slurps on the cheese a minute and says, almost in a whisper, "God made the Virgin Mary pregnant . . . and God, as everybody knows, is faster than the speed of light."

Howe Letourneau reddens.

Beal looks out through the speckled glass. Jet is hunkered down on the piazza, scratching. Thump. Thump. Thump. Thump.

Beal creaks back over the slanted floor and Merry Merry opens her mouth wide. He fishes around inside Merry Merry's mouth with his fingers. Pete and the other men watch. Out comes Merry Merry's soft, warm old gum. Beal sticks the gum in the ashtray. Then he unwraps the new Dubble Bubbles and Merry Merry claps her hands. "Gummm! Beeee! Gummm!"

Pete says, "I expect she'll drop them pups any day."

Merry Merry's heavy braids swing, one knocking against Pete Bean's elbow.

"Whaddya got for jokes in dat Dubble Bubble, Beal?"
Howe Letourneau asks hoarsely.

"Ain't no jokes in this kind," says Beal.

"Bazooka Joe," says the bus driver solemnly.

Beal puts the new bright gums into Merry Merry's
mouth one at a time. Gently, her lips close up around his
fingers.

----------- 7 -----------

Merry Merry works the latch of Whitey's cage with her
fingers, and the thumbs straight as fingers. The brilliance
of sun and snow charges through the wire window onto
her back in a pattern of lines. The cage door comes open.
She lifts out a very old white doe with a pouch, a doe
large as a lamb. She finds Granville Pollard's pallet of
blankets, collapses onto them, laughing.

Pa lets the stranger off at the top of the right-of-way.
Granville Pollard comes sweeping down in his long
unbuttoned coat.

Meanwhile, Auntie K.'s eyes are glued to *The Guiding
Light*. Auntie Hoover sleeps off third shift.

Granville Pollard enters the barn.

Merry Merry looks up. She laughs. "Ba-heeeee!" She
drives her face into the white doe.

Granville puts out his hand. "You ain't supposed to be
out here," he says. "Or is it I'm supposed to be
somewhere?"

Merry Merry laughs violently, redly.

He kneels, crosses his arms on his knee. His beard
parts over his thigh and almost touches the floor.

Now she's rocking the top half of her body . . . laughing
that sounds like sobs.

He draws his pointing finger between the ears of the white doe. The doe's eyes show endless pink circles.

Granville focuses on Merry Merry's braids swinging in frenzied circles. He catches one braid in his hand.

"Gettin' gray," he says.

She smiles a slow eerie smile.

He says, "Me, too . . . goddam it. Ain't it a pissah!"

She scrambles her fingers more deeply into the doe's shoulders.

Granville rolls the braid between his hands.

Merry Merry kisses the doe. The kiss sounds like more laughter.

Granville stands. He gives a coil of rope a hard kick. "Well . . . they ain't got ta worry. No shit. There's too much watah over the dam . . . I don't even *like* you no more."

He turns and squints at the braids that are raking through the dusty-looking sun.

"They're makin' a hoo-ha over nuthin', for cryin' out loud."

8

Rosie cries out, "Auntie K.! Auntie K.! The dog is under Beal's cot!"

Bean can tell Rubie's just come home from another drunk. The whole back room smells like Rubie's wide-open mouth.

Auntie K. pushes the door panel aside, and the light from the hallway fire door explodes around her. Now Beal can plainly see Rubie's arm, the hand with the long and short fingers . . . the green workshirt ripped from a fight.

Jet's tail thumps.

Auntie K. snarls, "I smell a dog."

Beal sits up, tries to flatten his hair down. He rubs his eyes. "Ain't Jet that smells." He looks at Rubie.

Rosie says, "Beal's in trouble, ain't he, Auntie?"

The tail thumps.

Beal has been sleeping in his clothes . . . even his boots. His cot is covered in sand.

Lizzie and Annie and Rosie stand around Auntie K. in pajamas and gowns. Rosie simpers, "You sneaked her in the fire door, didn't you, Pimplehead?"

Auntie K. stoops to grab at Jet, but Beal blocks the way with his foot. He says, "Auntie . . . she's gonna have pups. Can't she stay indoor to have pups?"

Auntie K. puts her hands on her hips. "Ayuh . . . and get goo and crud all over my floors."

Rubie makes about six bull-like snorts in his sleep.

Lizzie chirps, "How'd *he* get in here? I just seen him out sleepin' by the steps."

Annie says, "Where was you, stupid? Pa and Ernest just lugged him through."

Beal's chin dimples. "Ah-aaaaah-ah-ah-auntie . . . please!"

Auntie K. gets a grip on the nape of Jet's neck and pulls hard.

Rosie says, "Beal's cryin'."

Beal pretends he's going to spit at them.

"Auntie!" Rosie screams.

Beal watches Auntie K. shove Jet out through the fire door.

Rubie's eyes jump under the lids. His shoulders quiver. One leg jerks.

Annie gives Rubie a sideways look. "What a dub. Even in his dreams he's makin' a nu-since of hisself."

_____ 9 _____

Beal and Jet are in the tree house, waiting for night.
Beal's left hand is spread on the tight convex belly that
now and then shudders from the pups. Beal's face is a
mess from crying. His pant legs are wet. He wears a
Lone Ranger bedspread over his shoulders. He has brought
six blankets, but these are heaped under and around the
dog.

Another hour. Total dark.

The wind picks up and the tree house sways crazily,
and through this wind, Beal's crying is a high ghostlike
scream.

_____ 10 _____

The sunrise makes red bars through the bony trees. Beal
hears the scuffing of snowshoe tails. He puts one eye to a
tree-house crack.

Rubie Bean.

"Get down!" commands Rubie from below.

The memory of Lizzie, Annie, and Rosie with hammers over his fingers flashes into mind.

Jet stands up and paws at the tree-house door.

"It's Rubie," Beal whispers huskily. "Pretend we
ain't here, Jet."

"Make it snappy!" Rubie calls in his raspy, grunty
voice. The voice hammers through the bony trees.

Jet gives the door another scratch.

Rubie spits hard, and the spit drives into the snow deep as a hot bullet.

"Beal! Get the hell down here!"

Beal holds his breath.

Rubie bends and unlaces the snowshoes with his long and short fingers. "I ain't fuckin' around, Mistah Man!" the raspy voice says.

Beal hollers through the crack, "I'll be home in a while. I ain't runnin' away . . . just campin' out."

Rubie moves up the ladder fast.

Beal's chin dimples; his face scrinches in a loud sob.

Jet whines. Her tail slowly sways. Rubie punches the little tree-house door and it jerks open, strewing the red morning light. Rubie comes in on his hands and knees. One hand of long and short fingers muckles onto Beal's right foot.

Beal shrieks with terror.

Rubie rises up on his knees, his huge head touching the ceiling of the tree house. He narrows his eyes close to Beal's face. "You make me sick, pussy face!" he snarls. "At least *my* boys *try* ta fight back."

Beal collapses, sobbing. And Rubie looks frantically from wall to wall . . . confused.

11

When he enters the barn, Beal hears a hose running. It's the stranger in a box stall with his head in a tub of water. The clothes are piled over a plank of the stall, the old coat, the dark shirt, empty pant legs dangling. The stranger jerks his head up and stands, the water pressing down the front of his body. The water flies from him in a noise, spreads on the floor.

"Sorry," says Beal. "Didn't know you was here."

The stranger stops bathing. The water drips. High up on the right arm is a tattoo of a leaping deer. A twelve-pointer.

"I come to get Pa a spare . . . right over h-hah-here," Beal stammers.

Twelve points. How can Beal count the points in a split second? He paws through the pile of tires. And the deer was done in blue, the trees and hills in red.

"Well . . . I *know* it's right in herè . . . I seen it here . . . last week," Beal murmurs.

The stranger tries to focus. The water drips slower now. The hose deep in the tub makes a sudden gurgle. The man pushes into the tub again as if to dive from a height. The water bucks out of the tub. The floor blackens.

The water divides, makes bright falling sheets down hard on Granville Pollard, like the hissing icy falls come down in Egypt Village, rocking, bucking, trembling over rocks and stumps . . . It also divides this way around the gray penis, in and out, around and down.

Beal's fingers cleave to the worn tread. He rolls the tire into the light, keeping his head down.

The man drives his head into the tub another time, and when he rears back, the water explodes from him . . . and terror rises thickly in Beal's throat . . . terror that Granville Pollard with indescribable morals could be in one glimpse a kind of Santa Claus . . . that Beal in one glimpse would *love* him . . .

"This ain't no sixteen-inch. What the hell's Pa talkin' about?" Beal drops the tire. He raises his head. The stranger is squinting, in his half-sightedness, looking with one green, milky eye at Beal.

12

Beal walks along the newly plowed road. He pictures Death to be a place of no pain, no shame. His pant legs are frozen and they scuff together like heavy canvas. Beal considers the dying part of suicide, those moments between life and death when the body lets go of those shreds of soul. His body perhaps will also be shreds.

His pant legs hit together . . . thwank, thwank, thwank.

Roberta Bean opens the door of her wee blue house, and Beal is swathed in heat and the smell of baking potatoes.

He sleeps on the floor next to her mattress, is wakened in the morning by Roberta's warm old baby, fruity-smelling baby, jumping on him, making wet echoey half-words in his ear.

He's glad he isn't dead.

EARLENE

THREE

The Sons of God

Daddy comes in wearin' his khaki carpenter's clothes and goes straight to the couch and sets on it with his arms folded.

I says, "You ain't mad, are you?"

He says, "I'm sorry, Earlene, but this is goin' ta be a stinky Christmas."

I sit next to him on the couch and put my hand between his shoulder blades. I feel the bumps of his spine with my thumb. I says, "What do you mean, Daddy?"

He says he's been laid off, and there won't be any presents. He jiggles his leg and blows his cheeks in and out.

I pull up his shirt to scratch his back. I scratch shapes of flowers between his shoulder blades. He always likes this. His leg stops jigglin'.

Daddy is the littlest man anywheres. As he sets there on the couch, his shoulders wing out and his proud body

curves inward . . . so from the back he looks like a piece
of celery. He always has a hard time finding his khaki
carpenter's clothes in his size. His belt is always cut off
at the end to get rid of the extra. Lately, I've been
growin' right and left. "A growth spurt," Gram calls it.
I'm almost as big as Daddy. When I'm next to Daddy, I
draw myself down to be smaller.

I look out the picture window. I don't say nuthin'. He
don't say nuthin'. We watch Pa Bean come out on the
steps of his mobile home overway. Daddy's backbone
stiffens under my fingers. Daddy has said a million times
that the Beans breed like flies. I must admit I can't count
'em. The Beans are the only neighbors here on the
right-of-way. And there's Beans all up an' down the road,
and all along the highway to East Egypt. Daddy says even
the Letourneaus got a gallon of Bean blood in each of 'em.

Out there on his step, Pa Bean's got a box and a brown
bag. The wind slices sideways through Pa Bean's stand-
up gray hair. The wind gives the brown bag in Pa Bean's
hand the look of a flutterin' hen.

Daddy's eyes are on Pa Bean. His backbone can
almost cut my hand, it's so sharp and stiff.

Pa Bean takes Christmas lights and a brand-new exten-
sion cord from the bag. Then he lets go of the bag and
the wind takes it. The bag skips, leaps, runs . . . through
the tires, radiators, and parts to old bicycles . . . around a
skidder motor covered with a rug . . . over the right-of-
way . . . into our yard, where it catches on Daddy's wee
gardenia bush.

Daddy narrows his eyes.

We can see a lot through our picture window. We can
see every move the Beans make when they're outdoor.
What they do inside is a mystery. Daddy says what the
Beans do inside their mobile home would make a grown
man cry. In the summertime you see them Beans' plastic

curtains risin' and fallin' in their windows . . . and now
and then a loud grunt or a screech . . . but mostly just the
tinny little crackle of their TV.

Daddy's leg is jigglin' again. I say, "Want me to
make you coffee, Daddy?"

Daddy says, "If there's any left."

I get up and run water into the kettle.

Not only did Daddy build this house and most the
furniture in it, but he also whittles. He whittles little
fishermen, horses, deer, and gulls for Gram to take to the
church fairs. He makes these things right on the rug in
the living room, his legs crossed Indian-style. He hardly
ever sleeps.

I see Pa Bean out through the kitchen door, stringin'
up the little lights to the exact shape of his mobile home.
He scoots along the top of the mobile home on his all
fours, tightening all the little blue bulbs.

Daddy hisses, "They are the tackiest people on earth."

I see the blackberry bushes clawin' up the side of the
Beans' metal walls. Pa Bean looks like a sailor left
behind . . . feelin' over the top of a submarine for a way
to get in, like on TV . . . He doesn't lose control of
hisself.

Daddy's got his face in his hands, like he's fainted into
his hands.

-------------------- **2** --------------------

A couple days have gone. Daddy says he's got me a
Christmas surprise . . . the best thing in all the world.

I says, "Is it an English bike?"

"Better than that," he says.

I squint. I'm dumpin' jelly on toast.

Daddy says that the surprise is a surprise to him, too . . . that he just found out about it. He says, "The Lord is good to us, Earlene."

I press the jelly jar cover on, lap my fingers. "What COLOR is it?"

Daddy shakes his head. "Unh-unh! No guessin'. I'll just say that on the day you get out of school for Christmas vacation, I've gotta drive a hundred miles to get it."

I look into his pale eyes. "Is it somethin' we gotta SHARE?"

He says, "Yes."

There's a thunder out on the right-of-way, the hiss of brakes, the grunt of gears.

The jelly and toast, not even chewed, goes down my throat whole. I see the loggin' truck backin' into our driveway, the giant tires squatted down from the weight of the logs big around as supper tables, mashin' down Daddy's crushed rock. On the door of the truck it says, RUBIE BEAN LOGGING, EGYPT, MAINE, and gives his phone. The boom sways. The mud flaps flutter against the fenders of Daddy's little khaki-color car. Then the truck slides out onto the right-of-way and idles while Rubie Bean goes in to eat dinnah with his mother.

Daddy says stiffly, "Earlene . . . where's your crayons?"

"Whatchoo want 'em for?"

"It's a surprise," he says.

When I come back with them, he's pacin' the kitchen, circlin' the table in quick little steps.

———————————— **3** ————————————

It's the last day of school. Daddy's car's in the yard.

THE SURPRISE IS HERE, I say to myself, steppin' down off the bus.

Comin' down the right-of-way, I stay on my side. The Bean kids stay on their side. The biggest of them is Beal Bean. He's got pimples big as plums. He watches me with his orange-ish eyes in black lashes. Weird eyes. The others keep their eyes down, carrying their battered dinnah pails. They are big and hunched like bears.

Beal Bean says, "Earlene."

I pretend I don't hear that.

He moves to the center of the right-of-way, walkin' in the wheel ruts. Rain has taken all the snow. There's just frozen muck everywheres. "Earlene."

I say, "Go eat a rat."

Daddy's in the picture window lookin' out at me, his face weirdly gray, lines around his mouth.

SOMETHIN' HAS GONE WRONG WITH THE SURPRISE, I say to myself.

Daddy's new sign he made with my crayons is on a good-lookin' lathed post. It says, NO TURNING IN DRIVEWAY!!!! KEEP OUT!!!!

The Beans got a sign, too. It's painted on a metal drum at the edge of their yard. It says, WORMS AND CRAWLERS. It's always been there. Always.

Lizzie Bean and Annie Bean and Rosie Bean and Greggie Bean slow up, narrow their fox-color eyes on Daddy's new sign.

I say, "Hey, you! Ain't you never seen no sign ba-FORE?!!!"

All the fox-color eyes slide onto my face, then scrinch up like the words of the sign are on my forehead.

Then we part ways, them to their trailer, me to the white ranch house with black trim which Daddy built.

A woman is in our livin' room in the rockin' chair, the springs goin' woinka woinka . . . 'cause she's rockin' so fast and hard. Smoke goes out of her cigarette in a tornado shape up to the ceilin' where clouds of smoke roll along. She's got a RED RED mouth.

I says, "Hi."

She says, "Hi."

By her foot is her pocketbook.

I stay in the archway to the kitchen, kneading in my coat pockets. Daddy stays by the picture window.

She springs up, charges at me, waving her arms. "*Look* at that towhead!!!" she gasps. Her voice is hoarse, a sore hoarse. She pulls me to her, and she smells like cigarettes. She mashes my face into her white turtleneck sweater. She's got a cigarette in one hand, Pepsi in the other somewheres behind my head. What a squeeze! Daddy watches.

There's a box of little unpainted sea gulls and fishermen near my foot. Gram will paint them. Gram always handles Daddy's whittled-out birds and things with respect, her eyes on fire behind her readin' glasses. Gram says Daddy is a genius.

The woman kisses me, my face, my hair.

Now she lets me go, veers back to her chair. Her red mouth is smeared now. I imagine some of it is smeared on me. I finger the inside shape of my coat pockets. Her short reddish hair is messy. She drinks off the Pepsi, smokes off the cigarette. She rocks hard and fast, woinka woinka woinka.

"Where's my surprise?" I says to Daddy.

Daddy points at HER.

Woinka woinka woinka.

I look at her . . . the red red mouth sucking, gulping.

Daddy undoes the top button of his shirt . . . lets out his breath.

"Are you Daddy's new girlfriend?" I says.

She laughs around the spout of her Pepsi.

Daddy cries, "EARLENE! This is Mumma! Home for a visit . . . for Christmas. She's with us for Christmas."

"Ain't you *sick*?" I says.

She laughs. She smokes. She rocks.

Daddy says, "Mumma has pills and they make her feel better."

"Oh," I says. I'm startin' to feel hot in my coat. I don't leave the archway. Daddy don't leave the window. He's jigglin' his leg.

"You're all better?" I says.

She smiles, draws from the cigarette, drops the ash onto the rug.

Daddy says, "Mumma feels well enough for a visit."

I squint.

Daddy says, "The Lord is good to us. Praise Him!"

The smoke squirts outta her nose like two side-by-side exhaust pipes. She sets the Pepsi on the table and stops rockin'. "Lee . . . what girlfriends do you have?"

Daddy moves away from the picture window. "None," he says.

She laughs. Starts rockin' again. I see her coat on the couch. And Beatle records. Some still got cellophane on 'em.

"Earlene just *said* that," Daddy says.

"How does she know what a girlfriend is?" she asks. She drinks and smokes and rocks.

"She don't," says Daddy. He goes to the newspapers spread on the rug, kneels, picks up pieces of soft pine, one already showin' the head and shoulders of a gull.

"I ain't STUPID!" I says. "I know what a girlfriend is, Daddy! You think I'm STUPID!"

"Earlene, does Daddy have any girlfriends?" the woman asks.

I squint. "Daddy don't have NO friends."

She laughs. She leans forward into her pocketbook. "Is it four o'clock yet, Lee?"

Daddy nods. With the whiskbroom he swishes some shavings into the dustpan.

She pops off the cap of four or five plastic bottles and lets some pills out into her hand.

I move into the room, over the rug. "When we gettin' the Christmas tree, Daddy?"

Daddy says, "Soon." He stands, then looks around like the living room has become a dark closet.

"When?" I ask.

"Oh, boy! A Christmas tree!" she cries out. As she speaks, her eyes flutter like words hurt her throat. Maybe her throat is why she stays in the hospital. Gram always says that what's wrong with my mother is the works of the DEVIL.

My mother swallows the pills with her Pepsi and sets her pocketbook back on the floor.

I take off my coat, throw it on the couch. I sit on the couch and look at Daddy, slide my eyes over to her. "Can we get the tree now?" I ask Daddy.

"Soon," Daddy says. He paces a little, leans on the wall. He's sweatin' under the arms, on his ribs, like a hot day.

I pull off my boots, throw 'em into the corner. I swing my stockin' feet over the edge of the couch.

She says, "What a pretty outfit."

I says, "Thank you."

I look out the picture window, see Beal Bean by hisself on the steps of the mobile home, throwin' a fan belt for his dog. Beal's hands are bare. In school in the cafeteria, he spreads his big hands around his Thermos and pours brownish stuff into his cup. His nails are dirty, chewed up. The pimples on his face are like volcanoes gettin' ready to bust and drown the world. In school under them lights, all Beans are purple. You sit next to a Bean, you can smell their hot black upright hair giving off the smell of a kerosene stove. I think if you tossed a match at a Bean, they'd burst into flame.

"Want a Pepsi?" The dry sore voice. She's holdin' her Pepsi up. "Your daddy got me a whole carton," she says. Woinka woinka woinka.

Daddy leaves the room. He goes into the bathroom and stays forever.

She rocks. I swing my legs.

A loggin' truck crashes down onto the right-of-way, the empty bed rattlin', clackin'. Our picture window ripples. The pictures of Auntie Paula's new baby and all my cousins in their school clothes swing on their nails. The lamp quivers. My mother looks around. "Christ! What's *that*? . . . For cryin' out loud!"

"Ain't nuthin'," I says. I swing my legs.

Rubie Bean, he's comin' so fast he could be a jet rippin' into the side of this house . . . if you didn't know. Hissss . . . bearing its shadow down on Daddy's little car. I get up and look out at him, Rubie Bean. He's high up on the seat . . . I see him through his gummy side window. She gets up, carries her soda and cigarette to the window. Rubie Bean's got his hat down on his nose so his mustache comes out of it like a black rag. And the mouth chews on itself.

"Jesus Christ," my mother gasps.

Rubie Bean pushes his hat back so he can squint at Daddy's new sign. Then he moves them fox-color eyes over to the picture window with me and her standin' in it. He revs the engine so hard his truck rocks, and the boom in back slices back and forth good as the pendulum of a clock. Then Rubie Bean looks into my mother's eyes and flattens his mouth on the glass like a plunger.

"Holy shit!" she chirps.

I say, "You sure swear a lot, dontcha?"

Then he pulls the loggin' truck outta Daddy's crushed-rock driveway . . . leavin' behind him a dust . . . and parks on the right-of-way facing out. All the little Beans get off the step fast when they see him comin'. They scramble over fan belts, a shovel, plastic toys. When the metal mobile home door slaps behind him, I says to my mother, "He's goin' ta eat a rat."

4

Comes night, it's windy. Leaves and trash from the Beans' yard beat against the front of our house. SHE'S there on Daddy's bed, snorin'. The night-light makes its cheese-color glow on the knotty pine walls. Her pocketbook and white turtleneck sweater are over the chair along with Daddy's clothes.

Daddy opens my door. "Earlene?" He snaps the light switch and the hundred-watt bulb up there comes to life. I cover my face.

He sets on the bed. He's wearin' only long-john bottoms. His hair, usually combed with water, is ragged fluff. He rubs his face.

I says, "What's goin' on with HER?"

He says softly, "Sleepin'."

"She sleeps a lot," I says.

He raises his knee, cups one heel with his hands.

I says, "Ain't we ever goin' ta get a tree?"

He closes his eyes.

"DADDY! Ain't we gonna celebrate Christmas? First you say no presents. We gonna skip havin' a tree, too?"

"I can't think," he says softly. Opens his eyes. "I'm goin' *crazy*."

I sit up. "Me, too," I says.

He looks through the open doors at HER on the bed.

"Ain't you goin' in there?" I says.

"I been in there," he says.

"Ain't you goin' in there again?"

He looks at me, drops his foot to the floor with a thump.

"Well," I sigh. "You ain't GOTTA go in there."

He slumps. I find his backbone with my fingers, press it and knead it. He stops breathin', draws back his shoulders to make the celery trough in his back.

I say, "Is it all right with Gram you go in there?"

"Earlene!" He swings around to look at me.

I feel my face get hot. "But Daddy . . . what I mean is Gram knows what God wants. You KNOW! You wanna know what's on God's mind . . . Gram knows . . . Gram's smart! I was only thinkin' about what GOD wants."

Daddy shrugs. "Well, it's all right with God if I go in there with my wife."

I say, "Are you scared, Daddy?"

He don't talk, just blows his cheeks in and out.

I say, "I'm scared. She *is* creepy . . . ain't she, Daddy? Ain't she creepy?"

"Oh, she's all right," says Daddy. "It's not as bad as they all make out."

"I'm glad I'm not YOU!" I says. "I'm glad I don't gotta go in THERE."

He closes his eyes, rocks his head and shoulders slowly back and forth.

Then he leaves . . . and for the rest of the night I hear him out there on the living room rug, sawing and hammering on the colonial bread box he's making Auntie Paula for Christmas.

5

In the mornin' Gramp drives Gram over to bring my angel suit for the pageant. When they leave, I sit on the couch and watch TV, swingin' my legs . . . wearin' my angel suit. My mother comes out for the first time, in the same white sweater. "Brrrrr! Ain't it cold!" she snorts.

Daddy flicks up the thermostat.

I says, "Daddy! When we goin' for the tree?"

He leans against the archway, watching her settle herself in the rocking chair with a Pepsi. "Don't you want breakfast, Jeanette?" he says softly.

Woinka woinka woinka woinka. "Naaa. This is all I ever eat. Pepsi freak, you know." And she laughs, deep dry moans of laughter.

"DAAAAAADDY!" I scream.

"What, Earlene?"

"Ain't we GOIN'?"

"Not right now."

She gets up, puts a Beatle record on Daddy's record player with her left hand, Pepsi in her right, cigarette in her teeth. "Hey!" I narrow my eyes. "How'm I gonna hear this TV?"

Daddy cuts off the TV.

I give Daddy a raw look.

Daddy goes back to the archway.

The Beatles start singin' their latest. "Well . . . I guess we can FORGET Christmas," I snarl. "No tree." I jiggle my body so my flower-print angel wings flap.

She looks square at me, but don't say nuthin'. She don't seem to notice what I'm wearin'. So I work the wings some more. She slouches back in her rockin' chair, nods, and sorta sings along with the Beatles. Her eyes are closed and her mouth moves. But no REAL singin' comes outta her RED RED mouth. Woinka woinka woinka.

"Is it ten yet, Lee?" she asks.

Daddy says no.

I gotta yell to get 'em ta hear me over the Beatles. "DADDY! WHEN WE GET THE TREE, WHERE WE GONNA PUT IT? USUALLY IT GOES WHERE HER CHAIR IS!"

She don't open her eyes.

Daddy says, "Earlene, let's not worry about it, okay? You're makin' an issue."

I make a fart noise with my lips. Everything I look at is through the furry blue lines of her smoke.

I start walkin' around on the rug in my angel suit. She don't open her eyes. "PEACE ON EARTH GOOD WILL TO MEN!!" I scream. I spread my arms. This is durin' the silence between Beatle songs. Then the Beatles start a new song. A fast one. I walk faster.

"It's turned off quite cold, Jeanette," Daddy says.

She don't answer. She makes her lips go to the words of the fast Beatle song.

"PEACE ON EARTH GOOD WILL TO MEN!!!" I scream again, jumpin' up and down. My cousins' pictures sway on their nails.

Daddy says, "My mother says it's goin' to snow. Don't it seem too cold to snow?"

I jerk to a stop in front of Daddy, my flower-print wings saggin'. "Snow!"

But he's lookin' hard at my mother.

Suddenly her eyes open. She says, "Who's your favorite Beatle, Earlene?"

"Ringo," I says.

She says, "I love Paul."

Daddy takes his hand from the archway frame.

Woinka woinka woinka woinka . . .

Daddy says, "Get your coat, Earlene."

"We gettin' a TREE?!!"

"Yep."

She says, "Is it ten yet, Lee?"

He says no.

I says to her, "Are YOU goin' with us to get a Christmas tree?"

"Naaaa. I'm not much of an outdoor girl." The Beatles are singin' another slow song. It's Paul. She looks at the record player, closes her eyes, hugs herself.

Daddy puts on his parka and goes to the cellar stairs for his axe.

I throw my angel suit on my bed . . . She turns up the music . . . Her smoke rolls down the hall and follows me into my room.

------------------------------ 6 ------------------------------

Daddy ain't waitin' up for me. I say, "Daddy! Daddy!" He passes the mailboxes, holdin' the axe close to his body. Little Beans huddled on their front steps in their snowsuits laugh at me while I'm runnin', while I'm callin' "Slow up, Daddy!!" wavin' my arms. I scream at the Beans, "NOSE TROUBLE!!"

They look at each other and giggle wildly.

My socks sag around my ankles. I reach in my boots, pull my socks up one at a time.

I scream, "Daddy! Wait up!" but he don't.

The Beans tee-hee and snort with laughter . . . Them

and their dog come to the edge of their yard ... narrowing their fox-color eyes on me, their snowsuits sliskin'.

I run.

"He's sure anxious to get a Christmas tree," I mutter.

I look back and the Beans've lost interest in me. They've gone to heave a fan belt to the dog.

As I pass the mailboxes I run hard.

But Daddy ... he speeds up, too.

"Daddy! I'm HERE!" I call.

Big white rags of snow start ploppin' down. The ground gets white quick. My socks drop.

I don't see Daddy nowheres. I yank up my socks. In a while I see his tracks in the new snow. The tracks turn into the woods, over a stone wall, down a steep gully. Then in the blackness of softwoods, I hear Daddy's axe. I pull up my socks. I zigzag through bushes and then I see him cuttin' a spruce taller than three houses. I say, "JEEEEZ!"

His breath comes out like white cabbages. I sit on a rock, my chin in my palms, my eyes on him. I say in a low voice, "This is BEAN land." I take a breath, narrow my eyes in the spaces between trees. Somewhere Beans are out there watchin' us.

Daddy stops hackin'. Takes off his parka. His khaki shirt is wet all up and down. His hair is like a wild man. Then he moves toward the spruce, swings the axe with his whole body.

"Maybe they'll hang us in their barn. EAT us. Beans will eat anythin'," I say to myself. I pull up my socks.

Daddy gasps, the axe takin' out big bites. Snow sticks to the fine hair on his arms. His back twists in a kind of fit. The snow drops all around like white mittens, white hats. It fills in the land. I never seen such fast, big snow. Daddy goes around to the other side of the tree and hacks on that side. His face is red and wet.

I say into my fingers, "How's he plan to get that thing into the house?"

I hear the tree crackin'. It drops like a hundred trees. It fills the path with branches and an explosion of snow. Some of the snow flies in my face.

Now there's no sound, just Daddy standin' there with his pale eyes like dimes, lookin' at me. I don't say nuthin'. Then the wind lifts with a hiss and a howl. Snow drops from limbs of other trees with a thump. I look at Daddy through the blowin' snow. Daddy leans on his axe.

Birds fly out of a balsam and I see Daddy's eyes follow them. He's motionless except for his turning eyes.

I chirp, "Jeez, Daddy! You call THAT a Christmas tree!"

He moves his eyes back from the birds to my face. He looks at the tree like it had a mouth and just called him a name.

I say, "Daddy, we need a better tree than that! Jeez, Daddy!"

But he's still lookin' at the tree, kneading the axe handle with his fingers. His eyes get big, then bigger and BIGGER and BIGGER.

He jumps on the Christmas tree, his mouth a savage curl. He holds the tree down with his foot. He hacks. Slivers splash up. The arms of the tree quiver, struggle. He bashes those limbs with his heel. He jumps all over. He don't stop actin' this way till the tree's in a million pieces.

7

After the Christmas pageant at church, Auntie Paula drops me off at the top of the right-of-way 'cause it ain't plowed yet. It's pitch dark. I wear my coat over my angel suit. The wings make enormous blobs on my back. Down on the right-of-way, the blue Christmas lights of the Beans blink and wrinkle so the mobile home changes shape before my eyes.

Daddy said he's sorry, but he had a headache and couldn't make the pageant. When I left with Auntie Paula, he was on the couch with his hands between his knees, lookin' at my mother's snorin' red red mouth. I imagine he's still there now, limp hair, limp half-smile, watchin' her by the light of the kitchen coming through the archway.

My knee hits a drift.

Then a flashlight flutters over the snow and trees, burns between my shoulder blades. I turn around fast. It's Beal Bean . . . with a new haircut . . . nearly bald . . . his head and face big and bare as the broad, white Bean land behind the mobile home.

"Quit it!" I scream.

He makes a snowball. It splats between my feet.

"MISSED!" I scream.

"I missed on p-peeeee-pah-purpose!" he screams back.

"You hit me with any more snowballs, I'm callin' the deputy!!!" I says.

The jaw. Daddy says Beans got the Cro-Magnon look. Bean mouths always got slack. And in the slack is their chunky yellow teeth.

Beal Bean says, "Earlene, you wanna see somethin'? A m-m-mah-miracle?"

I says, "No-suh. I don't wanna see no miracles. I HATE miracles!"

"You'll like this miracle. Honest."

I stop, let him catch up. He is in fifth grade . . . stayed back a million times . . . big as a man. He looks down at my angel suit hangin' out under my coat. He puts the flashlight there.

"Quit it!" I roar.

He moves the spot of light over the snow. He's breathin' through his mouth.

"What color is this old miracle?" I ask.

"You'll see," he says.

I watch his back as he lunges ahead of me, leadin' the way. I can make out in the darkness the white curve of his Sherpa collar.

He is goin' to get me behind the trailer of Beans where ten big Beans, ten big ugly Beans, will grab me and kill me. They are probably mad about what Daddy did to that Christmas tree on their side of the brook. "PEACE ON EARTH GOOD WILL TO MEN!" I scream.

His long legs drive through the snow with ease. I try to use his footprints . . . but his footprints are deep like dug wells.

"PEACE ON EARTH!" I sing.

He don't say nuthin'.

I say, "That was my lines in the pageant, you know. At church. I go to church. I know Beans don't never go to church. You prob'ly ain't never heard 'bout peace on earth 'n' stuff."

He stops and looks at me. He don't say nuthin'. In school in the cafeteria he don't never talk. Just chews his lunch and looks at his hands. I think how if he keeps stayin' back, I go past him, and graduate, and Beal Bean will just go on forever in fifth grade . . . eatin' rat sandwiches and gettin' bigger and BIGGER and BIGGER.

I says, "At church we sang Christmas songs. 'Silent Night.' And 'Hark! The Herald Angels Sing'!!"

The brownish spot of his flashlight moves over the snow, near the hem of my angel suit.

I say, "Gram says Hark! all year long. If there's a

noise in the yard...you know, a noise...she says, Hark! And you gotta listen. Ain't that a funny word?''

The brown spot moves even CLOSER to my hem. I says, ''Do you think all old ladies say Hark? Does your aunties say Hark?''

''I guess,'' he says softly. He springs the light onto my angel suit.

''GET THAT OFFA ME!!!'' I scream.

He says, ''You're weird.''

He knees into the snow, aimin' the flashlight on the hills of snow which is the junk Beans always keep in their yard. When we're at the back of the trailer, Beal Bean moves his eyes over me. He puts the flashlight on an opening in the trailer skirting. That's where the pipes are under the floor. ''In there is th-th-thaah-the miracle,'' he says.

''You ain't gettin' me in there,'' I says, trying to hold my angel suit out of the snow...This suit is actually Gram's old lace tablecloth.

His fox-color eyes hold mine. My skin prickles with fear. ''It's neat in there,'' he says.

We hear squeaks.

My eyes widen. ''Rats. You call that a miracle?'' I back away.

He smiles. ''Ain't rats. It's something you'll laww-law-love...Honest.''

Even as I duck down to look, somethin' ugly sloshes down the Beans' drain above my right ear. ''I don't see nuthin' in there,'' I says.

''Go in,'' he says. He puts the flashlight in my hands. I hear him breathin' through his mouth. My heart shakes in my chest. I go down on all fours.

There's a low growl...the thump of a tail.

Then I see the black dog with the bluish-whitish eyes. Around her a mound of moving parts...like smaller pieces of herself. Puppies. They charge toward me, flying at my face. They box at me with their little feet. They pass over me from all directions . . . seems like fifty of them. They lap and suck my eyes. They tug on my soggy angel suit. They are everywhere, dragging me down.

Overhead, the Beans walk over the mobile home floor in heavy parade.

The mother dog keeps her eyes on me.

I am on every inch of me stingin' with pain . . . a trillion needle teeth.

Beal comes up beside me on his knees. He says, "These puppies don't have no father."

"So what?" I gasp, a puppy snatchin' away my holly halo.

He says "No father" in a deep manlike voice. He cradles the mother dog's head in his hands.

I blink up at Beal Bean, the flashlight laying in the dirt making only the undersides of his face show, the Cro-Magnon jaw, the two holes of his nose.

He says, "Wouldn't that make 'em the sons of God?"

I work my breath up slow. I work my fingers in the dirt.

THE BEANS

FOUR
Buzzy Atkinson's Paper-Plate Kiss

What's that racket?'' Artie asks.

Marie Bean keeps a couch in her kitchen . . . and this is what Artie usually does . . . lays on it and looks at magazines . . . the kind with black-and-white pictures of women motorcyclists with their shirts around their waists . . . and Artie eats. He's broad across the chest and has a double chin . . . the only one of Marie's boys who hasn't quit school to work in the woods.

Artie eats baloney sandwiches, peanut butter on a spoon, carrots, ice cubes . . . anything he can find.

"That's one of them Letourneaus comin' for the junks," Marie says, squinting through the glass oven door at her pies. She sees herself. Pats her hair. Adjusts her glasses.

Artie sits up, pitches his magazine onto the end table littered with magazines and a wagon-wheel lamp. He lights up a cigarette. "Ma! You're gonna get a bust in the head when Dad hears this," he says, standing up, pulling the yellow curtain aside.

Down the crumbly road roars the car hauler, says, LETOURNEAU'S USED AUTO PARTS on the door.

Suddenly, the back part of the house shakes. It's Otis out on the glassed-in porch. He rolls his nose along the panes. He sees the junkman riding with his arm out, wearing gloves. Reflections of overhead maples drizzle over the car-hauler windshield.

"Which Letourneau is it?" Marie asks her boy, patting her hair again . . . her ten-dollar permanent . . . with a black rinse that doesn't quite cover up all the gray at her temples.

"Damned if I know . . . Can't make him out," says Artie. He blows smoke out of his nose. Rubs his stomach. Yawns.

Otis sniffs under the porch door. A growl flickers low in his chest.

The kitchen smells of mincemeat. It's Marie's day off from working at the office of Allen's Oil. Her cooking day. She goes to the window herself and stands behind Artie, peering past his wrist . . . her cold blue-eyed stare . . . her rimless glasses reflecting the car hauler as it sweeps by them. "It's Buzzy Atkinson," she almost whispers.

"They prob'ly sent him 'cause they don't wanna throw away one of their better mechanics," says Artie, turning from the window. " 'Cause if Dad comes around while he's messin' with his rigs, there's gonna be broken bones." He sniffs, goes to the refrigerator, drags out a new jar of green olives.

Marie says, "I got bills to pay. If Rubie Bean thinks he can prance around with that ticket he's shacked up with now . . . and stick *me* with the bills, he's got a surprise comin'."

Otis doesn't know one Letourneau from another. He

gallops from one end of the glassed-in porch to the other, his nose sucking along the outside wall.

Marie takes two mincemeat pies from the oven, sets them on cutting boards. She can smell the exhaust of the car hauler here in the kitchen as Buzzy Atkinson backs up to her ex-husband Rubie Bean's fifteen-year-old Caddy in mint shape with its wheels on concrete blocks. Marie still wears her wedding ring, a brutish silver band with hearts slashed into it. She says, "Don't touch these pies, Artie."

Artie is looking at the pies.

"You got two of 'em!" he says, his voice croaking inside his double chins. He has a softness across the eyes that the other two boys don't have. Although he shows no interest in logging with Rubie and has Marie's taut, unplayful mouth, he has rages ... He is his father's son.

He gets a fork for the olives, sits at the table ... slides a magazine in front of him.

Otis is shaking the porch with his wish to get out. Sometimes, Otis makes messes on the linoleum. The glass porch is cold. He doesn't want to be there, ever. He is only happy with Marie ... to drop his bread-box-sized muzzle into her lap, to have her twirl his ears. Marie. Her whisper.

Marie says she has plans for the pies. She goes into the bathroom, which is off the kitchen, closes the door.

Artie listens to Buzzy Atkinson working the winch ... the whine of the winch ... knowing the Caddy is rearing up. He says, "That Buzzy Atkinson's married to one of Willie Letourneau's sisters. He's got the brain of a flea. Did you hear what he did at Gaston's last summer? Dad was tellin' ... Remember?"

"No," she says through the door. She is brushing her hair, her heart racing.

"Yee-hah!! Ma! You gotta see this one . . . a broad fuckin' an eel!"

"You ain't handlin' them pies, are you?"

"No!" he croaks. "I'm settin' right here!"

"You been known to throw your voice."

He whispers to himself, "Wonder where they get eels that Christly huge . . . prob'ly some rare ocean kind . . . Jesus . . . I can't stand it." He whimpers. Jiggles his leg.

The winch stops.

Otis mashes his face to the glass . . . the juices of his lips hanging like stalactites.

Outside, Buzzy Atkinson looks at the house for the first time, looks right into Otis's eyes. Otis's nose is steaming.

Buzzy Atkinson has let his crew cut grow out the front of his orange tie-up hunting hat, and the hair sticks out and up like the gray horn of a rhino. He stands in a way you'd think he has cement in his gloves . . . pulling forward . . . like his back is about to give out from the weight of them. The gloves are the orange fuzzy kind with blackened fingers and palms. He scratches his loose, stubbly cheeks, his massive lips, with the glove of his right hand. Then he scratches his ribs. He moans. In his left glove is a receipt book, the cold wind flapping at the yellow sheets.

Marie comes out of the bathroom. Artie's with the mince pies, feeling them. He says, "Don't Buzzy Atkinson have ten kids?"

"That's what I heard," she says. She crosses the room.

"That's stupid," Artie croaks.

He gets himself a paper plate and the stainless-steel pie server. "Well, all them kids are goin' ta be fatherless soon." He chuckles.

Marie goes through the front room. She pulls open the

front door and goes out on the step with her arms folded across her white shirt, the wind slapping at her ten-dollar hairdo. "Hey! Mr. Junkman!" she shouts.

The sun shows behind the haze like a flashlight behind lacy curtains.

Buzzy lopes up over the grass, his gloved hands leading the way. He walks from the knees, and his loose lips and cheeks flutter. He scratches his belly as he hikes along. He doesn't look directly at Marie, avoids her cold, blue-eyed stare. "Ayuh," moans Buzzy. "You got a bear out behind. Charge extra for the worry."

"Mr. Atkinson...wouldn't you like some mincemeat?"

"Prob'ly," he says. He stops, pawing at his opposite shoulder, looks back at the car hauler. "To take with me?"

"Why don't you come in? You a coffee drinker?"

"Ayup." He follows her inside.

He smells like the underneath of a car. His smell swells to fit the whole front room, billowing from his orange work gloves and green work clothes like a stinging, puckery, black smoke.

When they enter the kitchen, one pie is gone, Artie is gone.

"Have a seat, Mr. Atkinson," says Marie, patting her hair. "How do you like your coffee?"

"Half coffee, half can milk." He looks at the table, the magazine spread open showing a young woman with an enormous eel passing into her deepmost parts...a look on her face of fatigue. Black-and-white. Buzzy's eyes widen. Then he looks away fast.

"Oh, I'm sorry. I'm fresh out of canned milk," says Marie. "Had a chowder couple nights ago. Want some reg'lar Oakhurst?" She studies him with eyes so pale they seem at a glance to be aluminum behind those metal-rimmed glasses.

"Ayuh," says Buzzy Atkinson. He scratches the back of his neck. A wooden clothes rack over the hot-air register catches Buzzy's eyes. Wool socks and T-shirts and dishtowels lifting up on the blowing heat show in fluttery miniature on his eyes. He moans.

"You can sit down, Mr. Atkinson." She smiles.

"Oh, yuh . . . I know . . . in a minute." He looks at her, his loose cheeks quivering. He has green eyes. Broad shoulders. Looks like two pencils along his neck, such startled-up veins. He leaves on his hat, leaves on his nasty gloves.

Marie turns away, thinking about his green eyes.

Meanwhile, a suspicious silence comes from the glassed-in porch.

"How many kids you got, Mr. Atkinson?"

"Ten."

She turns with a glass cup and shoots her icy eyes into his green ones. "Sit down. Sit down!" she commands. Not smiling.

He sits. He rests his elbow directly over the eel and the legs. Marie sets his coffee by his gloved hands and his yellow receipt pad. "Ten," she says softly. "Your wife sounds like a wonderful woman."

Buzzy Atkinson stirs his coffee.

"You must have a wonderful relationship," Marie says softly, cutting into the pie. The steam explodes from it, fogs her glasses. She wipes them on the sleeve of her white shirt. She says, "You must be very *close*."

Buzzy says, "Ayuh." He sips his coffee. A quiet flutter of the big lips . . . nothing like Rubie Bean's evil snorts.

She lowers a piece of pie onto a large blue-print plate with mincemeat and crust sprawled to the very edges. The steam roils up and is divided into two steams by Buzzy's horn of gray hair. He wriggles his gloved fingers. Moans.

She thrusts a tarnished silver fork at him . . . wild-rose pattern . . . He opens his gloved hand for it.

"Take off your gloves," she says.

He looks around. Panicked.

She brings herself a tiny wedge of pie and sits.

"Do you know my ex-husband?" she asks, her blue eyes hammering his gloves.

"Heard of him," Buzzy Atkinson says. He has a voice as soft as her own, the two soft voices meeting together over the table like the two steams from the two pieces of pie, entwining.

He paws violently at his ribs.

"Thought you might," Marie chuckles. "Well, he's a no-good bastard."

Buzzy puts his gloved hands together to wring them a time or two, lowers his enormous lips to his cup. The lips flutter over the cup like the lips of a gentle cow.

"He's livin' with a young girl now, up off Seavy Road . . . You heard about that?"

"A little," he says softly. His green eyes draw the kitchen into them. She can see little kitchens on each of his eyes, green kitchens with dewy refrigerators, mossy stoves.

"And of course the girl is in the family way already." Marie sniffs, raises a fork of mincemeat to her open teeth. "This mincemeat is from a deer Rubie caught seven years ago . . . Don't that man *love* to kill . . . don't matter the season . . . son of a bitch."

The mincemeat in Buzzy's mouth tosses over his tongue, crashes upon the walls of his enormous cheeks. He moans.

"Don't worry, Mr. Atkinson . . . The seal was good. I used all brand-new jars that year." She isn't smiling. She almost never smiles. She pats his gloved hand. "Mr. Atkinson! Take them gloves off, heavens to Betsy!"

He looks at his gloves.

She says, "Good riddance to bad rubbish, right? Let him go an' make an ass of hisself. Right?"

His green eyes show two Maries melting, soft as squash, Marie with her mouth ajar.

"Ayuh," says Buzzy.

Marie says, "I tell you I couldn't live no longer with his rages. He would get ugly over the teensiest things. You know Bernie Merrill?"

"I don't think so," says Buzzy.

"Well, tell me what you think of this, if this is something you could live with. This happened when the kids was small. In fact, I don't think Stephen was born yet. Well . . . Bernie . . . Bernie Merrill . . . I bet you do know him . . . He was comin' up through the village in an empty trailer rig . . . runnin' chips for Dunlap . . . You know Jimmy Dunlap, dontcha?"

"No," says Buzzy. He moans.

"Well . . . anyways . . . we're in Rubie's old beast . . . his loggin' rig . . . You seen it, ain't you? It's red . . . the fenders all stove up from Rubie goin' out each mornin' and punchin' it with his fist first thing. You know the truck I mean?"

Buzzy slumps. "Ayuh."

"We were goin' up ta Pa's . . . I think Rubie was gonna drop us off at Pa's that day . . . an' Bernie comes along an' passes us on the straight-away, you know. And our mirrors touch." She squints. "Bernie taps his horn . . . you know? And guess what? Rubie *rams the gas!!* Imagine that! I say, 'Rubie, he was just bein' friendly; he didn't mean to hit your ol' mirror.' Rubie's face ain't got a sprig of color."

Buzzy's working the fork quite smoothly with his gloves. Marie watches the gloves.

"After Bernie gets clear of us, he . . . Bernie . . . steps

on it. He's got a newer rig...a *lot* more horsepower, leaves us in the dust. Rubie practically stands on the throttle...*Both feet*. I says, 'Reuben, the man was just bein' friendly. He don't mean for you to act like a baby.'

"You won't believe this, Mr. Atkinson, but my husband was so pissed off he was *droolin'*. Spit springin' from his mouth like a dog. Spit foamin' off his mustache. Honest. I swear on ten Bibles. Christopher was cryin'. And I'm screamin' at Rubie, 'You're gonna kill us all!'

"Well, I couldn't believe it...The old beast catches up with Bernie's rig...Maybe Bernie let him. Bernie's just as crazy as Rubie, anyways. Are you sure you wouldn't know Bernie if you saw him? Ol' Duck Eyes, I always call him...and he's got a nose out ta here."

"No," says Buzzy. "Can't place him." Buzzy's plate is almost clean. He leans down and scratches his shin.

Marie studies Buzzy: his neck with the puckered arteries. The smell of auto parts, black and thickened by cold, seems to churn out not only from the gloves but from his open collar, his dirty T-shirt.

"Well," sighs Marie, hardly touching her pie. "The two trucks are side by side...really honkin'...and there's a hill, a *curvy hill*...Can you believe that? And from my window, I look over at Bernie. He's lookin' in at us. So of course, he sees Rubie droolin'. And you know what I felt like, Mr. Atkinson?"

"No," says Buzzy, setting down his fork.

Marie shakes her head. "It weren't fear. It was *shame*! I was embarrassed to have that fella see my husband droolin' like a Christly hound." She sniffs.

There's a thump on the glassed-in porch and Marie howls, "ARTIE! IF YOU ATE THAT WHOLE PIE, YOU'RE GROUNDED FOR A YEAR! AND NO MOTORCYCLE!"

She narrows her eyes on Buzzy, who's finishing his coffee. "More coffee?"

He shakes his head.

"Well," she says, "Bernie Merrill...he lets up...slides back...prob'ly took pity on me and the kids. When we get to East Egypt, Rubie pulls over, goes into the store for somethin'...and you know?...he walks into that store like nuthin' happened. His color come back...His drool's wiped up. He's smilin'. A normal man, you might think."

Another thump. Buzzy turns his head toward the door to the porch. "Sure that noise ain't your dog?" he says.

"No...that's Artie plannin' to sneak out here and scoff up this other pie. Have another piece."

"No, thanks, Mrs. Bean." He looks at the door to the porch, swallows. "You know...me an' dogs...we don't get along."

She pats her hair.

"Well," says Buzzy. He stands up. "Gotta get the Caddy back to the yard. I'll be back for the others Monday. It's too late to do much more."

She stares at his gloved hands.

His eyes go everywhere but to the eel and the languishing legs. He stands behind his chair with his gloved hands on the back. "You wouldn't mind, Mrs. Bean...if I...I...I used your flush a minute, would you?"

"No! Of course not...Help yourself. There it is." She points to the door, partly open, revealing a shower curtain with leaping dolphins.

"I wouldn't bother you...but...it's wicked bad." He rubs his lower stomach.

"No problem," Marie assures him. She goes to the sink with the plates. "Just be sure you jiggle the handle after, or it will trickle all day."

He leaves his yellow receipt pad on the table, nods,

disappears, his gloved hand pushing the door shut, engaging the hook and eye.

She rinses the dishes.

Then from the glassed-in porch, Artie Bean lunges...and a piano-sized black dog pushes past him. Otis, terrific nose, traces the junkman's bootsteps to the bathroom door. Otis flexes his lips. Then he rams his shoulder, gorillalike, to the door.

"Mrs. Bean?" says the voice in the bathroom.

Otis stands taller than any man with forepaws on the door. A gurgly growl.

"Mrs. Bean?"

Artie's wearing a brown leather jacket now. It says Harley-Davidson across the back. Artie says, "Is that the fella in there that Dad's gonna cream? Is that him in there?"

Otis digs at the bottom of the bathroom door. Linoleum peels up.

Something goes dark in Marie's heart.

Otis covers the keyhole with his nose...snorts.

"Mrs. Bean...are you out there?"

The smells of mincemeat, the junkman, and the messy porch suspend her. Her mouth is stuck on the half-syllable of a word. Artie chews his thumbnail. "Yes, Artie, that's him," she says softly at last.

She walks with rubbery legs to the glassed-in porch to clean up the fresh dog messes...and to fetch the empty pie plate, pie server, and paper plate from one of the porch chairs.

2

When Marie gets home from work Monday, Rubie Bean's unloaded logging truck is in the yard and he is sitting on the well cover looking up at Artie, who's smoking. Artie is wearing his leather jacket, unzipped. When Marie shuts her engine off, Rubie stands up. His black mustache retreats from twisted teeth only when he smiles. She drags a bag of groceries across the seat with trembling hands.

Otis, who is lying at Rubie's feet, springs up.

From the distance Rubie's eyes look like two lighted candles.

Artie throws down his cigarette, walks on it.

Otis pounds down the driveway toward her and jumps on her camel-color coat. "Down!" she commands. He drops down.

Rubie's hands rise from his body. And Artie has the same rigidness come to his limbs and terrible terrible grinning mouth.

Her camel-color coat flaps against her legs as she hikes up the driveway to the glassed-in porch. The smell of dog mess lands in her face as she enters.

Rubie runs up behind her, puts both hands on her shoulders . . . feels to Marie like the two squeezing feet of a hawk readying to lift her, Marie, a mouse, away.

She closes her eyes.

"*Why* are you here now, Rubie? I ain't seen you in *three* months."

He is breathing raggedly from running. Otis pushes between them, tries to sniff in the bag.

Rubie twists her around, but she keeps her eyes shut.

His tobacco-smelling voice: "Think you're smart, dontcha?"

Artie is somewhere beyond her closed eyes . . . past Rubie's shoulder . . . Artie, with his muscled arms cocked in the sleeves of his motorcycle jacket . . . pacing.

Marie says, "I sold them because"—she opens her

eyes—"because I had to pay off those loans...the taxes...and get the furnace cleaned, okay?" He is still grinning.

She sighs. "Reuben...I *had* to. You did not..." She cannot stand looking into his boiling, fox-color eyes. She looks away. "You did not want those cars and trucks until you realized they were gone. Who told you they were gone?"

Rubie grins bigger. "Artie."

Marie won't look at Artie. She can picture him, but she won't focus.

She says to Rubie, "I'll call the deputy if you touch me...This is not the old days...Go maul your new sweetie pie."

Otis hunkers down to scratch. The floor seems to shake out from under them.

Rubie looks down into Marie's grocery bag. The haggard mustache closes down as if there were no mouth. "There's *one* rig left...down in the alders," he says. "Miss that one?"

"No...I guess the junkman didn't have time to pick that one up today. But I see while I was at work, he had no trouble with the others."

Rubie strokes his mustache with his fingers and stumps of fingers. "So you think he's comin' back, huh?"

She backs away, reaching with her free hand for the kitchen door.

But he moves with her like they're dancing. She catches sight of Artie, lighting up another cigarette, the orange glimmer of the match scuttling over his cheeks and the palms of his hands.

She sees herself reflected on the many glass panes... dozens of panes, dozens of gray-templed, blue-eyed Maries...

"Rubie, go home!"

The hands crush down, gathering up the camel-color coat.

Her glasses leap, clatter to the floor. Rubie's plain wool shirt becomes a black-and-red blur.

Somewhere Artie is watching, perhaps taking a step forward. His leather jacket squeaks.

Otis rises taller than a man, sawing the air with his forepaws, rakes Rubie's sleeve. Rubie elbows him. *"Yipe!!"* Otis falls away.

Rubie draws the plastic gallon of milk from the bag. Under Rubie's boot the metal nosepiece and earpieces of Marie's glasses change shape with a *chirp*! Rubie squeezes. The jug explodes.

Loops of milk stretch in all directions...mostly on the camel-color coat. Otis gets a faceful. He blinks and yeowls. On Rubie's wool shirt, there are bluish-white stars. He is screaming with laughter. He twists the empty plastic jug above her head and it drips into the ten-dollar permanent.

He pinches her cheek, almost lovingly. "You was always *fun*. No one can say you ain't a *fun* woman." He wheels away.

After the logging truck clatters down onto the main road, the limbs of trees shaking behind, Artie comes onto the porch and sits on a chair by a giant Christmas cactus, watching Otis lap up milk, lapping around the mangled eyeglasses, and through the cactus he also can see his mother holding her face.

3

The next day Marie calls in sick. While brownies are in the oven, she showers, then shakes baby powder on.

Most of it splatters her feet. She buttons up a blouse she rarely wears, pink with tiny red dots; close up, the dots are wee hearts. She yanks on a pair of tight jeans, a narrow belt with horses tooled into it. She slashes the brush through her perm.

Artie's in school.

She drinks coffee in the front room, watching *As the World Turns* through the blue blur of having no glasses, and twirling Otis's ears. She gets up during commercials to squint down the road.

When the car hauler grumbles to a stop in the yard, she drags Otis to the glassed-in porch. She sees through the panes of the porch the car hauler backing slowly down into the alders. She can see in a fuzzy way the orange glove, the face in the side mirror. She knows he plans to make it quick. He will never come in her house again.

She puts on the old pea coat she wears for dirty jobs. She wraps the brownies in aluminum foil, lowers them into a grocery bag, adds a jug of milk, two paper cups, paper plates, napkins, and the yellow receipt pad he left on the table.

She hurries through the front room and out.

He is winching up the last car; his back is to her, the sleeve of his green workshirt showing, a glove on the lever.

When he sees her, his green eyes widen, Her face is grave, gray. He eyes the bag.

"Hello!" she shouts over the yowl of the winch. He averts his eyes.

"Would you like a brownie?!!"

He works his tongue behind his thick lips. "Can I take it with me? I'm in a rush!"

She frowns.

His green eyes drop. "Well, I ain't goin' in *there*!" he shouts, thrusting his head toward her house.

"I know! I know!" she cries. "I'm sorry about that."

With his free hand, he scratches his chest. "Me and dogs . . . we don't get along," he says.

"I know!" she says. "What if we sit out here under this tree?!" She points at a maple that's growing out of an old foundation where a barn once stood. The rocks are heaved about like dinosaur eggs in the high, gray grass.

He frowns.

When the car is in place, Buzzy Atkinson cuts off the winch and the engine. The silence is spoiled only by a woodpecker giggling in the alders and by Otis's low, evil growl from the glassed-in porch.

Marie hurries to the maple, stepping over tne rocks. Buzzy ambling, moaning. She kneels, spreads out the paper plates, pours milk.

He doesn't sit. Stands. "Won't you get cold?" he says softly.

"No. *Please* sit down."

"I guess," he says dully. Squats.

"That ain't sittin'," Marie says.

So he sits. Raises his knees.

She puts a brownie on his plate. "You like milk?" she asks.

"Ayuh."

He takes off his orange hunting hat, which has the flaps tied up, and he digs into his outgrown crew cut with his gloved hand. Then slaps the hat back on.

He swallows all his milk.

She pours him more.

The brownie moves inside his mouth like the fibrous cud of a cow.

"Help yourself!" chirps Marie. "Let's eat all these brownies right up."

"All of them?" he whispers.

"Mmmmmm." She chews fast and noisily. "Don't you just *love* brownies?"

"I like 'em okay."

"Does your wife make brownies?"

He looks her in the eye. "We have Jell-O."

Marie makes a face. "Nuthin' like a hot brownie."

He chews. Marie sees him glimpse the car hauler as if it were a car full of kids, all ten of his kids, waiting for him, blowing the horn.

Marie swallows some milk. "Did I tell you my ex-husband used to beat the shit outta me?" Her eyes burn. She misses her glasses.

"No," he says. Then he moans. Chews. "You didn't." He spreads his gloved right hand over his thigh . . . makes a fist . . . then opens the hand . . . makes a fist . . . like when you give blood.

He is watching his yellow receipt pad lying among the paper napkins.

"See this?" She opens her mouth, chewed-up brownie wrinkled on her tongue. "See them two miserable fake teeth? He busted the real ones. And see this tongue? It almost come off! And wow! Don't the ol' tongue bleed! By the pails!"

He sets down his empty paper cup. "Can't eat no more."

"Oh, there's *tons* left!" she cries.

"I know it . . . but . . . I feel sick."

"Sick?"

He pats his stomach with his gloved hand.

"Oh," she says softly. She puts her own cup and plate down. Shifts her legs around. Wipes her mouth with a paper napkin. She says, "I had a nervous breakdown, you know . . . had to go to the hospital. Pills, pills, pills, pills. Pills for shakin'. Pills for cryin'. Pills for night-

mares. He was always gone. He'd be gone for *weeks*.
Sometimes I'd be in the kitchen . . . even the bathroom!
. . . and get this feelin' like Rubie was there . . . but he
weren't there . . . He was nowheres. The kids would be
asleep and I'd be downstairs with a little snack on the
table . . . lookin' at my bills, you know . . . or listenin' to
the radio real low . . . and I'd hear him breathin'. But he
weren't there. That's when I'd get the shakes. I'd make
the kids come in and sleep with me . . . and that helped.
One time he come home in the night . . . they was in there
with me . . . and when I see them headlights on the walls
I get to shakin' . . ."

"Mrs. Bean . . . please stop."

She pries her hands between her thighs.

He scratches the back of his neck.

She whispers, "Mr. Junkman . . . why don't you ever
let me see your hands?"

He looks at his gloves, says, "I just got a habit, I
guess. You know . . . like Linus has a blanket."

"There's nothing wrong with your hands, then," she
whispers.

"Nah!" His cowlike lips smile. He slides the gloves
off one at a time.

Marie leans forward, squinting.

He spreads a hand on each of his thighs. "See?"

As with old hardwood trees the roots break up, through,
make a coy leap, then plunge, so it is with the colorless
veins of Buzzy Atkinson's hands, the knuckles softly
swelled like the bodies of women in early pregnancy.
Cakey, curry-color nails. No pores, no spots, no hairs. A
wedding ring the width of a yellow hair.

Marie looks away, draws herself back against the tree.
"Your hands . . ." Her eyes sting.

He looks at his hands, blinks.

Inside her throat comes the feeling of a blade. "What are your ten kids like?" she asks.

He squares his shoulders. Smiles. "Well . . . I dunno."

She goes up on her knees, walks on her knees, puts her hands on his shoulders. He draws back.

The hardness in her throat doubles in size.

He keeps himself from tripping backwards by flattening his bare hands on the matted gray grass behind him. Marie whispers, "If you kiss me once, I'll never bother, never never bother you again."

Her face in his green eyes, one face to each eye, is two swans afloat, baring their throats, adjusting their wings across their backs, shaking down the dough of chest feathers, trumpeting, the water ruffling for miles.

"I can't," he says, lowering his eyes.

"Am I horrible?" she asks, her voice squeaking.

He shakes his head. His right hand retrieves his paper plate, shakes the crumbs off. He seems shy, even of his plate. He closes his eyes as his lips touch the plate, making a tiny rodentlike sound. He passes her the plate. "Now you do it," he says. She feels nausea. She kisses the plate.

He pulls his wallet from his pants. Counts out bills with his bare hands. He writes on the backs of a handful of receipts. He says, "I took the serials from the motahs for you. Most of these rigs"—he glances at the fenderless Ford on the hauler—"we're gonna part out an' crush . . . All I need is your signature on these . . . where I put them X's." He hands her a grimy ball-point pen. She signs her name on all eight slips, her hands steady, her eyes unblinking, bitter blue.

"Thank you," he says, averting his eyes. He stands up, knees creaking. Scratches his chest. Steps over the rocks, winding his way to his truck, sliding the yellow pad into his rear pocket, then tugging the dirty orange gloves back on. Pulls himself up onto the seat.

Marie squares her back against the maple, the paper plate between the vise of her knees.

The car hauler rolls down the grade. Buzzy Atkinson pops the clutch, and the engine makes a dragonlike snarl. The gloved hand hangs from the window.

FIVE
Tall Woman Love

Beal comes in the night. "Auntie!" he says softly with his lips against the glass. The door is latched. Just a thin latch, not meant to keep out something big. Beal taps the glass with his knuckles. "Auntie! It's me!" Among the hairs of a young boy's beard, pimple scars have been carved, concave as cellar holes. He's wearing a new jacket with a Sherpa collar, one with longer sleeves than the last. He never seems to stop growing. His weight makes the top step sigh.

In another room, a greenish light appears. Beal waits.

She comes to the door wearing men's long underwear. The greenish light tumbles along the dimpled cloth, the white, unshaky legs, bare feet. In the dark, her deep eyes are like no eyes. Just eye pits. Her black hair, in a bun, strains against a strip of kerchief tightly wound.

"You run away again?" Her voice is reedy like a tall-legged, tall-necked bird.

He pushes in around her, stands by the supper table in

the greenish half-dark. He breathes like he's been running.

She closes the door.

"Ain't you too big to run away?" She faces him, folds her arms across her chest.

"I got a job," he says. He looks around suspiciously. In the greenish light her smile is dark and slow-coming, like the unlatching of her back door.

"What kinda work?" she asks. Her arms drop away, long Tinkertoy arms, flashing white.

"Drivin' for Libby's." He gets out a dark rag and wipes his face.

"Logs?"

"Eyup. Got my second-class now, ya know."

"Good. That'll be good for you."

In the other room there's a rustling, like eggs hatching . . . feet scraping along the linoleum. The greenish light flutters.

"Well," says Auntie Roberta Bean, "guess you don't call it runnin' away when you're an all-growed-up man."

Beal watches the room of greenish light. "I j-aaah-aaah-ust wanted to see how you're doin'," he says.

"Doin' good," she says.

They come to stand in the bedroom doorway, five look-alike babies in diapers and crinkly plastic pants. They stare at Beal Bean with eyes deep and black as their mother's. They raise up and down on tiptoe, flex their calves.

Beal frowns. Avoids their eyes. "They're big," he says, making his voice low.

She smiles.

One baby picks up something from along the mop-board and hurls it at Beal. Beal sees it flutter down onto his left boot, a piece of Christmas tinsel. The baby hisses at him.

"We ain't seen you in a long time," the tall woman says more soft, more reedy, almost flutelike.

Beal nods.

The babies scuttle to their mother's legs, bunch up handfuls of her long johns. They dangle from her, squinting at Beal.

"Well . . . I guess you can stay here, if you gotta." She turns toward the greenish light. Beal sees the bed of grayed crazy quilts. He knows the smell. It is a low bed, raised on stumps of pine with bark still on them. She says, "But you ain't sleepin' in here like you think . . . not no more."

As she moves, the babies hug her legs. Her bare feet scuff the pink-fern linoleum. She turns and Beal looks at her long neck, her purplish mouth. "I'll get the little foam mattress for you from under the stairs," she says.

Her black black eyes glitter on him.

Beside her bed is the green globe electric lamp. Beal knows there are more children in the attic. Lying on boards, wrapped in their quilts and coats. His mouth trembles. "N-n-neh-eaaah-ever *mind*!" he says hoarsely. He glances again at her bed. She never sleeps with sheets. There's never any pillows. She always rolls up caterpillar-style in her quilts. Beal remembers a dozen mornings there. The room is always dark . . . and he would never have known it was morning except for the quickening blood in his body.

Tonight he looks long at her face. He pulls out of the greenish light. He opens the back door. "See ya," he mutters.

He closes the door. She can hear his feet on the frozen mud . . . thud thud thud. She knows in the morning she'll find him with the hens. Through the gray straw, she'll touch his dark hair.

2

The door opens and the new neighbor, March Goodspeed, the celebrated highway engineer, hurries down the hot-top path to the hot-top driveway in his pointy dress-up shoes and asphalt-color suit.

Across the road, the tall woman, Roberta Bean, is dressed in a man's ribbed undershirt and green wool pants. She is circling a piece of bare ground with an axe, her babies in yellow raincoats. The babies ornament her ankles, dangle from her pant legs. Thwank! Thwank! Thwank! Her axe beats upon the chopping block.

March Goodspeed picks open the door of his forest-green Lincoln. He lays a folder of papers on the seat. He does not say good morning to Roberta Bean. He quickly dives into his car. The tall woman circles the chopping block, her babies moving as she moves.

Roberta Bean has the smallest head of all Beans, her head being about the size of a fifteen-cent turnip with a blue knit cap stretched over the top of it. The hat has a chrome-yellow cuff. Nowhere does her black black hair show.

March Goodspeed shuts the door of his Lincoln.

Roberta Bean's axe goes Thwank! Thwank! Thwank!

March was to be in Portland by ten . . . a site walk for a new shopping center. It is 10:03. He turns the key. The Lincoln breathes almost like a human being. March pats the folder of papers on the seat. He clicks on the news He starts to back out of the yard.

The tall woman is so tall she divides March's rearview mirror into two clean halves, white grass to the left, white grass to the right. And everywhere, shuffling and darting, are babies and the tall woman's peach-color hens.

The Lincoln stalls partway into the road. March twists the key.

Out of the openings of the undershirt, Roberta Bean's assiduous, straining, bony neck and scarry long arms work the axe on the stringy wood. Faster. Faster. Now and then one of her dark eyes turns onto the Lincoln Continental.

The Lincoln whispers, "A-herm hm hm hm" . . . little burps, little giggles. "Start, damn you!" the highway engineer demands.

Some of the peach-color hens have come to his lawn, poke in his short grass. March rubs his eyes.

The tall woman moves all over the Lincoln's rearview mirror as a prizefighter moves around the ring. The white wood is spewed into the pile . . . faster, faster. Her back is to March now. She seems to ignore him.

March checks his watch. 10:09. He twists the key. *"Start!"* he commands.

The Lincoln only laughs.

The man slumps in his seat, his heart scrambling inside his dress shirt like a pillowcase full of puppies.

The babies seem unconvinced of the possibility of being stepped upon by one of the tall woman's mighty boots. Dazed by their love, they keep in step.

March squints at the mirror.

Roberta puts down her axe. She looks at March Goodspeed.

March can smell gas.

Roberta Bean crosses the road. With her flutters an army of boots and yellow raincoats, a hollow tromp tromp tromp tromp.

"Why is this happening?" March breathes. He picks a ball-point pen from his breast pocket and snaps it fast. He takes a breath of his Lincoln's rich interior.

Roberta Bean's tiny head is smiling at him through the glass.

March has blond hair, the color of faded newspapers. You'd never know he had been a redhead as a child; you'd never have known he had *been* a child. His eyes show leadership, are fibrous as salad olives. Green.

Her eyes look tired.

Reluctantly he scratches at the button. The window glass disappears as naturally as a lake thaws.

March says, "It's just flooded. It'll be all right in a few moments."

Roberta Bean redistributes her stature, somewhat to the left, and simultaneously there's the rumble of ten oversized boots, each boot to the left.

Long feelerlike noses sniff up at March. He looks down just in time to see one baby pick up a small piece of broken glass and aim it at his Lincoln. "Make that child behave!" March shouts.

Roberta's dark, close-together eyes move onto the child.

The baby puts the glass in its raincoat pocket.

Another baby spits. The foamy wob slides down the door of the Lincoln.

"You need a jump," the tall woman says. Then her mouth opens for a smile, the teeth like the far-apart teeth of a Doberman, long, fat, yellow, sharp.

March says, "It's flooded. That's all."

Roberta says, "Eyup . . . gas stinks." She puts both hands on the window frame and rocks the Lincoln so that March and the Lincoln move in great waves on the luxurious springs. "Ain't she a dandy!" the tall woman says.

March's eyes rest on the front of her undershirt, its rapt, fat flowers of spilled coffee, and some year-old blood shaped like the paw of a cat.

She says, "You set there, mistah, an' I'll getcha some help."

"No. In a few moments the gas will dry out. You just go back to what you were doing." He is as commanding as a trainer to a huge but humble dog.

"Yes-suh," she sneers, withdrawing her hands. "If it was just flooded. But you cranked on your throttle till she don't hardly turn over . . . does she? . . . You've run your batt'ry down. I'll getcha some help." And she veers away in the horrible scuffing of many boots.

He hangs his head.

One of the peach-color hens steps up and hammers with her beak on her reflection in the Lincoln's hubcap.

On the same side of the road as Roberta Bean's wee blue house is Beans' Variety Store. With sweaty dread, March anticipates four or five of those woolly, squinting Egypt, Maine, men over on the piazza of the store—fluorescent vests, black nails, wagging beards—loping toward him, hailed by Roberta Bean. And they would study him frankly through the tinted windshield, the way visitors to hospitals gape through Plexiglas at newborns.

But no. She returns without them.

Her black truck is parked by the front steps of her wee blue house like you tie a dog out to pee. She and her babies get into this truck, and she backs it out onto the pavement with a clanging like a half-dozen cowbells. The yellow-raincoated shapes of her children bounce around beside her on the seat.

She lines up her hood with his hood.

March closes his eyes, opens them slowly.

He turns in his seat and there's the tall woman, hurrying, helpful, steam rising out of her like what rises on the backs of straining spotted oxen. He squares his shoulders, pats the knot of his asphalt-color necktie.

"Shit!" he cries as his folder of many papers slips to the floor, covering the pedals and his pointy, shiny shoes.

Roberta flings up both hoods and uncoils jumper cables from around her neck and shoulders, cables which she carries there with the exuberance of one who wields pet snakes. He opens his eyes to see her fingers strum the cables' silken skins. And how gracefully she capers between the vehicles, her eyes misting in a joy March cannot fathom.

A half-dozen hens are now pecking at the bright hubcaps.

Meanwhile, the babies storm out of the black fenderless truck, three of them fastening to one of the tall woman's calves, two the other.

March sweeps open the door of his Lincoln, authority written on his face, knotting him up hard.

She is clasping the cables onto the terminals as he drives his own arms through her long long bare ones. "I'll do that now," he says.

But she is done.

The babies glare up at him. One is looking at March's left pointy black shoe.

March's arms are still parallel with the tall woman's bare ones. He is drawing back in slow motion, in disbelief. His heart is just one of the babies' oversized boots . . . tromp tromp tromp tromp. Roberta Bean's smell is in his face, a smell he is convinced is the smell of the inside of her wee blue house. Because of this smell, he sees the long fingers worrying the rubber from a Mason jar of cloudy green beans, boiling them hard, doling out baggy white yeast rolls, everything of a hotness that is injurious to the lips and gums, while this brood with crew cuts and long noses, like a bizarre litter of moles, tries even at the table to get close to her, forever close, madly close.

He backs onto the short grass of his yard. His necktie flounces.

With curling lips, the babies stare at March Goodspeed's pointy black shoes. "YUKK!" one of them says.

A small hen sees her reflection in his heel, jabs at it. March re-enters his Lincoln.

In a matter of moments he is shifting into reverse, giving the Lincoln the gas. It lurches over the road, backwards. Hens squawk. The babies look up at the tall woman, their eyes wrinkled up with love. The big car lunges up the grade and springs into the sun.

3

Beal waits out on the step with the big battery lamp across his knees.

Roberta Bean handles her old boots lovingly, then slips them sockless on her long, silvery feet. She loads her twenty-two with a clip of seven cartridges and fills her housedress pockets with a dozen more. The babies sleep in a wreath of blubbery snorts and sighs around the TV on the kitchen linoleum.

She latches the door of her wee blue house. Beal stands up. They enter the moon-whitened fog, fog so thick it seems to hold them back at times. He carries the high-powered lantern in one hand. The tall woman turns her face down, as if peering to the bottom of a warm, shoulder-deep pond. Water drips from the pines, from hemlock, from hardwood. A bunny dives around her boots, maddened by the feather atmosphere. Beal turns the lamp on him a few yards away. The bunny freezes. Roberta fires her twenty-two. They find others. The night is filled with the squeals of bunnies and the clap of powder making the droplets churn.

Back in the blue house, they stand side by side with their hips to the sink, the tall woman and Beal Bean. They clean the bodies in enamel basins, with two slender, dark-bladed knives. They pile the oozing hides in a cardboard box. They mound the bunny vitals in a bowl, and these look like strawberries with buds of rainwater on them.

Then Beal sits at the table, wiping his hands, watching her.

He frowns because she is putting the best bunny parts into a bread bag, crowding them into careful sticky intercourse so they will fit—footless, handless.

"What are you doin', Auntie?" he asks.

She moves her small head in his direction, the strange dark eyes squirming beetlelike. "Ain't your business," she says softly.

She goes outside, leaving him at the table.

She tapes a note to March Goodspeed's front door . . . a childlike scrawl: WELCOME TO EGYPT HERES A LITTLE PRESENT.

Then she ties the bag of bunnies to the doorknob.

She is silent out there in the fog, careful not to scuff against the hot top so she won't wake the man who wears the shiny shoes, her consideration bordering on love.

Then she strides away.

---------------------------------- **4** ----------------------------------

Back at her house, she picks up the babies one by one and arranges them in their shared crib in the kitchen. She turns off the TV. She takes down her hair and brushes it hard with water by the sink. There are still bits of bunny in the corners of the sink. On the supper table there are small white eggs mounded in a Tupperware colander under the shaded kitchen lamp, a peach-color feather stuck to one. She turns off the kitchen lamp and enters the weak, green light of her bedroom. Beal is in her bed, pretending he's asleep.

She comes up to the bed slowly, knees the bed hard. He doesn't move.

"Get outta my bed!" she snarls.

He rolls onto his back, his dark, bare arms spread like a crucifix. "Please," he murmurs.

Her close-together eyes wriggle. "Ain't you got a little girlfriend yet, Beal?"

He shakes his head.

She sits on the bed. Her housedress is a cornflower print. There are still some twenty-two shells in the pocket. Her smile is just this crack in the wax of a fifteen-cent turnip so small, so strange her face . . . and yet, so long a woman.

"So you drove a big truck today, eh?" she says.

He nods.

"Not bad for nineteen years old. All grown up now . . . Ayuh . . . You're big."

His eyes grow rounder. He moves his fingers.

She gives one of his fingers a little tug.

Her voice rises. "Don't want no parta you, Beal. Ain't messin' around. You're just so tricky. You're hurtin' me every time you come here . . . you stupid kid."

He jerks himself up on his elbows. "Ain't hurtin' you, Auntie! I make you feel nice! What kinda shit you slingin'!"

"You're good and you're bad. Ain't messin' with you. Get out!" She yanks at his wrist.

"Auntie! Li-eh-aaah-listen! I ain't bad!"

She tears at the grayed quilts that smell of a thousand sleeps. She works to pull him to the edge of the bed. "Get dressed!" she cries.

"Please!" he cries.

She picks up his clothes. "Put these on!"

"Pah-ah-aaah-palease . . . I think of you all the time. I can h-hah-help you now, Auntie! I got a job. I can buy stuff . . . for *them*!" He points through the bedroom door and to the upstairs.

His body spilling to the floor from the quilts is nothing like it used to be. Now there are dramatic dark ravines between the muscles, hair big as an apple on the groin . . . tornado-shaped on the chest.

He hugs her legs, the endless bare legs, the old boots.

She doesn't talk to him anymore but pulls him up and stuffs his clothes into his arms. He says, "I ain't *never* comin' back, Auntie. You're not gonna ever see my face again, no matter how wicked bad you beg!"

She leads him to the back door, opens it. He grips her wrist. Her black eyes turn crazily in on themselves. Then she pushes him out. She knows in the morning she'll find him in the gray straw. She'll shake him awake. And she'll have fried rabbit and canned apples and runny scrambled eggs on his plate waiting for him. And while he eats, nobody talks.

_____ 5 _____

Forty-five miles per hour. He is coming up the crumbly road in the lavender twilight, the window down, his tie off, his sheaf of papers flapping and fluttering on the seat beside him.

He steps on the gas. Fifty-five miles per hour.

At times, the Lincoln seems to be lunging through an upper atmosphere. There's no sensation of earth being rolled under tires. He is aware only of the sweet, almost sinewy, night air. The speedometer reads sixty. He takes sharp curves with an intermittent yelling of tires.

The Lincoln pounces onto a bridge, the one that straddles the railroad bed. There's a straight-away after that which seems to end in the dead center of the moon.

Sixty-five miles per hour.

The huge radials catch the soft shoulder. March yanks on the wheel . . . but the wheel seems disengaged . . . a kind of toy wheel. "Arrr!" he cries. The Lincoln bucks. He sees the blackness of an embankment rear up, saplings dancing, a sideways sky playfully appearing, then disappearing.

The forest-green Lincoln stands at last stock-still in the culvert, its front end high like a motorboat. March's heart beats in his back, beats in his head, and on the palms of his hands. He strains to get the door open. It is heavy at this angle.

Once outside, he feels the Lincoln all over, squinting in the lavender twilight for dents. His face is wet. His shirt is wet. He reaches inside the car for his suit jacket . . . sets the flashers.

He waits.

6

The moon rises slightly like a self-luminating craft idling up there to observe the town of Egypt, Maine. And out of it clamors the black fenderless pickup . . . making the sound of a half-dozen cowbells.

He says to himself, "Oh, no! Not again."

The truck squeals to a stop.

Then there's the face with the squirming beetle eyes. The mouth opening: "You in the cul-vet, huh mistah?"

"Yes, I'm in the culvert," he says softly.

He sees beyond her, lighted by the greenish dash, the babies all asleep in a pile.

She opens the door, leaves her truck parked in the road with the headlights splayed dimly on a wall of trees, the moon behind her rising another half-inch off the ground.

He sees she's wearing a light-colored housedress and no shoes. Close to him now, he swears he can smell boiled dinner on her: cabbage, potatoes, carrots, and ham.

"Eeeee-yup, she's in the hole," says Roberta Bean. She wears a visor cap which says, MERTIE'S HARDWARE. She puts her hands on her hips. "Mistah . . . I got a chain on me, but my little Chevy ain't no match for that . . . that *thing* . . . what is it there . . . oh, a Chrysler?"

"A Lincoln," he says.

"Same thing," she says.

He narrows his eyes.

As if the moonlight were blinding, she shades her eyes with one hand and studies the Lincoln. "Why, ain't that a tool!"

Up on the crown of the road her truck sputters, like it's about to stall. The lights flutter. But it regains its composure.

"Well, mistah, the best I can do is give you a ride ta my nephew Rubie's place. He's got a loggin' rig an' all the chains your little Lincoln desires . . . Aye? Just hop right up here an' I'll give ya a lift."

"I've got Triple A," he says flatly. He glares at the open door of the truck. "I just need a phone."

She nods, says no more. She strews her long legs up over the seat and her bare feet clasp the pedals.

When he opens the passenger door, the heads of all the babies go up. Their eyes grow enormous. Their teeth grate, and popping noises come from the walls of their mouths. They flatten themselves against their mother, leaving him a bit of room. Where they've been lying is wet. They're wearing only soaked diapers and the deep creases of the truck's upholstery stamped on their skin.

March hesitates.

Roberta's face is turned toward him, but there are no eyes. Just pits of eyes.

He hops up, drapes his suit jacket over his lap, slams the door. The truck lurches forward. He notes the greenly lit console. The gas tank reads empty. The speedometer registers zero. He imagines he is riding backwards. Indeed, the trees seem to move that way at first. His stomach swells like a big cake baking.

The babies' eyes are on him, and out of their little mouths come the grating, popping noises.

Roberta's broad scarred hands grip the vibrating wheel.

March Goodspeed smiles stiffly. "Well, you can take me right to my place. I'll call from there."

Roberta doesn't respond.

His torso shifts. His white shirt is as wet as if he'd been swimming in his clothes.

He sighs. "Miss Bean..." He hesitates. "This would be a good time to have a little talk."

She still shows no response.

He says, "I've been meaning to ask you... although I've been too busy to get over... but I was wondering if you might happen to know which locals might be wanting to tease me?"

Roberta doesn't move, or speak. The babies hang off all her parts, equally motionless.

March clears his throat. "Do you know anything

about . . . someone fastening a bag of . . . chicken meat on my front door?''

Roberta's head turns. There is glittering in the backs of her eyes. ''Ain't chicken,'' she says grumpily. ''Was rabbit. Don't you like *rabbit*, Mistah Goodspeed?''

All at once the babies scramble. A foot cuffs his cheek. He ducks away, puts his arm up—which only makes them scramble all the more. The tall woman seems unflustered by this, but March Goodspeed is against the door with his eyes closed.

After a while, Roberta says, ''I know you been livin' in the neighborhood almost a year now, but you know how it is, you're still the new fella to us all. Massachoosits an' all.''

March sees that the MERTIE'S HARDWARE cap has been knocked back on her head. It is the first time he has seen her hair. It is parted in the middle. Lovely hair.

''Look here, Miss Bean . . . or is it Mrs.?''

She smiles.

''I have a wife, you know,'' he says.

Roberta's long neck swallows.

''She's a paraplegic . . . having a bad time adjusting. She's with her mother in Amesbury. I'm going for her when I feel she's ready for this place.''

''A paraplegic,'' says Roberta.

One of the babies pulls a clump of stuffing from the seat and throws it at March Goodspeed. It falls on his suit jacket. March leaves it there, ignores it.

Then another baby, together with the first baby, yanks two or three even bigger pieces out, and these hit the side of his head. Some sticks in his hair.

Before they reach his house, March Goodspeed is snowed over almost completely.

When the old pickup clangs and wheezes to a stop in

front of his house, he looks up at his unlit windows with an expression of near panic.

—————————— 7 ——————————

It is noon. There is no view of the hills. The fog is low and dark. The black truck is parked on the narrow bridge. Both doors of the truck are open and Roberta Bean's long legs stick out from the seat, the boots propped up on one truss. She is eating an Italian sandwich with double cheese and ham. Some of the babies are in the truck. Some are out on the bridge, throwing little stones and little sticks down onto the railroad tracks.

The logging truck takes the curve with a screech. All the babies look up with expressions of welcome. The logging truck horn fills the air with a startling blast. The great truck heaped with pine screams to a halt a bare six inches from Roberta Bean's black truck's puckered-up, dimpled tailgate.

When the babies see that it's Beal Bean up on the seat of the truck, their expressions of welcome disappear.

Roberta sits up, leans forward. Her dark eyes slowly creep to Beal Bean's face. Then she leans back and rearranges her feet on the truss.

Beal drops to the pavement and walks toward her, squaring his shoulders in a dark blue workshirt that says LIBBY'S LOGGING on the pocket. "Fuck you!" he shouts. "You crazy broad . . . You wanna be dead . . . thuh-aaaah-that's the way ta do it . . . parkin' on a one-lane bridge!!!" The logging truck idles. The fog is so thick the top of the load of logs is only a fuzz.

The babies hiss at Beal. They close up in a huddle and dangle from the tall woman's long legs.

Roberta smiles. Her teeth, like yellow ball-point pens, catch the dismal gray light of surrounding fog. "Want me to move?"

Beal is red-faced. "You scared the shit outta me!" he snarls, wipes his sleeve over his eyes. His black hair is in a turmoil, upright like a newborn baby's.

The babies squint up at him. One of them picks a sliver of green pepper off the seat and hurls it at Beal. It misses.

Roberta is wearing her other housedress. A pale green print. Beal can hear change jingle in her pockets as she shifts on the seat. "Ain't seen you in a while," she says. Her eyes don't meet his, but dangle somewhere near LIBBY'S LOGGING on his pocket. With the yellow teeth, she tears off a few inches of the sandwich.

Beal says, "What's it to you?"

She points at a sign that they can't see the front of. "Six-ton limit," she says with her mouth full.

He shrugs.

She takes a roll of blue toilet paper from the dash, snaps off five or six sheets, wipes her mouth. She's wearing no hat. Her head is small and hard-looking, and right in the middle are the two eyes jumping out at the words on Beal's pocket. "You're gonna die young, dear boy . . . I hate to say it," she says, and rips off another few inches of the sandwich with her teeth.

He puts his shoulder against the cab of her truck. "It's got to be better when you're dead," he says.

She says, "We're havin' us a little picnic, ain't we, kids?" She smiles, balls up the Italian sandwich paper and tosses it over the bridge. Her arms are long enough to reach from the truck all the way to the green trusses of the bridge.

Beal squares his shoulders. "I won some money last night, Auntie."

She stuffs in the last of her sandwich. "Good boy."

A baby tosses a black olive. It whizzes between Beal's knees.

Roberta says, "Been over Chet Letourneau's barn, aye? Don't Auntie Hoover make a stink over that?"

He flushes. "Ain't none of her business."

She smiles. "As long as you're under her roof . . ."

He says low in his throat, "I been stayin' over at Rubie's."

She chews. Looks into the fog. Her eating noises are self-satisfied. "Rubie Bean's a pig," she says.

He grips her wrist. "I'll d-uh-do what I damn well want, okay?"

"You gettin' his ways," she says.

"Ain't *his* ways . . . It's *my* ways. He's him. I'm me."

"All in the blood." She laughs deep in her long neck.

When he lets go of her wrist, he gives it a push into her body.

"Well," she says. "We was goin' ta wait for the train. The kids wanted to see the train before we left. But you never know when the old train might come. It's a kinda free 'n' easy train." She peers down the foggy tracks that have been laid through two dynamited walls of ledge. She takes a huge breath.

Without opening his mouth, Beal makes something like the belch of a bullfrog. His hand goes for her shoulder, closes down on the green, flowered fabric.

"Well . . ." she says. She rolls up one of the babies' sandwiches. "The worm turns."

Beal tightens his fingers. There is only the bone of her shoulder. How fleshless a woman!

She says, "Now, Bushy, look what you done . . . You took all the stuff outta that sandwich. If all you like is

bread, I ain't purchasin' you no more loadeds.'' She
gives the paper with the vegetables a heave over the side
of the bridge, and it flaps down like a white dove shot in
midflight—with an explosion of onions and tomatoes and
so forth.

"I won sixty bucks, Auntie,'' Beal Bean says. His
beard is still soft, still sparse, silly-looking.

She ignores him.

He pats his pocket. "Sixty bucks . . . Four of a kind
and a full house . . . It was pure hell on Chet. Ruth come
out and blew out all the lamps. We figured it was time ta
go.''

She seems not to hear.

Beal kneads and kneads the shoulder, the skin tight on
the bone.

The babies click their teeth at him. One of them chews
on a piece of Italian sandwich paper . . . then spits it at
Beal. It hits Beal's chin, then ricochets.

The tall woman shifts her boots on the bridge. "Too
bad we don't get to see the train, kids . . . but we gotta
let this man's load through.''

Beal steps around and faces her, straddles the long
legs. He has fox-color eyes. He is like all Beans. There's
no difference in Beans. The tall woman sighs.

Beal says, "Auntie . . . sometimes you want me . . . Why
you *get* like this?''

She squeezes her eyes shut like she's in the middle of a
little prayer.

One of the babies scuttles forward on the truck seat
and bites Beal's forearm, leaving spit and a bit of chewed
bread.

"Jesus!'' Beal shakes his arm. "Little smartass!''

He stands back.

When she starts the truck up, it sounds like a half-

dozen cowbells. It lurches forward. All the babies stand
in the back window and stare at Beal.

"Goddam . . . caaah-c-crazy woman!" Beal hisses to
himself as he lets the brake go in the logging truck, then
creaks onto the six-ton bridge. The smaller truck travels
the crumbly road at twenty miles an hour, and the big
truck tailgates till the straight-away, where it passes in a
roar.

—————————— 8 ——————————

After sunset the tall woman lunges out of her wee blue
house on Tinkertoy legs. The blue of Roberta Bean's
little house is the blue of a plastic fork or cheap blue
comb . . . a tacky blue. Her old pickup is parked close to
the door. Her housedress is made for a much shorter
woman. Her visor cap says, MERTIE'S HARDWARE. She
carries a cardboard box of laundry. Hens hunker on the
limbs of an apple tree by the road, hens not much bigger
than apples, soundless as apples.

Over the grade, a forest-green Lincoln moves in silence . . . almost human breathing. In the dying pink light
the car looks black.

The tall woman sees the Lincoln and sighs reedily in
her long neck. She hangs up diapers and her own huge
socks. She is barefoot. Her long, silvery toes pry at the
mud. She racks her tallness to a further tallness to reach
the clothesline that is up out of anybody else's reach,
screwed to the back of Beans' Variety Store, as taut and
important as a power-company cable. Her hard fingers
march along this rope.

The Lincoln comes to a halt at the edge of her grass.

She turns her head. Around her head and shoulders, the big socks and gauzy diapers suspend without motion. She holds three clothespins in her teeth. She is skeletal, eerie. The Lincoln's automatic window whispers down. The tall woman pulls the clothespins from her mouth and goes to the edge of her grass.

"Miss Bean," the voice within the car says.

She nods, steps closer.

"How are you tonight?" the voice asks.

She squares her narrow shoulders. "Fine."

"I have something here I picked up . . ." The hands put into her hands a box of glazed donuts. ". . . for your kids. I thought they might like them."

She looks down at them.

The man chuckles.

She says, "Thank you."

The dark smell of the Lincoln's interior embraces her.

"You're entirely welcome," says the voice. "It's something I've wanted to do . . . for your kids, your young ones."

His arm stretched along the top of the door shows a sleeve the color of a Coke bottle. He fingers the flawless paint. She squints at his cuff links shaped like little eagles. He has a wedding band and another ring, a school ring colored like a ruby. His hands look brand-new, never used.

Every night after that, the Lincoln stops at the edge of the tall woman's yard. Sometimes, she sends out one of her two oldest children, but usually she goes out there herself to get the gift of donuts, turnovers, or fig squares. The man has his arm out the window on warm nights, now and then his jacket is off, on the seat, the sleeves of his damp light-color shirt rolled to the elbow. His face looking up at her is silvery, eyes that never close, watchful, fishlike. Sometimes, if there is a wind down off the mountain, the tall woman's housedress bends around her body. And the man in the Lincoln watches this eerie thing happen.

But nothing changes after this.

Every night is the same. The donuts are carried into the wee blue house, and the forest-green Lincoln swings away.

9

It is noon and she sets the metal tub out in the yard because it has just sprung a leak. She fills it with teakettles of hot water and the steam heaves up, climbs among the branches of a poplar and its new coin-shaped leaves. It is the first really hot day of the year. The hens make a frenzy in the sand. One of the tall woman's oldest children sits on the back step in cut-off jeans, turning a red felt cowboy hat in its fingers. Its chest is narrow, and the dark nipples are as close together on its body as its eyes are on its face. The tall woman steps around this child and drags a trash bag of laundry from the house.

"Ain't nuthin' ta do," mutters the child.

"It's a hot one," says Roberta Bean.

She squirts pink dish soap into the tub and washes her two housedresses. What she has on today she got at a SALE. It used to belong to a much thicker woman. It is pink paisley with buttons shaped like little hearts. The breeze kicks up and the new pink dress twists and turns like nothing is in it.

The babies are in the house with the TV. You can hear strains of *As the World Turns* through the open door, but the babies are quiet babies.

When the logging truck parks on the shoulder of the road, the tall woman doesn't stop what she's doing. She squeezes the water from a dress and drops it in a cardboard box. She pulls a crib sheet from the trash bag.

Beal Bean comes around the corner of the tacky blue house with his dark blue workshirt tied around his waist. His T-shirt is messy. He steams like the laundry tub steams. Sun is on one half of his body, shade the other. Deer flies swing near his head.

He carries a sandwich wrapped in wax paper. A Thermos. He stands by the steps, unwrapping his sandwich. He watches the tall woman. She ignores him. She bears down upon the sheet, water heaving out of the tub onto her feet.

Beal sits on the top step with the child and eats his sandwich, hunkering over it with his body as if somebody might try for the sandwich. After he is finished, the child with the close-together nipples and close-together eyes gets up and brings Beal Bean a honey-dipped donut on the palm of its hand. Beal's beard comes to a point now and is thickening. The diesel smell of the idling truck moves around the corner of the house.

Beal eats the donut. Sips coffee. He and the child watch the tall woman wash clothes. Beal's eyes strike the tall woman's back like rocks pitched hard.

After he is done with the donut, the child goes back in and gets him another. And then after that another—each one more glistening, more sticky, more golden, more plump.

SIX

Moon on Cole Deveau

The game warden, Cole Deveau, parks his new gray truck on the shoulder of Seavy Road and gets out. He is wearing mirror cop glasses, although there's no sun. His pistol lays on his thigh like a cast-iron pan. It is a cold, damp day, the hardwoods iron color, still leafless. But the logging road is soupy. Mud splats the pants of the warden's uniform as he hobbles along among the ruts, headed toward the sound of Rubie Bean's logging truck loading up.

A red squirrel rustles the leaves, then scolds the warden explosively.

The warden's neck is as big as a chopping block Black and gray hairs stick out along this neck like the businesslike whiskers of a cat. He's broad-shouldered, big-bellied. His weight makes sucking in the mud.

When Cole Deveau reaches the landing, Rubie Bean's oldest boy is on the seat of a ratty mud-splattered skidder, drinking an Old Milwaukee. The boy is just as mud-splattered as the skidder. He sees the warden coming and his cold blue eyes grow wide.

Over the warden's mirror sunglasses reflections of overhead limbs slide like protracting claws.

He walks straight to the open door of Rubie's truck and jumps aboard. The enormous growl of the loader on the back is like a wall, and so Rubie has no idea the warden has come, so he keeps working, his fox-color eyes on the jaws of the boom.

Cole Deveau pulls Rubie's rifle out from under the seat and stands on the running board with his legs apart, looking into the loading gate.

The boy tosses the Old Milwaukee empty into the bushes, pounces from the skidder, moves toward the warden. Another Bean boy, limbing a log, works in a T-shirt, his neck red and vaporous. He has not seen the warden. Rubie still works the boom, the log sliding through air, making a hawklike shadow.

On the floor and dash and seat of Rubie's truck are the uncountable ready cartridges. The warden rolls them in the fingers of his hairy hand. Then he jacks those inside the rifle out onto the ground.

As Steve Bean approaches, the warden jumps down from the cab and shoves past him, strides to the back of the truck. Rubie's eyes widen. Cole Deveau squares his shoulder, points at Rubie.

Rubie's ruddy face drains white.

The other boy turns, sees the warden, stands with his saw idling. The boys, like Rubie, are broad, bow-legged, and dark, tall as the warden, perhaps taller. All around is the sound of sucking mud as they raise their feet.

"Move!!" Rubie bellows. The muscles in his neck twist like snakes. The suspended log creaks, slips from the boom, and rolls thunderously toward the warden's feet. Deveau jumps back, his face coloring.

Rubie pushes his felt hat back on his head. He is grinning broadly with many twisted teeth, the black mustache hanging heavy as a pelt. "Sor-ree!" he sings out. Then stands. He climbs the high half-load tigerishly slow, pauses to light a cigarette, then jumps with the cigarette in his teeth. The warden stands with the butt of Rubie's rifle between his feet, the barrel up into his cupped hand.

Rubie comes near, eyeing the gun.

The boy in the T-shirt cuts the saw off and stands in the middle distance with open mouth, fox-color eyes pressed on the warden's neck and flabby ears.

The warden lights a cigarette. Cole Deveau and Rubie Bean, not looking into each other's face, stand side by side smoking within the idling whine of the hydraulic

Rubie says, "Shit," softly.

The warden squares his shoulders in his splendid grayish-green uniform, grunts, "For chrissakes, Bean, why can't you control yourself?"

Rubie chuckles, smokes.

The warden says, "It ain't what's hangin' in your shed, Rubie. That isn't why I'm here. It's what's strewed all over the power line, drawin' flies."

Rubie smokes. His hand shakes.

The warden smokes.

Rubie's boys watch. They stand suspended in mud, their arms raised somewhat away from their bodies as if the mud were a tide rising.

Cole Deveau sighs. "I can understand bein' a glutton for meat, Rubie, but what you left on the power line isn't meat . . . it's a friggin' holocaust. Haven't you got a sprig o' conscience?"

Rubie smokes without hands, the cigarette fluttering on his bottom lip, hands on the hips of his wool pants. "I ain't been nowheres but here . . . right here, Cole,'' Rubie says.

The warden nods. Turns the rifle on its butt like an augur in the mud. Rubie narrows his eyes.

Cole says, ''I wouldn't bother a man at his work if all I had was a hunch. Sorry, Rubie, but I got my case squared away.'' He is looking into Rubie's eyes, but Rubie can't tell because of the mirror sunglasses. Rubie brings his hands together—fingers and stumps of fingers— and cracks his knuckles.

The warden turns the rifle. Rubie squints. The warden puts his foot up on a mossy rock. Rubie watches the warden's foot.

''Ayuh,'' says Rubie. ''Son of a whore.''

The warden smiles, big square teeth. ''Some people call it a waste of deer meat. Others would go to pieces to see those bleatin' motherless fawns. But when I came upon that puking scene, I says to myself, Cole, you've shot good dogs for less . . . and there's that Rubie Bean out there still at large. Go round him up, Cole. This is what I said to myself. And that's what I'm doing.''

Rubie smiles with twisted teeth, but the bottom lip trembles.

The warden twists the rifle down into the mud. The butt sinks deeper, deeper. Rubie eyes the sights.

''I'll treat you fair 'cause we're old friends. I'll recite you your rights while you're walkin' back with me to my truck. I won't handcuff you.''

Rubie snorts, then spits into a skidder rut. He turns, strides tigerishly slow to the logging truck, his dark wool clothes almost blurring into the trees. He cuts off the hydraulic and the motor. He tugs out a red bandanna and wipes his face and heavy black mustache. The warden watches him hard. The boys watch, their big shoulders stooped.

Rubie spreads one hand on the purplish dented fender of his old truck, fumbles with his wool pants, and pisses onto one of the tires.

The warden keeps twisting the gun, mud riding up over its loading gate, splaying around the perfect full buckhorn sight. Rubie turns. He trots back to the warden, his eyes on the rifle. "Gimme my gun," he pants.

"It's not your gun anymore, Rubie. It's the state of Maine's gun. Pretty little thing, ain't she? Don't see many of these old Model Ninety-fours anymore. Real nice."

Rubie's eyes blink crazily, almost like a child holding back tears. "You know Pa gimme that gun," he says deep in his throat.

The warden turns the gun with one hand, runs his finger in the barrel with the other. "You don't see one of these octagon barrels every day, either. Amazin'. Lever's good 'n' tight. Hardly a scratch." He caresses the gun. "Might need a little bluing. Jesus Christ almighty, ten shots . . . You gotta respect a thing like that." He turns the gun. The mud heaves over the sights.

Rubie's eyebrows go up. The mutilated fingers of his right hand scramble spiderlike. "You ain't convicted me yet . . . Give 'er ovuh."

"Now you know better than that," says Cole Deveau. He pulls the gun out of the mud. "Let's head down." He starts walking, swinging the muddy rifle.

Rubie makes a horse whinny. He dives, his palm connecting with his rifle. The warden pivots with his arms out. Rubie has the rifle.

With both hands he swings the unloaded gun like an axe, making a blump blump blump with the muddy butt against the warden's face bones, his ribs, the bones of his fingers. From the warden comes an unearthly bellow. He flips onto his back, his great belly up, his face black with mud.

Rubie's boys don't move, their faces studious.

Rubie rolls the warden over and over, a large soft round mound of gray . . . smashing and spearing at the softest parts with the rifle butt. The warden tries to cover his face with his uncrushed hand. Rubie finds his mouth with the gunstock and drives it home. The crying mouth fills with blood, fills with broken teeth. Rubie snatches Deveau's pistol from the tangle of bloody muddy uniform and pitches it among the skidder cables. Then Rubie, crying too—not with pain but with a ghoulish rage—aims the empty rifle at the warden's neck, big as a chopping block, and dry-fires over and over and over until Steve, the blue-eyed Bean, comes up behind, saying softly, "Come on, Dad . . . *Dad*, come on . . . Let's go!"

2

A shaky moon lifts out of the hills. Its pink light seeks out Cole Deveau. He lies on his side, his rib cage rising and falling, rising and falling. Through gummy eyes he can almost not see the fairy light. He cannot distinguish himself from the pinespills and mud he is bleeding into. He feels as though his lungs and twisting, turning bowels are gorged with mud. His mouth is immovable. But a voice clear in his head says, "I'm dead, I guess." He knows that somewhere right now on some power line, some meadow or orchard, a deer is also lying, on his side, the great rib cage rising and falling, broken to bits by one of Rubie's meteors of lead, this queer cold pinkish moonlight trespassing the hide.

3

Cole Deveau's bride loves a straight-back chair. Her knitting lies black on her knee like a sleeping cat. She wears a flowered apron, the kind that goes over the head. It is dark out now but she doesn't need a light to knit by. She is just a pair of pale hands and number-three needles, a gray face in moonlight. She sits by the window where she can look out, waiting. Her eyes look straight into the yard, somewhat turned in on themselves like the eyes of the dead. Her lips move, counting stitches. But otherwise she is like a big doll, unrelenting perfect posture. But no one comes. The moon lifts clear of Cole's caved-in barn . . . feeble, shaky.

4

Earlene Pomerleau stands in the picture window, brushing her long pale hair, and putting it up with pins. It's the first hot hot day of the year even though there are no leaves yet. Strands of her pale hair stick to her face. "Daddy! Look! Cops! Millions of cops!"

Lee Pomerleau is on the couch most of the time since his back surgery. An afghan of variegated golds covers his legs. He lies with his face to the wall, his arm over his head. He is a small man, wearing khaki, with unadult proportions, flexing angry pale fingers against the wall. "Millions?" he says dully.

"Practically," Earlene says. "It's like on TV when the cops come, you know."

The air this day is thick, almost yellowish, like dog's breath. Through it moves the warden, Cole Deveau. He carries his fat belly differently than usual, with a stiff straight-legged gait. Another warden stands beside him, shouting into his walkie-talkie and looking over the hood of his Land Rover up at the paved road.

There are other cars and trucks, deputies, a uniformed sheriff standing beside a brown sheriff's cruiser . . . and now another warden just arriving in a mud-splattered car. They stand around on the Beans' "lawn," and two big Bean women and large Bean babies are watching from the open mobile-home door. The women have their hands on their hips. They have fox-color eyes.

Earlene says, "Daddy, you gotta see this. Get up!"

Earlene's father moans.

Earlene can see through the Beans' open windows, the plastic curtains rising and falling.

Cole Deveau wears a short-sleeved gray uniform, which is blackened with sweat at the ribs. One of his hairy hands is in a cast. His face is no face, just a lot of purple, and on this purple crouch the mirror cop glasses so you can't see his eyes.

Earlene's voice is high and cheerful like Minnie Mouse's. "Daddy! The warden's been in some kinda accident. You oughta see his face." She lays her hairbrush on the TV.

"I don't want to see his face," Lee Pomerleau says, and tries to massage his own back. "Ahhhhh!" he says, kneading at the incision. "None of them cops are turnin' around in my driveway, are they?" he says darkly.

"Not yet," says Earlene.

"You'd think my driveway was Grand Central Station sometimes," says Lee Pomerleau.

"They ain't. They're all just standin' there, lookin' up the road," says Earlene.

Along the frame of the mobile home are the blue Christmas lights the Beans leave up all year; every night after dark for several years, some Bean hand flips the switch that sets them to twinkling. Around the dooryard are plastic toys of Bean babies and the oil drums and car parts of Bean men and a chicken-wire pen of five or six silent, statuesque, blue-eyed black dogs.

"Look what's comin' down the right-of-way now, Daddy!" Earlene folds her hands. "*State* police."

The walkie-talkie squawks. Cole Deveau doesn't look interested in talking.

Earlene squeals in her Minnie Mouse voice, "Somethin' happened to Cole Deveau's teeth, Daddy. He looks like an old man."

"Did he have 'em out?" Lee asks, still facing the wall.

"They're gone, Daddy."

"Well, it ain't my business," Lee mutters.

"Daddy! How's he gonna sing Sunday . . . without no teeth?"

"Ain't *my* business, Earlene. Ain't *your* business."

Earlene is in her midteens. She has a long, pale neck, pale eyes, and tiny nervous hands. She wears a little sleeveless top with a print of tiny kittens.

Cole Deveau is wearing his warden's hat, the hair on his huge neck gleaming thornlike and gray. He wears a gun that hangs on his thigh.

"Now, wouldn't you think Cole Deveau would take the day off when he's not feelin' good, Daddy?"

"He's a devoted lawman," says Lee Pomerleau.

"Wait'll Gram hears this!" Earlene exclaims, then whistles sharply. "*Somebody* is in trouble at Beans'!"

"It's about time," sighs Lee Pomerleau, rubbing his back. "Hope this is the big dragnet that's come ta scoop 'em all up."

"Here comes another sheriff, Daddy. Can you believe this?"

"Earlene, sit down and stop starin' . . . Praise the Lord."

"Daddy! I can't help it!!!"

One of the deputies reaches through the open window to the cab of a truck and pulls a carbine from the gun rack. He pushes a few cartridges into the loading gate

"WOW!" gasps Earlene.

The warden's walkie-talkie spits and clicks.

"Daddy, don't you think Cole Deveau oughta be in bed?"

Lee Pomerleau sighs. "The day old Deveau takes a day off will be a cold day in . . . you know where."

"Yuh, but Daddy . . . he can't prack-tickly walk!"

Lee Pomerleau blows his cheeks in and out a time or two. "That man is so devoted, he'd nab his nanna if her nose looked like an undersized salmon." Lee pulls up his shirt and paws furiously at the incision.

A deputy, who is picking his nose, abruptly looks alert. Up on the paved road, Rubie Bean's loaded truck swishes through the low-hanging bare maples, grinds down onto the right-of-way. He's coming to have dinner with his mother. There's no shadows. Rubie Bean is as good as a clock. When he comes to eat dinner with his mother, you know it's noon. When you hear those brakes hiss, the gears snatch and rake, you know it's time to set the table.

Rubie Bean backs into the Pomerleaus' crushed-rock driveway, an inch or so from Lee Pomerleau's little car with the JESUS SAVES bumper sticker and a brand-new one: HONK IF YOU LOVE JESUS! The picture window ripples. The NO TURNING IN DRIVEWAY!!!! KEEP OUT!!!! sign, very faded, flaps on its lathed post in the sudden breeze made by the truck.

One of the deputies tosses an empty Fresca can into the Beans' yard. It rolls to a stop among the plastic toys.

Cole Deveau looks through the windshield of Rubie Bean's old truck: Rubie's fox-color eyes meet Cole

Deveau's eyes, which are underneath his mirror cop glasses.

"Daddy! Get up 'n' see this! Somethin's gonna happen."

"I don't want to see it. It's just another tacky day in the life of the Beans," says Lee Pomerleau.

Rubie revs the engine of his truck. He looks down through the spotted windshield at the warden moving stiff-legged toward him, the assorted others also closing in. The deputy keeps the carbine close to his body. Another deputy pulls a gun with a worn strap off the seat of a pea-green car. Cole Deveau's handgun rides his leg. The sun flashes on his mirror glasses. Every bit of flesh not covered by his uniform shows up the color of canned plums.

Rubie revs the engine again. He makes the loaded truck buck and rock. The mountain of logs sways ominously.

Lee Pomerleau says, "What's going on in my driveway?"

"The usual, Daddy . . . except for all them cops comin' *our* way."

Lee Pomerleau sits up. "Why're they comin' *here*!"

"They're gettin' ready to arrest Rubie Bean, looks like."

Lee Pomerleau turns the gold afghan in his hands. "It's about time. *Praise God! Praise Him!*"

Earlene looks into her father's eyes. "Praise Jesus," she says softly.

Cole Deveau points his plum-color finger at Rubie Bean.

Rubie Bean's mustache hangs heavy as a cat over his twisted teeth. His green felt hat is wet around the crown. He isn't wearing a shirt, just a frazzled blue bandanna around his throat. Over the truck door where it says RUBIE BEAN LOGGING, EGYPT, MAINE and his telephone number, his tawny left arm hangs, the long and short fingers spread.

He makes the truck rock crazily.

The state police talk into their car radio before getting out. Then the two of them slide out into the heat.

Cole Deveau walks stiffly in front of the truck and stands before the dented grille, pointing up at Rubie. The other guys spread out, one tripping over the Pomerleaus' wee gardenia bush.

Both state cops have drawn their revolvers.

Rubie pushes open the door of the truck, stands on the running board. His chest and arms are white-hot, glassy. He hangs from the door frame.

Cole Deveau's voice is strained, like Donald Duck's: "Okay, Bean! Maybe you're ready now?"

All the lawmen squint. The purply red of Rubie's rig and the steamy glare of his body are too much for them. Rubie crouches.

Earlene whispers, "Rubie's goin' ta jail. It's almost over with."

Lee Pomerleau stands up.

Rubie drops, arms spread. He scrambles around on all fours among the ankles of the lawmen. The deputy with the carbine tries to take aim. Handcuffs appear in a state cop's hand. Another man springs at Rubie with both hands, but Rubie is slippery, slimy. Hands come from all directions . . . trying.

Cole Deveau finds Rubie's felt hat next to the Pomerleaus' wee gardenia bush. He raises his foot and stomps it.

The deputy with the carbine raises it and punches the butt between Rubie's shoulder blades. Rubie goes down with his face in the crushed rock.

Another deputy draws his foot back and gives Rubie his boot to the cheekbone, while at the same time another guy is kicking from the other side. Rubie's head and neck give a shudder in the middle. But he flips to one side, spits on the deputy's boot

Then, just as Lee Pomerleau comes to the picture window and puts both hands on the glass, Earlene says, "Daddy," in a whisper.

Rubie climbs up the front of Cole Deveau. Cole Deveau stiffly closes his arms around him the way sweethearts embrace in reunion, Rubie's face gashed and liver-colored. They stand eye to eye in stock-still silence. One of the state police deftly yanks Rubie's hands behind his back and clinks on the cuffs.

"It's about time," says Lee Pomerleau. "Now maybe they'll hog-tie the rest of them heathens."

"Not the babies and little kids!" Earlene croaks.

"Yes, all of 'em. Get 'em while they're harmless. Before they're full-blown Beans."

After they all drive up the right-of-way, Rubie Bean's truck with the door hanging open is still chugging in the Pomerleaus' crushed-rock driveway. Nobody comes for it for a long while.

_____ 5 _____

At the church with the square steeple there are only two men in the choir. Cole Deveau is the *big* one. He stands in the back with his maroon robe rising and falling upon his bearlike and tuneless bellows.

Earlene Pomerleau sits with her father and grandfather in the front row. She wears a little pink, child-sized sundress, and her hair splays over the back of the pew. She smells of the hot steam iron. Her body is round and narrow at the top like a Coke bottle.

Lee Pomerleau holds his face in his hands, the pain in his back and legs a dull red.

The choir sings madly. Gram Pomerleau plays the

organ, the narrow shoulders pumping, the blue curls
pumping, the feet in black prescription shoes running
over the pedals.

"Daddy, the warden is as devoted to singin' as he is to
arrestin' people, ain't he?"

Her father gives her a sharp look.

Earlene's eyes, which are vast like pastures, move in
long, rolling waves around the room.

Nobody seems to stare at the warden. The congregation acts like nothing's different. You hear a few "Praise
Gods" here and there. One or two moans. Meanwhile,
Cole Deveau sings toothless. All the way from the
corners of his mouth to each ear are the uncountable tiny
stitches. Where are the eyes in the black-and-yellow
wreckage of his face? He holds his hymnbook inches
from his face.

Earlene squeezes her eyes shut. "Praise Jesus," she
says. She can feel her father jiggling his leg next to her
leg.

Earlene says, "Daddy."

He gives her a sharp look.

"Daddy," she says.

"What?"

"I'm goin' ta be sick."

"Do it outdoor," he says.

_____ 6 _____

Outside, the rain is smoke-colored and cold. Cole Deveau's
bride sits on the seat of the new gray truck, knitting, as
usual. Nobody in the town of Egypt knows her name.
Cole Deveau never speaks of her, never brings her
inside. You never see her at beano or in the drugstore

waiting and pacing with all the others for the pill bottles to be filled. You only see her in his truck, knitting, knitting up a storm.

Earlene Pomerleau dashes through the rain, her hair a white flash. She dives into her father's little car, slams the door. "Phew!" she gasps.

The rain thuds all over the car.

Earlene paws through the bag of groceries her father picked up along the way. She finds a jar of black olives. "My favorite!" She eats the olives and listens to the rain. She switches on the windshield wipers. Slisk. Slisk. Slisk.

Now she sees the gray truck parked facing her, with Cole Deveau's bride in it. Earlene chews the olives and watches the bride's rain-blurry face. "What a queer-actin' woman."

The rain thrums. Earlene slowly chews. The pits have built up in her cheek.

Earlene waves at the bride. The bride seems not to notice, although her eyes are on Earlene.

Earlene blows the horn.

Nothing. The woman is raising one hand with the knitting needle in it. With her longest finger she dabs at the corner of one eye.

Earlene giggles. Blows the horn again.

The woman continues knitting.

Earlene gets out, carrying the olive jar. The rain increases, knocks her face and shoulders . . . like olives, the hard, green ones. She looks in the truck window at Cole Deveau's bride. The woman's hands working the needles show the frequent glint of a wedding ring. Her skin is unlovely, white, like three-day-old frosting on a wedding cake. Her dress is a charcoal-color satin with charcoal-color-satin covered buttons and a narrow belt of the same.

"Creature Feature," breathes Earlene. She eats another black olive. The bride keeps staring straight ahead.

"Maybe she's blind," Earlene whispers to herself. She puts her hand in front of the windshield, waves, splashes some rain.

The bride looks away.

Earlene notices the bride is knitting mint-colored baby booties. She knocks on the glass. "Havin' a baby?!!" Earlene shouts. The woman turns her head slightly, but her gray, satiny eyes come short of Earlene's face. The woman's lips move, counting stitches.

The rain thickens. It darkens Earlene's hair. It darkens her dress.

"Ain't FRIENDLY!" Earlene screams. "Ain't FRIENDLY!" She glances up at the church windows. Then she climbs up on the bumper and wildly waves her arms. The truck rocks. The bride's eyes look into Earlene's. Color comes to the woman's cheeks like two tiny spots of strawberry ice cream. She closes her eyes.

Earlene hops down. On the other side of the strumming rain the choir is singing "He Abides," and the congregation does the refrain. Earlene hums along. "Hallelujah, He abides with meeeee! . . ."

Earlene glances over at the church door, the forsythia bushes churning in the rain on either side. One by one, she flattens black olives on the bride's window. She arranges them like constellations of stars. They hold fast. Purple. They smell of salt.

SEVEN
Earlene's Yellow Hair

Since the stroke, Earlene knows Gram's body by heart. She rubs her with cornstarch every morning and arranges her in the wheelchair in her new violet print dress or one of the other dresses, always steam-ironed. Tied to one armrest is a loud silver bell, which Gram rings if Earlene gets too far off in the house.

Earlene's small wallpapered bedroom is upstairs. She leaves the door open at night and imagines every sound is Gram's bell.

Today is the hottest day in memory. They sit together in the sticky gloom of Gram's screened piazza. Earlene smokes filter cigarettes while her father is at work. Gram hates cigarettes. Back when she could talk she said a million times, "Tobacco is the work of Satan. It wasn't a Christian that invented tobacco, was it? No sirreee! It wasn't a Christian. It was them wild Indians . . . planted it everywheres . . . and the worst of our lot took it up. Don't you know your history?" And then she would bellow in her big voice, "YEA, DOGS ARE ROUND ME! A COMPANY OF EVILDOERS ENCIRCLE ME! DELIVER MY SOUL FROM THE SWORD, MY LIFE FROM THE POWER OF THE DOG! SAVE ME! SAVE ME! PRAISE THY POWER!"

Gram likes it when Earlene reads the Psalms, over and over and over, the favorite ones . . . and Ecclesiastes of Wisdom and Folly Compared . . . and when Earlene hums hymns or tries a few stanzas in her Minnie Mouse voice. She is singing now between long drags on the filter cigarette.

Earlene's father drives into the yard in his new yellow VW Squareback, home early because of the heat. The construction company he works for has the lowest bids on three new schools. This means no layoffs for at least a year. Lee seldom sleeps, never tires. Earlene drops her cigarette through the floorboards on the piazza. Gram moans.

Lee Pomerleau crosses the yard with his khaki shirt around his waist, a bag of groceries in each arm. When Gramp died, Lee sold his other house, came here to be in charge of grass cutting, in charge of repairs. He is more exacting than Gramp ever was. The old old place has taken on a new bright look.

Earlene rocks nervously in her upholstered spring rocker: woinka woinka woinka. Her father pushes the screen door open with his knee. He glares at Earlene as he passes. His eyes are pale like dimes. "*Who's* been smoking?" he asks Gram. Gram moans. "Has Earlene been smoking?" he asks. Gram closes her eyes.

He puts the groceries away.

Earlene pats Gram's hand.

He comes out and sits on a green-painted rocker but doesn't rock, just jiggles his leg and blows his cheeks in and out. He has just run cold water over his face and hair.

Earlene hums a hymn.

Roberta Bean's wee blue house is on the same side of the road. All the Pomerleaus turn their heads to the left as the tall woman strides across her yard with a basket of green tomatoes. She is barefoot and wears a thin, worn-out housedress with print nearly the same hue as the green tomatoes. She arranges some of them on a card table on the shoulder of the road. She unfurls a stained blue-and-yellow beach umbrella to shade the tomatoes and other produce, then places her folding chair in the sun. She sits, picks up her sewing. She crosses her ankles. Her feet aren't bony like the rest of her. They are staunch and silver-color, and the long toes handle the grass like deft fingers.

"I wouldn't buy a three-cent radish from that insane woman," says Lee Pomerleau, jiggling his leg furiously.

Earlene rocks: woinka woinka woinka.

Gram feels the skirt of her new violet dress with the fingers of her good hand.

Before Roberta Bean, giftlike, are the peppers, eggplants, red tomatoes, ears of corn with copper-color tassels, summer squash, green beans, wax beans, and a cardboard sign: VEgtiBles 4-sale CHeaP.

As cars pass on the road, Roberta Bean looks up from her sewing and gives them each a long, hammering stare. She wears no hat, just an egg-sized black bun right on top, and a ring of tortoiseshell combs.

In the thickness of this summer day only she looks unsticky.

"There should be a law that after you've had nine kids and no husband, you get the knife," Lee mutters. He looks into Earlene's eyes. "They call it tyin' the tubes."

He points at the tall woman with his thumb. "Hers... They should cut 'em, then tie 'em in twenty knots."

Earlene looks at her father's red face, the jiggling leg.

In the tall grass, Roberta Bean's two most recent babies toss and toil in a seething giggly pile... nude... both of them... right by the road. One scampers forward on all fours... the other falls to its back... both males, their privates wagging. Yet sometimes all that is recognizable of their anatomies is four grass-stained feet.

A logging truck makes its slow, growling ascent up the grade and Lee Pomerleau gives an annoyed red red look in that direction. The truck hisses, pulls to the shoulder, stops. The doors open. Two men get out, one a Letourneau Earlene remembers from school... He wears a messy T-shirt, his elbows are black, his crew cut has a bald spot. The other man is Beal Bean.

Earlene stops rocking. She closes her mouth in a tight, self-conscious line.

Beal wears aviator sunglasses, the darkest kind, and a railroad cap. As he crosses the road, he wipes his bare chest with a dirty bandanna. It is hard to tell where the hair on the chest begins and the great hulking beard ends.

Lee Pomerleau stops puffing his cheeks.

Earlene's deepest wish is for a cigarette.

From her seat in the sun, the tall woman raises up on her toes to stretch, worrying her body back and forth, baring her dark teeth in an ungracious leer as if she were waking from a nap alone in a small room.

Beal stands in front of the vegetable stand and runs the dirty bandanna into one of his ears.

Earlene's eyes slide down, and she sees that her father is barefoot. He has perfectly shaped feet, the nails lavender crescents, always clean.

Beal Bean and the Letourneau lean into the shade of

the umbrella and paw around in the baskets of the tall woman's perfect vegetables.

Seeing the men, the babies dash to their mother and engineer themselves into a heap on her feet. Two of her older babies come to the open door of the wee blue house and look into the light.

Beal Bean turns from the umbrella with a red tomato. Then he feels in the front pockets of his dungarees for loose change, each coin warmed by its closeness to his body.

"Hot enough for ya?" Beal yells over the snarl of the idling truck.

One baby throws grass at him. Beal laughs.

Roberta doesn't speak but only watches Beal hard.

The Letourneau studies the tall woman with awe. She is taller than either man. His eyes rest on her silvery feet, her most beautiful part. One baby makes popping noises with the walls of its mouth, pats its mother's feet. The other baby snatches a balled-up paper towel dangling in the grass, hurls it at the Letourneau, but the thing only arcs crazily back into the grass.

Beal Bean feels in his pockets for more change. Warm pennies. He puts his hand out. The pennies are brand-new, almost pink. The babies' eyes grow bigger than pennies. They approach Beal on tiptoe as if to steal the pennies from his hand . . . one penny to each baby . . . one quick darting swipe.

"There, by God, you're rich now!" Beal tells them. "Don't sp-speeeh-e-spend it all in one place."

The babies hiss at him.

The men walk over to the store, Beal carrying the tomato, the Letourneau stooping to pick up a small rock, winging it at a road sign: *Thwannggg!!!* and both men laugh.

Roberta Bean returns to her chair.

Both the babies jab the pennies into their mouths at the same time. Although the tall woman sees them do this, she doesn't wrestle the pennies from those tongues. She straddles her folding chair all the more comfortably and rearranges her tortoiseshell combs.

The babies swallow the pennies.

_____ **2** _____

Earlene counts her change on the table. Gram drinks orange juice in a paper cup with her good hand. Earlene whispers to herself, "Wax paper, peanut butter, batt'ries, milk, English muffins . . . and . . . hamburg."

Gram moans.

There is a lamp on the table, a bull Earlene's father carved when he was in high school, a hundred-watt bulb on the hump of its shoulders, which shines on Earlene's hands as she lays pennies in groups of fives, nickels in twos. There are several windows in this ell kitchen, yellow check curtains, but it's such a dark day with muggy, slanted, grumpy light.

Earlene scrapes the coins into her change purse. "Be right back, Gram," she says, pulling a noisy plastic dry cleaner's bag over her yellow hair.

Only after she is out in the downpour does she realize she's got her fuzzy yellow slippers on. "Oh, no!" But she keeps running. She runs past the tall woman's wee blue house. Of course, the vegetables are not on display today.

Two empty logging trucks idle along the road in front of Beans' Variety. A white dog smells their tires. Rain slaps the plastic bag on Earlene's hair. On the open piazza of the store she sees Beal Bean and a red-haired man squatted down by the door, drinking beers. She pulls the plastic low over her eyes.

She scampers up the three wet steps in her slippers. A freckled arm stretches out and grabs her ankle. "Well, I wouldn't know it was you, Earlene, 'cept for that yellow hair in the back . . . Give us here a look."

"Quit it!" Earlene snarls. She kicks at him. It's Fred Brown from school, only somewhat older, more weathered, quicker. He wears a T-shirt with a marijuana leaf, baggy army pants. His hair is the reddest of reds, but his eyes are dark. On one forearm is a colored tattoo of Donald Duck in mid-quack. He howls, "Earlene! It *must* be you!"

Beal's not wearing sunglasses today. His eyes avoid her. He opens another beer, flips the cap into the grass.

"You want a kick in the mouth, Freddie?!!" Earlene hisses, then lunges for the door.

Her hands are shaking as she pulls wax paper from the shelf and then peanut butter. She looks over the soups. Decides on tomato.

Behind the store, thunder makes a crackle, then a boom.

"Jesus!" chuckles the Bean ringing up Earlene's things. "I think it hit my trash can."

"A packa Kents, please," Earlene says.

He reaches for the Kents, adds them in.

The rain outside the piazza thickens, an impassable wall of water.

The door opens and Fred Brown comes in, watches the Bean putting the groceries in the bag. Earlene keeps her eyes on the Bean's hands.

Fred Brown looks at Earlene's slippers. "I can't allow this!" he shrieks. "It ain't right!!"

Earlene gives him a scorching look.

As she reaches for the bag, Fred Brown picks her up . . . She is child-sized, easy to move about, except for the flounce of massive yellow hair that rakes across his face.

He passes Beal, who is still scooched on the piazza, gallops through the rain. Beal is opening another beer, studying something almost invisible on one of the far-off gray hills.

When Fred reaches the screen piazza of the Pomerleaus', Gram's bell is ringing wildly inside the house. Fred puts Earlene down with a flourish, then says, "Ain't you gonna thank me?"

Earlene sniffs. "If you squished this wax paper and my cigarettes, there will be nuthin' to thank."

He is turning away. "Don't thank me, then!" He giggles, dashing into the rain. The hills whiten as electricity stretches down, touching the open field like a tickling finger, withdrawing with a loud CRACK! CRACK!

"What *is* it, Gram?" Earlene says as she comes into the kitchen. "What's all this fuss?"

Gram pitches the bell. It skids on the painted boards, rolls between Earlene's feet.

For the rest of the afternoon Gram sits by the window, looking out into the rain.

_____ **3** _____

Gram doesn't go to church anymore. She doesn't go anywhere. If you ask her to come along, she shakes her head. She sits in her wheelchair on the piazza and watches Earlene and Lee moving along under the dead elms and the almost dead elms. The road is spotty with

leafy light. And the shoulders and faces of Earlene and
Lee are spotty, too. They walk along, not talking. Earlene
carries her hymnbook. She wears a sundress of pale
green check and a real yellow rose in her hair, cheapy
rubber sandals that go between the toes, and a sullen
half-smile. She sees Beal Bean on the steps of Beans'
Variety, dark blue LIBBY'S LOGGING shirt buttoned to the
throat, his black beard burying the word LOGGING. He's
sitting with his knees up. Nothing in his hands. There's
no logging truck in the parking lot this time . . . just
Beal's old pickup with spotty light on the roof and raised
hood. On the ground beside his truck are some black rags
and a tin box of tools.

Lee wears his new pale-color suit jacket, his shoulders
back, swinging his arms.

Earlene says huskily, "Daddy, there's that grimy Beal
Bean that used to have pimples."

Lee reddens. "Look at the scenery on this other side
of the road. See how Mr. Goodspeed's fixed his place up
over here."

"Yes, Daddy. It looks good, don't it?"

Earlene feels something hit the back of her leg. It
burns. She looks in time to see an acorn rolling to a stop
on the pavement. She looks back and Beal Bean's fox-
color eyes move in deft circles over her sundress. She
looks away and keeps walking, tossing her yellow hair.

— **4** —

Uncle Loren stops in for a visit with Gram. He parks his
new pumpkin-color pig truck out on the road. There's a
handsome, long-legged hog painted by a sign maker on

the truck doors: POMERLEAU FARMS in a crescent underneath. The hog is black and white, his expression one of
supreme understanding. He is the prince of hogs.

Uncle Loren sits at the table for close to an hour
without talking. He smokes. Now and then, he leans
back on the two legs of his chair and pulls open the
refrigerator door. "Earlene . . . got any bread 'n' butters?"

"They ain't ready," says Earlene, standing with her
hands on her hips in the door to the dark hall.

"You plant too late?" Uncle Loren asks.

"What's late?" Earlene asks.

Uncle Loren lowers his chair legs and grins over his
shoulder at Earlene. "When they ain't here when I want
'em." His hands are big red scaly pig-farming hands. He
lights a cigarette with a wooden match. Gram moans.

Gram always used to say you can't get the smell of
pigs out of the house after one of Uncle Loren's visits.
Gram always used to say her boy Lee is a genius. He can
do *anything*, you name it. She liked to add that her boy
Lee has accepted Jesus Christ as his Savior.

"What about Uncle Loren?" Earlene used to ask
her.

"I'm afraid, Earlene, that the Lord will lose patience.
Ain't no sneakin' in the back door."

Uncle Loren uses his hand as an ashtray, wipes each
ash into the knee of his striped overalls. The smoke of his
cigarette is thick and curved.

Earlene sits down in a chair next to him. "How's the
pigs?" she asks.

"Good," says Uncle Loren.

Earlene lights up a cigarette by pushing the end of it
on the element of the stove. Loren's eyes widen. He
scratches one of his huge, freckled, sunburned arms.
"Well, well, golly gumdrops," he says deeply.

Earlene sits in the chair across the table from him and smokes, tapping the ash into a teacup.

Loren breathes noisily in and out of his mouth.

Earlene says, "Uncle Loren, how long have you smoked?"

"Since I was seven," he says.

Gram moans.

Earlene smiles. She tosses her yellow hair. "Your lungs must be pitch-black," she says.

"Ayuh," he says. "But I'm supposed to . . . I'm a man."

Earlene giggles. "Uncle! That's old-fashioned!" She shoots the smoke out her nose, leans on one elbow, and looks out through the glass in the door to the new pig truck. "Uncle Loren, don't you ever get lonesome livin' with just dirty old pigs?"

"Ain't dirty!" Loren says. "Pigs are clean. Ain't you never seen a litter of bitty pigs in fresh hay?"

"Ain't never been to your place, Uncle Loren."

"Well . . ." He leans forward, his pale eyes bright as open windows. "Sweetheart, pigs and hogs is superior to folks. Folks are ratty messed-up back-stabbin' sons-a-whores."

Gram moans.

Earlene blinks.

He adds, "I'd rather be a born-once hog than a born-again Christian any day . . . you name the day!" Then he bares his little teeth. "Pigs was created in the Lord's image."

Gram leans forward with a shriek . . . then something like the kai-yai-ing of a little puppy. Her good arm makes a graceful arc. She sweeps everything off the utility table. Everything: bread box, napkins, tea-bag cannister, a bouquet of plastic yellow flowers, sugar, salt. It all settles on the kitchen floor in a cloud of white flour.

---------------------- **5** ----------------------

When Lee gets home, the pig truck is gone. His mother is sobbing. Her glasses have flown off somewhere, and only her eyes are human. The rest of her is floured . . . ghostly. Her good hand twists in the lap of her dress. All around her is the flour-coated debris.

"Mumma!" Lee cries. He dusts her off. "What happened! Who did this?"

Gram howls.

"Where's Earlene? Why isn't she here lookin' after you? Has something happened to Earlene?"

Gram waves her good hand matter-of-factly.

Lee collapses on his mother, hugging and holding. "Praise God!" he sobs.

Gram pats him. Her maroon mouth grins.

---------------------- **6** ----------------------

Earlene is upstairs with the sewing machine, hemming a sundress with eyelet lace. Her room is small and crowded with things. There is a gray haze from many cigarettes.

Something hits the door like a punch.

She stops the machine, stares at the door. "Who is it?"

"Your father."

"Be right out."

"NOW."

"Daddy, I'm almost done." She puts out her cigarette, covers the ashtray with scrap fabric.

Again he gives the door one furious single bang.

"Okay. Okay." She unlatches the door.

He has a tall bottle of honey and wheatgerm oil discount shampoo in his hand. He twists the top off. They look into each other's eyes.

"Oh . . . jeez," Earlene croaks.

His eyes are ringed with sleeplessness, tears bulging.

"Okay, Daddy . . . what'd I do now?"

He tosses the bottle cap down. It rolls under Earlene's bed.

"Daddy! This is almost funny!" She giggles. "You an' your soap." Her laughter becomes almost like singing, eerie, high, and sweet. "I'm grown up!"

He races at her and grabs her sleeve, stretching her shirt away from the neck.

"Daddy!"

He turns, still grasping her sleeve, and kicks the bedroom door shut, tears hanging off the end of his nose.

Earlene yanks away. He chases her around the bed. She pushes at him. Struggling, they are like two awkward children, tiny, twisting figures at play. He drives the bottle into her mouth and a cold thickness fills her throat.

"Praise God for His mercy . . . Praise Him! And ye shall have everlasting life!"

He presses her to the corner. She is dizzy, wild, gagging.

"Praise Him!" he howls.

"Bein' sick," she gasps . . . red-faced. "Bein' SICK." And over his shoulder she vomits . . . a foamy wob of orange . . . and as she vomits again . . . again . . . she clutches his khaki shirt . . . and he prays with his eyes closed. Prays for truth.

_____ **7** _____

She stands on the weedy shoulder with her thumb out. A

half-dozen cars pass with their windshield wipers swishing. As each one passes, she screams, "Pig!"

The hard rain makes tea-color streaks in her yellow hair. The rain runs off her chin. Another car passes. "PIG!" she cries into the rain. "Pigs . . . all pigs. Daddy's a pig. Gram's a pig. All fat pigs." She burps up the taste of shampoo.

When the logging truck hisses to a stop, she looks surprised. He pulls her by the arms up into the high seat. He wears his railroad cap low over his eyes. Nothing shows of his face. He is just all hair.

"I'm running away," she says dully and lights up a soggy cigarette.

He watches the road through the windshield wipers, cranking high speed.

She looks at him. His soft denim shirt is patched in a dozen places, lays on his body like a ratty dishtowel.

She draws on her cigarette, makes a curtain of smoke. "Mind if I smoke?" she says in her high Minnie Mouse voice, almost tunelike.

He shrugs.

She looks out at the trees blurring by. "High up, ain't we?"

He nods.

"We goin' to the mill?" she asks. She blows smoke in a long, hard, ruler-straight line.

"That's right," he says.

They strike a frost heave and she is jarred almost off the seat. She puts her cigarette out on her shoe. She burps up more shampoo taste. She sees a long stone wall rising-falling and leaves being beaten by the rain. "We sure are high up . . . I never rode this high up before."

He smiles.

8

She stands behind him in the doorway, lighting a Kent with nervous fingers. Rain drips from the eaves of the wee blue house. She turns and looks at the windows of her own house next door, wondering if, in the hours she's been gone, her father is sorry yet . . .

There's a comedy routine on the black-and-white TV, but nobody looks at it. The top of the tall woman's head nearly scrapes the ceiling. She wears a housedress made for a much fatter woman. Behind her is a fat yellowish refrigerator with black smudges around the door handle. The tall woman is cutting hair. The babies and older kids wait turns. A baby with an adult-sized red T-shirt low on the shoulders sits Indian-style on the supper table, and the tall woman clips away at this one.

Beal says, "Auntie . . . thiii-is is Earlene. She's running away from home."

The house smells of soft, rotting, wet wood.

The tall woman looks blankly at Beal. She doesn't stop working the scissors.

Earlene smokes.

Beal says, "It's raining out, Auntie. She needs a place." He pulls the door shut behind them, and a few of the babies give Earlene dark looks.

The rest of them ring closer around the table, watching their mother's hands. She snaps the scissors, working the crew cut into a shorter crew cut. The scissors are those orange kind they say you can cut pennies and dimes with.

Beal says softly, "Just one night, Auntie?"

The baby on the table drives its fingers around in its

soft red mouth. The tall woman draws its hand down. But the fingers just go back again.

Earlene looks around frantically for a place to put her cigarette out.

The tall woman drinks from a jar on the table. Between the times she drinks from the jar, other hands reach up and take the jar to drink from, then set it back.

Earlene spits in her hand and touches the cigarette to her palm.

The scissors clack and the hairs seesaw downward.

A warm hand closes around Earlene's wrist. Beal says, "It's okay, Earlene." He steers her through a room with a low bed and cold greenish light. They go up lightless narrow stairs. "Watch your head," Beal whispers.

At the top of the stairs Beal feels for a chain. The attic blooms into a hideous, glaring gray light. There are blankets strewn on the unfinished attic floor, pink Fiberglas still in rolls in one corner. Two young boys are asleep here.

Earlene moves her eyes cautiously.

Beal scrapes up some blankets from directly under the swaying light bulb. The single dormer is curtainless, busy with spiders. Beal makes a pallet with the blankets.

"I'll make a pillow," he whispers and takes off his shirt, rolls it up. Then he sits on the blankets. Earlene stays standing.

"Well, here's yaaaw-your hideaway, Earlene. How long you runnin' away for?"

Earlene frowns. "I don't know."

He pulls on his beard.

She glances at the sleeping boys.

The light seems to scream from the bulb.

She says, "You're gonna sleep here, too?"

He nods.

He looks like an upright BEAR. She thinks of her

father's childlike frame. Shakily, she sits on the blankets next to him. He smiles with yellow teeth within the tumbling beard. He takes some of her hair into his hand.

A hardness comes to her throat.

She twirls a corner of a blanket in her fingers.

He laughs. Deeply. "I like your hair," he says.

She stares into the light till it almost blinds her.

He rubs his palms together, parts them, looks into them.

"What are you thinking about?" she asks.

He laughs. "Wicked work." He unlaces his boots.

Earlene watches the huge feet emerge. She says, "I ain't gonna do nuthin', you know . . . you know . . . with you."

The heads of the sleeping boys stir. Faces appear. They watch Beal pull off his dungarees. There's nothing under the dungarees. Earlene covers her face. Beal laughs. He says, "Earlene . . . you are grown up, remember? You c-ah-aaah-can handle this!" He goes down on his knees.

"Turn off the light!" Earlene screams.

"Jesus fuckin' Christ, Earlene!"

She looks over at the boys, who are looking over at her. Their eyes twinkle.

She clasps her hands as if in prayer. "Beal! Please!"

Beal stands and heavily crosses the floor to the light, yanks the chain.

She adds her clothes to the pallet. The elastic of her underwear snaps, and one of the young boys snickers.

Somehow, when Beal straddles her, they miss the pallet, and Earlene's shoulders drive into the floor and the head of a nail. His body weighs, it seems, like a stack of bodies. She rolls her eyes and thinks how Gram used to say, "You know, Earlene, God only gives you one chance. There's no sneakin' in the back door!"

Beal sniffs at her throat, blows into her yellow hair.

"You can live through it," Uncle Loren had insisted. "The black bear is only curious. You just gotta remember: *Never* scream. This one had Chuck Winters grippin' him in a muck hole up Piscataquis ten, twelve years back . . . pokin' him, lappin' him, rubbin' its head in his shirt . . . sniffin', snortin', grippin'. Ol' Chuck, he just kept what you call a low profile . . . just laid there *loose* in the muck hole. Well, after about fifteen minutes or so of checkin' out all the interestin' parts of ol' Chuck, the bear plants one powerful final snort in his ear, then ambles off into the fiddleheads."

Beal arranges Earlene's hips with four or five powerful tugs, his vast and hairy front raking back and forth.

"But then"—Loren had sighed—"they been known to rip you up. They're a lot like a dog . . . They go for the head . . . but . . . well, now Dick Cross . . . he's that old Maine guide Bertie used ta chum with . . . he says if you got a beer gut you're more apt ta live through mutilation . . . but the pain is enough ta make ya lose your mind . . . He said he'd rather be taw-tured with a white-hot iron . . . Yessuh . . . ol' Dick knows."

"Ohmagawd," says Earlene softly.

Beal drags his tongue up her cheek.

Her arms and legs struggle, but he pushes her harder into the boards, rocks his monstrous weight.

She screams in his face, a high-pitched wail.

The rocking of his body suddenly stops. She feels the hot arc of Bean seed. She pictures millions of possible big Bean babies, fox-eyed, yellow-toothed, meat-gobbling Beans.

"For God sakes, Earlene," Beal says.

He flips onto his back and makes a soft groan.

Earlene wildly jumps to her feet, gasping for breath. She feels her abdomen. It's intact.

Beal thrashes the blankets around, buries himself in them, head and all.

Earlene stands in the dark, pushing her damp hair back, anchoring loose strands behind her ears.

Beal is silent.

The young boys turn slowly in their bedding.

"I suppose that woman will be up here . . . to see what's the matter," Earlene says.

Beal is silent.

Earlene blinks crazily in the absolute dark.

Beal is silent.

"Well," says Earlene. "Maybe she won't."

Beal is silent, hardly breathing under the blankets.

Earlene puts her hands on her hips. "I weren't born yesterday, you know, Mr. Big Man."

Beal sighs.

She tries to make out his form in the dark, but she can't see anything. "Most the kids in this house're YOURS. Anybody can tell. ANYBODY! They all look just like you. It's no secret, you know. Maybe you think so, Mr. Secret Secret Secret. But you are wrong wrong wrong!"

He slides the covers from his head.

She says, "Ain't I right, Beal? Ain't they yours?"

He sits up. "You was always a smartass little twerp, Earlene. I'll give ya five seconds ta lay down and SHUT UP."

9

Yes, Daddy is a genius, Earlene thinks to herself. He can do anything with his hands. She watches through the living room doorway as he hammers and hacks out one inside wall of Gram's two-hundred-year-old farmhouse. She stands with a cup of almost cold coffee, watching the small self-conscious hands of her father measure and cut, and she says, "Daddy, thank you. It's what I've always wanted."

He looks up quick and his pale eyes pass over her. It is spring. She's pregnant.

He and she sweep up the floor, a frazzle of plaster and wallpaper. Lee stops sweeping now and then to flutter his fingers through his thinning hair.

Now he is grunting, lifting an enormous glass tank into the hole in the wall. He frames it with strapping. It becomes a wall of glass. Little doors open up in the wall on either side of the glass. Through these, Lee fills the glass tank with warm water.

"Come on, Earlene. Let's go see 'em!"

"Oh, Daddy . . . it's my legs. They got that ache."

"Horseradish!" he cries, and lifts her off her feet.

"Daddy, you'll throw your back out again!"

Gram is in the kitchen in her wheelchair, eating Chips Ahoy! with tea. Lee winks at her as he rushes through, carrying Earlene.

Hours pass.

They come in carrying big and little brown bags. Gram has wheeled into the living room and is feeling the wall of warm water with her one good hand. She smiles. They show her the little pumps. Lamps. Filters and heaters. Chunks of coral. A miniature sunken ship. Lee rolls up his khaki sleeves and fastens the equipment in the tank. He checks the temperature of the water. Earlene, cross-legged in a straight-back chair, rubs her legs and coos at her father's ingenuity.

He stands before them, his hands dripping. He bows, and Earlene applauds and whistles. Gram rings her bell.

After supper, the water is the right temperature. Here

comes the legion of white cartons, like Chinese chow mein to go. Lee untapes the flaps and looks in. "There they are!" he cries out. Jiggles his leg. "Yep! There they are!"

Earlene giggles.

Their foreheads come together over the white cartons.

At last, the wall of water becomes a black sky of cascading stars . . . wee fish . . . all of a kind . . . all of one size, navigating together down, up, across. Their eyes are pinpoints of red like the portholes of hundreds of deep-sea craft, envoys for distinguished missions.

After the last fish is added in, Lee Pomerleau pulls a straight-back chair between his daughter and mother, all chairs facing the wall of water. Lee turns off all the lights except those that illuminate the fish and the chalky coral landscape. He scurries through the dark hall in his stocking feet and returns with three cups of cocoa.

The three faces are lighted by the wall of water like faces in a movie house.

Earlene chirps, "Oh, Daddy! Your hand comin' down to fix the floor of the ocean was just like the hand of GOD!"

He sits on the straight-back chair, and she leans into him and kisses his clean-shaven jaw.

EIGHT
The Grave

Gram is in her wheelchair with her Bible on her knee, turning the tissuey pages one at a time with her good hand. She watches Bonny Loo climb up on a kitchen chair to tape a paper witch on the window. "Ma says it's two weeks till Halloween!" Bonny Loo says. She jumps to the floor on both feet and the glasses in the cupboards tinkle.

Through the kitchen windows, the afternoon dribbles in across Gram's cheek in a haunting violet.

Bonny Loo looks at Gram. "Halloween's the best, ain't it, Gram? 'Cept for Christmas." Bonny Loo's fox-color eyes widen behind her bifocals. "Ain't it, Gram?"

The Bible lies open, unwavering, on the butterknife-sharp knee. Gram's the first dead person Bonny Loo has ever seen, and yet Bonny Loo knows dead when she sees it.

_____ **2** _____

She is big, big in the knees, big across the back, and her face is a pumpkin-shaped wall of bone. Her dark hair stands out from the head to show her almost constant agitation, like someone who keeps getting poked with a stick. She tiptoes up the narrow stairs and says, "You ain't been up here before, have you?"

He says no.

Behind her thick glasses her eyes seem to fade in and out like two little TV sets with poor reception. She walks with her hands on her hips. Her hard shoes thunk on the stairs. She grips his wrist. "I'm a scientist, you know. Don't tell nobody what you see."

He hitchhiked here. His nose is red from the cold. He wears a fluorescent hunting vest, a fluorescent hat with the earflaps tied up. He smells of the cold. It's been a cold spring.

He is the biggest man Bonny Loo has ever seen. His nose is broad as a teacup . . . like the noses of other Beans. Bonny Loo leads him by the wrist past two closed doors. When she gets to her room, she picks up a flashlight from behind the door. "It's gotta be dark. Too much light could spoil 'em, you know." She never calls him Daddy. She calls him Beal Bean.

She clicks on the flashlight, leads him over the tops of Magic Markers, dirty clothes . . . around puzzles and plastic cars . . . parts to the Visible Man and the Visible Woman mixed . . . Her hard shoes crunch over Lincoln Logs, poker chips. He steps over a pink back scratcher shaped like a hand on a long thin arm. He can smell a urine-damp quilt. She points with the flashlight to a closet in the far corner. She whispers, ''You gotta kneel!''

He kneels, his monstrous beard almost touching the floor. She stands at his shoulder and her thick body bends, her large hand closes around a glass jar, one of ten or more glass jars on the pun'kin-pine closet floor. There's nothing else in this closet but these jars.

She raises the jar just a few inches from his face. ''See!'' she whispers.

''What is it?''

''This one is a coconut donut.''

''What ha-haaah-aaappened to it?'' he asks.

''It MOLDED!'' she chirps. ''I'm good with molds.''

''Ayuh,'' he says. ''You got a way with 'em.''

''Tall, ain't it?'' she whispers. ''And furry.''

He smiles. ''It's a beauty.''

She stoops, puts her mouth to his ear. ''I spend time here,'' she whispers. ''Hours.''

''What for?'' he asks.

''I watch 'em grow.''

He picks up another jar. She puts the light on it for him.

''Raisin bread,'' she says.

''You're really smaaaa-smart,'' he says.

She smiles. Her large square teeth have spaces. ''I can SEE 'em grow, you know. I put this flashlight on 'em and put my eye right here''—she holds the jar to her glasses—''and when it happens, I SEE it.''

''Jesus Christ!'' he gasps.

''It's a miracle,'' she whispers.

She shows him a jar with a lemon-filled donut. ''I started this one last night.'' She shows him an English muffin, a brownie, a tangerine. ''Fruit don't grow,'' she says grumpily. ''Donuts and sandwiches are best.''

"Where's your muh-uh-uther?" he asks.

She frowns. Sets down her jars. "Prack-tickly DEAD."

"What do you mean?" He stands up.

"I don't know. She's just come ta bones lately." Bonny Loo shrugs.

"Where is she?" he asks.

"Restin'," she says. She cuts off the flashlight. "Do you think I'm goin' ta be a scientist?"

"Shit, yes!" He looks around the room.

She looks at his black nails. "Do you fix cars?" she asks.

"Sometimes," he says. "But I ain't got very good tools."

"Oh . . . well . . . what *do* you do? . . . you know . . . for a job?" She narrows her eyes.

"Nuthin'. I'm outta work," he says.

"My gramp's a carpenter," she says.

"I know it," he says. He moves into the hall.

"Gramp says if he ever finds out who my father is, he'll KILL."

Beal puts his hand on a closed door. "She in here?"

"No . . . that one," she says, pointing to the opposite door. "You don't wanna go in there. It stinks." She wrinkles her nose. "Gramp NEVER goes in there. I'm the one that's gotta go in with stuff."

His face whitens. He puts his ear to the door. "I haven't seen her in a long time. She doesn't like me," he says.

Bonny Loo squints. "QUEER, ain't she?"

He taps on the door. No answer.

Bonny Loo's eyes widen. "Scary, ain't it? Sometimes I figure she's dead by now."

He turns the knob. Bonny Loo steps back, flattens her shoulders to the opposite wall.

"Earlene?" he whispers. A smell of darkness and stale food and of skin that sleeps and sleeps, never washes...and the haze of hundreds of cigarettes...leaps at the opening door. "Gawd!" he says, pausing in the doorway.

"I TOLD ya," says Bonny Loo.

The room is only big enough to hold a single bed, a sewing machine table, and a dozen cereal bowls with crescents of bad milk, a saucer with uneaten toast, a water glass, a heaped ashtray. Bonny Loo says heartily, "Look what I brought, Ma! The secret man...HIM!"

On an uncovered pillow is the face, onion-colored, skull-like, two great hunkering green eyes not quite open, glazed as in death. But the eyes see him. The lips part. "Get outta here before my father calls the deputy," a craggy, old-womanish voice says.

Bonny Loo grumbles, "He's at work, Ma! It's only dinnah-time." Bonny Loo goes to the window, yanks on the shade so that it flutters up. "I'll keep watch, okay?"

"Bonny Loo...please put the shade back down," Earlene moans.

Beal stares at Earlene with his mouth open.

Her yellow hair is matted, is almost like fingers around her ears, darkened by oils. "My Gawd," he whispers.

He has brought the smell of the outdoors into the room. It reaches the bed. Earlene turns her head away.

Bonny Loo stands on the sewing table to reach the shade. She yanks on it and again the room darkens.

Beal goes no closer to the bed. But he doesn't back out, either. He just stands and looks at Earlene, turning his fluorescent hunting hat in his hands.

Bonny Loo plunges to the floor from the sewing table, landing on all fours, chimpanzee style...then pushes past Beal into the hall, muttering, "See, I TOLD you she's prack-tickly rotten!"

———————————— **3** ————————————

Bonny Loo wears a reindeer sweater her great-aunt Paula made. She stands on the edge of her grass, trimming off a thumbnail with a jackknife. She watches the tall woman next door sowing her garden by hand. The sun is warm and lard-colored through bony trees and on all the rooves in Egypt Village. Bonny Loo waves to the tall woman. The tall woman waves back. The tall woman's dark eyes swim around Bonny Loo.

The tall woman's latest babies wake up from their naps and come to the sill of the front door, yawning. When they see their mother in the garden, they rejoice: "Yay!" They run and dive into the soft dirt with their knees and faces. "Weeeee!" As two babies stand up, another two go down. Bonny Loo takes a few steps into the tall woman's grass. The tall woman pitches rocks to the edge. The babies retrieve them and throw them back. Then the tall woman trudges from the wee blue house, giving a smooth ride to a shallow box of dinky tomato plants, plants that are yellowed by the darkness inside her house. Each seedling is in a Dixie cup. Behind Roberta Bean, single-file and solemn, march the babies, one Dixie cup to each, one silly, fainting-away plant.

Bonny Loo tugs at the hem of her reindeer sweater, agitated, kicking stones.

Roberta pets each seedling after its entry to earth. The babies follow, petting the seedlings.

When the planting is done, the tall woman and her

young ones troop past Bonny Loo...and Bonny Loo
waves, her fox-color eyes wild and wide...The babies
and the tall woman each give Bonny Loo a little
wave...Then they go into the tacky blue house and pull
the door shut.

————————————— 4 —————————————

"Maybe this will grow," Bonny Loo says to herself. She
stands on a chair in the kitchen, turning an onion over
and over in her hands. She lands on her feet, and the
glasses in the cupboard clink. She gets a dirty spoon
from the sink and goes out through the porch and around
to the back of the house. She plants the onion.

That night, she gets dressed in the dark and tiptoes
down the narrow stairs. She waits till she's outdoors to
click on the flashlight. She shines the flashlight on the
disrupted earth. "GROW!" she commands.

————————————— 5 —————————————

The steamy sun clamps upon the land for many days. The
evening is a dark bitter rose, heavy with odor, dim on
Bonny Loo's walls. She lies on top of her blankets with
her clothes on, her flashlight in one hand. She hears her
grandfather come up from the bathroom and step lightly
to his room. Through the screen she hears a golden robin
and a passing car. She waits.

Then she gets up and goes out. She carries the flashlight in the stretchy waistband of her shorts and walks
with swinging arms.

When she is only four or five paces from her onion plant, she hears low voices in Roberta Bean's garden. The tall woman is scooching among the squash vines in a light-color dress. The tall woman lifts a roly-poly pumpkin, still attached to the vine, and she coos at it. "This one will be the biggest. It's for your poor mother, Beal." She coos some more. "I can put her initials on it so it looks like nature writes. That's what I done last year, and she made a fuss over it."

Beal stands over her, swatting at mosquitoes that attack his face and neck. He wears no hat and his hair is in a dozen cowlicks in silhouette. He pushes his knee into the tall woman's back. He says, "I wish I haaaa-a-aad a m-mah-million bucks."

The tall woman says, "Me, too."

Beal says, "Ain't no way I'm goin' ta ever have a million dollars."

The tall woman says softly, "The meek shall inherit a hole in the earth. That's what Pa always says."

"Fuck Pa! He can just go fuck himself with his goddam sayin's," Beal snarls, and the mosquitoes dance on his beard.

"You havin' a tiff with Pa again?"

"Ain't no tiff, just tired."

"You stay away from Rubie's woman . . . Been hearin' some gossip 'bout you 'n' that one . . . Get yourself in a bind if you don't . . . I wouldn't hang around over there, Beal. Pa says you can come back."

He pushes his leg harder into her back. "I been takin' Rubie's guns to the cellar hole . . . bustin' up glass."

"Dontcha foul up no blue Masons or I'll crown ya myself."

"Crown me, Auntie." He pushes again.

In her scooching position, she swivels and pushes her face into his dungarees.

"Ain't foolin', are ya?" he says softly.

She stands, only a hair of rose-color light on the left side of her form, her strange small face. She opens up her mouth and her arms and fixes hard upon him. He paws at the buttons of her pale dress.

Then Bonny Loo hears Roberta chuckle, "You smell pure hot, Mistah Man. Ain't no way I'm gonna fool with these pretty little squashes in the ruttin' season of your kind."

She lets him undo the dress. She pushes herself into his hands. He makes a ghoulish howl and fumbles with his dungarees.

And Bonny Loo blinks as the two figures vanish in a whirl and whine of mosquitoes.

--------------------- **6** ---------------------

She stands with her hands on her hips. She wears shorts and a Red Sox T-shirt, bare thick arms. She is grass-stained, soggy, and bruised from hard play. She says huskily, "Ma, it's worse in here." In one hand is a single black-eyed Susan.

The room is near ninety degrees. Houseflies wheel against the ceiling. Earlene turns her head away from the light of the open door so that it only touches the outline of her razorlike cheekbone.

Bonny Loo goes to the foot of the bed and squeezes her mother's toes. "Feel that, Ma?" she asks.

Earlene nods.

"You ain't dead yet, then!" the child chirps.

Earlene closes her eyes.

Bonny Loo waves the black-eyed Susan in her mother's face. "Actually, these kinda flowers stink," she says.

Earlene's large eyes have begun to sink. The mouth looks huge.

Bonny Loo says, "Gramp's called the hospital about you. You're goin' there."

Bonny Loo sits on the bed. "It's awful in here, Ma!"

Earlene says, "It's okay. It's quiet."

"Ain't quiet," says Bonny Loo, glaring at the wheeling flies. Bonny Loo's shoulders suddenly stoop. She stretches her T-shirt up to wipe her face. She makes a little animal grunt and her face goes red. She sobs and her eyes are lost in tears.

She pitches the black-eyed Susan at the wall, then leaps up and runs for the window and yanks at the shade. It flies up with a ratatatatatat and an explosion of light.

"THERE!" she screams.

And she clatters out of the room.

7

The doorknob twists. The door opens. Roberta Bean's hugeness fills the doorway. Roberta Bean, pregnant again. And across the sill on both sides of this big Bean, an army of naked little Beans with contemptuous posture, their bellies flushed and tuberous, their navels—ruptured once—twisted like bows.

Earlene's eyes grow enormous.

The babies raise up and down on their toes. Like white, pointing fingers, their maleness is most teeming, most conspicuous.

Earlene's Minnie Mouse voice creaks, "I'm resting."

"Enough rest!" says Roberta. "What are all these shades down for? P.U.!"

Roberta wears her blue housedress without a belt, the

belly pumpkin perfect beneath the fabric of handsome blue clouds and cornflowers. She plunges forward off the sill and says to Earlene, "The whole town thinks you're at death's door. I don't."

Earlene feels the light from the hall stamp itself to her face and throat like a gloved hand. "Leave me be!" she cries.

"You must come out and get some sun. Come out and chat with me! Tell me about yourself!"

Earlene covers her face with bony hands.

The little boys swing on the skirt of their mother's blue cornflower dress. Their eyes are dark like little doggies' eyes. Their unfreckled, unmarred bodies stretch unselfconsciously, rippling nuances of coffee and cheese colors, the darkest being the shoulders where the sun most often drums.

"Please," Earlene whimpers, her greenish eyes flying to the walls . . . the ceiling. "I don't want to be with you."

"But we have things in common," says Roberta.

"Don't SAY that! Don't you EVER say that again!" Earlene screams, and her face reddens.

"Not even a TV in here," says Roberta. She smiles and her teeth are like a fort unto the darkness of her mouth. "You made yourself a nifty grave here."

The babies pad in on the old rug and their feet whisper. Their faces peer up over the edge of the bed. Earlene sees in the hand of one baby a TOMATO. Earlene's eyes widen with horror.

Roberta says, "Look here! We have a present for you, Earlene!"

The baby raises its hand. It is fruit at its most fit. The insides of coons and rabbits are like this just before being let out by a sharp knife. You see its readiness to come.

Earlene cringes.

Under the babies' long molelike snouts are the suggestions of smiles.

Then the fingers of the baby holding the tomato shift slightly. POP! The perfectly ready fruit collapses. Pale seeds in gel clobber Earlene's face and hair, fill one of her eyes.

"Ooooops!" say the babies in unison.

"Let me dwell in the house of the Lord!" screams Earlene. "Come for me now! Oh, Jesus . . . help me . . . I can't stand it no more."

The tall woman wipes Earlene's face with a corner of the sheet. She lifts her from the stinky bed. She carries her into the hall and down the stairs. On the screen piazza is Gram's wheelchair folded up. The tall woman plumps it out and squares Earlene in it. Earlene's sparrowlike legs squirm out from under her tomato-stained gown. The little boys go up on their toes and strain together like a team of tiny ponies and make the chair go.

Through a tunnel of trees, in and out of sun where the crumbly road scorches the pads of their feet, the wee kidnappers wheel and wheel and wheel.

And chirp, "Yippeee!"

Earlene moans.

The tall woman is a ship unto them all, carrying the afternoon on her light-color dress.

8

Bonny Loo is on her knees. "See! It's an onion."

The stalk is record length. The blossom regal.

"You think so?"

"I put it in the ground," Bonny Loo says, rising with

her hands on her hips. "So . . . will you help me make a scarecrow for it?"

Beal wipes his face with his bandanna. "Crows don't eat onions, Bonny."

"They'll eat THIS beautiful one."

--------------------------------- 9 ---------------------------------

He moves up the mountain like a packhorse, crunching many small sticks and branches underfoot. She rides on his shoulders like a child. She wears a child-sized summer dress, and her bare legs are almost lost in his beard. Her hair is almost a fluorescent yellow. She is still very bony, very white, very silent. She smells of her morning bath.

On the mountain are countless birches: gray, gold, and the white, some of the young ones bending from last winter's pitiless snows. There is not much shade here. Birds scream from all directions.

Earlene says, "I'm not like Roberta, you know."

Beal grunts over a stone wall and crashes through fern and over soggy ground. "I wish you were," he says.

Her throat tightens. She holds down a garbled scream.

They go into a dark pine grove and his boots hiss.

They can hear a brook. A dragonfly tests Earlene's hair, then veers away. Beal sways slowly toward the brook.

He carries her higher, higher, over a barbed wire. Her yellow hair attracts another dragonfly. This one buzzes in Earlene's ear. She swipes at it.

Beal wears his railroad cap, his dark sunglasses. She feels the packhorse muscles of his shoulders and neck working, and his arteries beat against her legs.

"I HATE Roberta," Earlene almost sobs. "Daddy says it's just a mattera time before the health department shuts her down."

He is silent. When he comes to the brook, he crosses on round, flat stones. He stops and looks up at the trees, at their autumnal mauve. He stands stock-still except for his hands, which stroke Earlene's ankles, prod the hardness of her nails. Then he turns.

Below are the tiny rooves, a tatter of field, the broad violet hills, here and there a ruffled pond. He stands and stands and stands, a shoulder muscle quivering now and then, his bearing unfriendly, packhorse silent.

EARLENE

NINE

Warren Olsen's Look of Love

Since we come to live with Madeline Rowe, Beal's found another job. Limbin' pulp. Less than minimum wage. "You gotta take what you can get," he says. "Pa always says that," he says.

His boots leak. One night last winter we sat up most the night with them toes. I hold 'em. Then he holds 'em. You roll 'em between your fingers. We take turns tryin' to warm 'em. He says, "They ain't gonna come out of it, for chrissakes!" I say, "Beal, you gotta get you some new boots next pay." He gives me a sideways look. "Shows hah-aaah-how much you know 'bout the price of boots," he says.

The next mornin' I'm in the kitchen with Madeline. We're pickin' up. I'm collectin' the kids' bowls. She's feedin' the stove. I'm singin' a hymn, one of Gram's favorites, and Beal comes out of the bedroom and he says, "Earlene, shut up!" He sets on the stool by the woodstove where Madeline's coaxin' the fire and he puts on his boots. I see them boots are still wet. He don't say nuthin', just puts 'em on, laces 'em up. Then he goes out and puts another can of thirty-weight in the truck.

I say, "He's in a bad mood."

Madeline says, "Frig him, then."

We hear the truck start, then he's gone.

That was winter, now it's summer. Black flies. Deer flies. He don't complain.

Madeline says, "Let's go to a movie! I'll treat." She wears her crazy frizzy black hair under a rolled bandanna like an Indian.

I say, "Maybe Beal's run outta gas again t'night."

I hope she will say, "Let's drive down one-sixty and see if we find him walkin'."

I can picture him in them awful boots, his shirt around his waist, pushin' his sunglasses up on his head as the sun gets lower, dogs runnin' out of houses at him, smellin' the backs of his legs.

Madeline Rowe is Rubie Bean's woman. She says Rubie's just a pretend man. "I made him up," she always says. "Only this missin' tooth is real!" She points into her mouth whenever she tells us this.

Tonight she's counting out dollar bills on the table. She says, "It's a Disney film!"

The kids go wild. Cookie, her youngest—Bonny Loo's age—comes in from the outhouse and asks me to do her safety pin. Cookie. I always wonder how Rubie coulda made Cookie, bein' away like he is.

Sometimes I love her so much, Madeline Rowe. She was maid of honor at our little wedding . . . Ernest Bean best man. Madeline and I carried matching bouquets of silk flowers. Daddy didn't come for the ceremony, said his back was acting up. But he gave us a neat owl lamp, one of his carving jobs. He's a little genius. After the ceremony, ol' Madeline Rowe kissed Beal long and wet on his mouth. He put his arms around her.

When we go out in the yard, carrying pillows for the kids, Atlas and Pinkie are on top of Madeline's old VW. Cookie and Bonny Loo run ahead, carrying the popcorn we made.

Madeline says, "I ain't seen a good Disney flick in at least five years. I think Disney is my absolutely all-time favorite."

I say, "Beal sure is late."

Madeline says, "Jesus, Earlene! He needs the overtime." She hugs me to her as we move through the mosquitoes, their deafenin' high whine. Madeline has huge, quaking breasts. They dangle under her peasant blouse like loaves of Wonder Bread. Her words always come like she's out of breath. I guess them big breasts crush on her lungs.

Bonny Loo tries to shoo Atlas and Pinkie off the roof of the VW. She runs around, wavin' her arms. Cookie dives for the back seat and the VW rocks like a boat. In a while, all of us are in, includin' Madeline's two long-legged teenagers and then Kaiser, who stinks awful. Mosquitoes drift over the windshield, trying to get in.

Bonny Loo says, "I ain't never been to the movies before."

There's a gagging sound. Teenaged Florence is holding her nose. "Ma! Give us a break! Make Kaiser stay home. He's wicked."

Madeline turns her hot face toward me with the monstrous black frizzed-out hair touching the VW ceiling. "Why ain't your Bonny Loo been to a show? Ain't got nuthin' to do with that God stuff, does it?"

Overhead we hear Atlas and Pinkie walkin' around.

I says, "No, Madeline."

Sometimes I despise Madeline. I despise her a million times a day. In the kitchen, she likes to put her big hip against Beal when she hands him a beer. She's always got a beer for Beal, lookin' into his eyes with her strange yellow eyes.

Beal says we can get our own place soon. But we always stay a little longer. With the money Beal makes . . .

Last winter, I wanted to ask Madeline for a loan to get Beal new boots. She was gettin' good hours at the cold storage. But I chickened out. And she never offered, even though she can plainly see them wet, torn-up boots dryin' under the stove.

We have a scarecrow who wears a green workshirt. It says REUBEN on the pocket. Beal says to Madeline, "Do you miss the real Reuben?"

She gives the scarecrow a strangling hug, kisses its pillowcase face. "You mean this gentle sweet one ain't the right one?"

She's told me a time or two about the beatings, how Rubie punched all the cupboards, punched 'em to splinters, then beat her in the corner of the kitchen. Then when she thought he was walking away, he runs back, comes down on all fours like a dog, and bites her in the face.

In the garden she mostly wears a halter of T-shirt material. Her breasts are all over the place. Sometimes one slips out. She laughs and stuffs it back in, never blushing. If Beal is on his knees weeding in the garden when a breast does this, he don't politely look away. I catch my breath, stand up quick, go to the edge of the trees to be alone. "The Lord is my shepherd, I shall not want . . ." And I say the whole thing. I say it two or three times. ". . . Thou anointest my head with oil . . ." And when I come back to the garden, they don't suspect a thing.

This is when I hate her. Madeline Rowe.

She hunts for the VW keys in her bag. Now and then the long legs of Madeline's teenagers push into the back of my seat. Kaiser puts a yellow paw between the seats and lunges at a mosquito.

Madeline starts up the engine.

Cookie screams, "Mumma! Atlas and Pinkie!"

"They'll take care of themselves, for cryin' out loud!" Madeline snorts, puts the car into first, and we lurch forward. One by one, Pinkie and Atlas spin off into the bushes. Branches whip the windshield.

As we ride along, I light up a cigarette and Bonny Loo looks at me and smiles. Her glasses don't fall on the floor anymore when she's actin' up. You know . . . jumpin' off chairs and things like she does, bouncin' in the bed . . . usin' her rope swing over the pond . . . 'cause her Special Ed teacher give her a black stretchy strap that goes around her head . . . holds 'em on.

I hum, "Swing lowwww . . . sweet charrrri-aaaw-t . . ."

Bonny Loo pushes at my shoulder. "That's enough God songs, Ma! Let's sing 'Abba Dabba'!"

A sad tightness comes to my throat.

---------------------------- **2** ----------------------------

There's no electricity in Madeline's house . . . Well, it's actually Rubie's house. Bean land.

I aim the flashlight beam into the bed. There's Beal with his arm hanging down almost touching the floor. He lays on top of the spread with his clothes on, even his boots. Bonny Loo marches over to her little bed in the corner of our room and lays on it with her clothes on.

"Take off your glasses, Bonny Loo, or you'll break 'em," I tell her.

I light the lamp with book matches.

Bonny Loo swipes her glasses off and puts them on the music box next to her bed.

I'll never get used to how big Beal is.

I say, "Where's the truck? It ain't out front."

His face is in the pillow. He says into the pillow, "Lost the fuckin' brakes. Okay?!"

I light a cigarette and stand lookin' at him.

"You all right?" I says.

He grunts.

I go out of the circle of light and change into my summer nightgown. I sit on the bed. "Want me to help you with your boots?"

No answer.

I light another cigarette. I take another stab at "Swing Low, Sweet Chariot" . . . softly.

Bonny Loo says, "Ma! Tell him about the movie!"

Silence.

"We went to a movie, Beal," I finally say.

Bonny Loo chirps, "Madeline said they shoulda hung Walt Disney by the balls for makin' a movie dull an' rotten as that. Didn't she say that, Ma?"

Silence. I put out my cigarette. He rolls onto his back. The lamp flickers. I unlace his boots. It is a warm night. His feet are hot, dry feet, the socks full of sand. I smile at him and get up on my knees. I press my fingers into the arch of his right foot, work all my fingers into the long bones. I rock the foot like a small baby in the curve of my groin. I feel the taste of the long day in my mouth. My hair dangles across the rolled-up cuffs of his dungarees. He's got the bed fulla sawdust and sand again. I kiss his feet.

3

Lloyd Bean's girlfriend's baby Bobby is in the highchair they brought for him, and Lloyd Bean's girlfriend smokes at the table. The yard is full with Beans and Letourneaus, Junior Atkinson, Larry Crosman, and some strangers, all puttin' away real bad cider from the back of Larry Crosman's truck, all watchin' Beal clean fish on a piece of plywood on the well. It's Sunday, Beal's only day off. Some of Beal's cousins look so much like him, I can't help staring.

Madeline's layin' hens and green-tailed gamecock feed on the fish guts Beal slings into the grass.

Beal is wearin' a T-shirt that isn't long enough, and most of his back shows as he kneels, scraping the pickerel with his jackknife. He ignores me when the men are around. He ignores them, too. I watch the thickness of the fish pass through his hands. He scratches a mosquito bite on his elbow with his knife.

Lloyd Bean's girlfriend, Bess, smells like Coppertone. She and Madeline and Rosie Bean Fecteau have had a few coffee brandies. Bess, according to Beal, is Passamaquoddy. She has a high forehead, frosted gypsy cut, and millions of rings on both hands. She says, "When's the baby due, Earlene?"

I say, "In four months."

She raises her eyebrows. "Really? You're big."

Madeline's oldest girl, Virginia, sets cross-legged on the floor against the wall. Motionless. Sullen mouth, the Bean nose sprawled on the face. Beal calls her Rubie's girl. You never see her twisted teeth. She's rare with words. She hates us all.

Madeline drinks, swaying around the kitchen in bare feet, jabbin' a big fork into the bubbling squash, pourin' a couple cannin' jars of dark string beans into a pan, her crazy hair in a red bandanna. She shrieks, "Earlene's gonna have twins! Any fool can see!"

Rosie smiles. Bess looks hard at my smock.

Madeline giggles. "Well . . . after all . . . look who the daddy is!"

My cheeks flush. I get off my stool and pretend to look for somethin' in a drawer.

Madeline drinks deeply of her coffee brandy. "Ahhhh!" she says. I turn in time to see Rosie and Madeline and Bess exchange glances. "Good lickerrrr!" Madeline says.

The baby, Bobby, drops his soggy Saltine on the floor. I pick it up.

Madeline says, "Yep . . . maybe *quads*! Did you hear! They're bringin' in America's top scientists to use their most . . . whaddya call it? . . . so-FISS-ticated scientific equipment to study this phenomenally fertile man . . . YOU KNOW WHO."

Bess blows smoke through her nose. "That's a hell of a thing." She smiles broadly.

A huge chickenlike squawk of laughter comes from them all.

I don't cry. I just glance around like I'm huntin' for a face but don't find one.

Virginia's eyes are closed, the lips pressed tight on the twisted teeth.

Bonny Loo comes into the kitchen dripping, wearing frog feet. "Ma!" she whispers. She wiggles a finger for my attention. "Ma!"

"What?"

Her bathing suit drizzles water over her square belly, down her legs. Her hair is flat and wet.

She whispers close to my ear, "Do chickens and fish go to heaven?"

"No," I say.

She whispers, "Why not?"

"Only man was made in God's image."

Bonny Loo screws up her face. "You mean NONE of Madeline's chickens are goin' to heaven?" A whisper. Her breath smells like the clean, dark pond.

"That's right, Bonny Loo."

"What about fish?"

"Only people."

She brushes my face with her fingers as she whispers extra close. "People are best, aren't they?"

"That's right, Bonny Loo." She's making the floor wet with pond water. But Madeline doesn't seem to notice.

They are all watching Beal come in with the fish on a board, his black beard spread over his T-shirt like some kinda dark and aimless overflow.

_____ 4 _____

The next night Bonny Loo takes my hand. "Ma! I got a secret. Come see!"

I put on my sweater. The sun going down behind the pines looks like a hundred lighted broom handles.

She pulls me along by the wrist.

The baby moves its fingers over the inside walls of me.

We crunch along on pinecones.

Then the path veers into walls of rock. Over us, heavy

tatters of gray mosses drip, and the path is soggy. I can't see Bonny Loo's eyes through her glasses, only greenish shards of light. She flattens her back to one wall. "Ma! Feel this stuff!" She squirms her fingers in it. "Feel this GREEN kind."

I reach out and my fingers disappear. "Yipes! It bit me!" I laugh.

Bonny Loo rolls her body against the rock. The rock seems to ripple affectionately. I narrow my eyes. "It's kinda creepy here, Bonny Loo," I say.

"No, it ain't!" she gasps, arching her back. "Hey, Ma! What's that thing you say about the pastures?"

"What thing?" I look up. Above and beyond the rock walls are softwoods with big bodies gorged on water. You can smell 'em dyin', crowding each other, spongy and black ... then beyond them more moss, everywhere in crazy colors ... turquoise and darker blues ... like rags of denim ... wools and cottons.

"The PASTURES thing!" she screams. Her hands are on her hips.

I say softly, "Oh." I clasp my hands.

Her eyes flicker on me.

"The Lord is my shepherd, I shall not want; He makes me lie down in green pastures ..." The sound of my own voice saying this makes me smile. Out of my smiling mouth, the words roll out like big, hard, musty-sweet Macouns. "He leads me beside still waters; He restores my soul. He leads me in paths of righteousness for His name's sake. Even though I walk through the valley of the shadow of death, I fear no evil ..."

She looks at me hard, real hard. I stop reciting a minute and look at her looking at me, with the dripping evil noise close to us, the darkness building.

"... For thou art with me ..." I swallow.

She swallows.

I see a kind of silly-lookin' tear come chargin' out from under one of her lenses. So there must be a tear in my eye. This is stupid. I put my eye to my sleeve. I am almost gaggin' with uncried cries.

"...Thy rod and thy staff, they comfort me. Thou preparest a table before me in the presence of my enemies; thou anointest my head with oil, my cup overflows..."

The drippin' of everything is crazy and awful. And yet, she's grinnin'.

"Surely goodness and mercy shall follow me all the days of my life; and I shall dwell in the house of the Lord FOR EVER."

Her eyes have been lost in my movin' mouth. Now she giggles. "That's it. You like it here, Ma? It's my secret place." She comes to me, puts her tough bare feet on my shoes. "Ma?"

"What?"

"Do you ever get so sad any more that you wanna...you know what?"

"Of course not."

She scowls, makes her forehead wrinkle. Her hair is such short, stand-up stuff. "I get so CURIOUS...Ma ...very very very curious about heaven. Do you think heaven is like this wonderful place?" She pats the rocks.

I gasp. "NO!" I say. "It ain't a thing like this... NUTHIN' like this...Certainly not. Bonny Loo, heaven has streets of gold!"

5

Madeline's got her tall boots on, and a swishy skirt like when she goes out. She's fixin' up some cupcakes with different-color frostings.

I say, "You look nice, Madeline." I'm in my robe tonight. Got that horrible business with my legs from the baby.

Cookie says, "Warren Olsen's comin' tonight!"

"Who's Warren Olsen?" I ask. I light a cigarette.

"Mind your own business!" says Madeline, her yellowish eyes jumping at me. Cookie looks like Madeline, the same yellow eyes in black lashes. Her hair is straight and cut like a Japanese doll. She watches her mother hard.

Madeline has gobs of eye makeup on tonight. She winks at me. "I'm sorry, Earlie."

Virginia watches me from her silent corner.

Cookie says, "Mumma's in a bad mood."

Cookie and Bonny Loo play with plastic cowboys and Indians under the supper table. Bonny Loo's Indians have Cookie's cowboys surrounded.

At the table, Florence slowly thumbs through a candy box of postcards.

Madeline takes another batch of cupcakes from the oven.

I smoke hard and fast. I rock hard and fast.

Florence says, "Earlene, did you know Daddy can't read 'n' write?"

I rock slower and stare into the kerosene lamp on the table. It's turned up high and hot. I say, "No, I didn't." I drag on the cigarette.

In the lamplight, Florence's freckles shift like stars. "But now he's got a . . . What you call 'em, Virginia?"

"Therapist."

"Yeh, that's it," says Florence. "Cousin Rosie says prison's the best thing that ever happened to Daddy . . . She says nowadays you don't get bread 'n' water there . . . You get reformed . . . you know, made nice. The therapist is helpin' Daddy do some cursive."

I says, "That's really neat."

"When's *my* daddy gettin' home?" Bonny Loo asks me.

"I don't know," I murmur.

"He prob'ly can't get the truck started, huh?"

"Prob'ly not," I says.

Florence comes over to my chair. "Here's these post-cards Dad sent Mumma." She puts the candy box in my lap.

Madeline gives Kaiser a cupcake with pink frosting. He eats it whole.

I pick a postcard from the box. It's written in fat tall letters like a little kid: DEAR MADELINE. I LOVE YOU. REUBEN BEAN.

Madeline's eyes are on my hand. I drop the card in the box.

Florence says, "Mumma, what's that they said Daddy's got?"

Madeline puts another batch of cupcakes in the oven and sets the timer. "Dyslexia," she says breathlessly.

Cookie and Bonny Loo make a massacre of the cowboys, giggling and scaling cowboys across the floor. A cowboy with a lasso wings Kaiser in the shoulder. Kaiser groans for another cupcake, paws at Madeline's tall boots.

"Lookit this one," says Florence, "a postcard of the Blaine House . . . Ain't it pretty?" On the back: DEAR MADELINE, WHEN I GET HOME I'LL MARRY YOU REAL. LOVE R.B.

"That's the best one," Florence says, glaring at her mother.

Cookie giggles. "Florence, read the baseball ones." She looks at Bonny Loo. "He gets home runs."

"I ain't marryin' that asshole!" Madeline snarls. And

she grabs the candy box, squeals open the woodstove door, and shoves the box into the wall of flame.

Virginia stands up, bares her twisted teeth. She folds her arms, her wee breasts pushin' out like arrowheads. "You are the asshole," she says to Madeline.

We hear a car in the yard. Kaiser growls, then skids to the door, barkin'.

Tears bunch up in Florence's eyes, stream over the freckles. "Mumma . . . I hope . . ." She sobs wildly, covers her face.

Warren Olsen comes to the door. Kaiser's voice is like cannon blasts. Madeline holds him back by the collar. Cookie and Bonny Loo are lapping green frosting from their fingers. Madeline says, "Earlene . . . you know Warren . . . from the Country Store? He owns it."

Warren puts out his hand. I stand up, tightening my sash.

Madeline says, "This is Rubie's cousin's wife. They've been stayin' here like I was tellin' you."

His hand is steady and cool. He has square Howdy Doody cheeks, freckles, auburn hair. I say, "Good to meet you."

He sits at the table with his legs crossed in Band-Aid-color nylon pants. He has a soft, soft voice. I gotta lean almost out of my chair to hear him.

Turns out he's only talkin' about the weather.

Florence and Virginia are in their room, bangin' drawers like they're packin' to leave. Kaiser lays at Madeline's feet, watching Warren Olsen. Madeline drops him a cupcake with blue frostin'.

Madeline pours coffee. Warren says, "Madeline, this kerosene light . . . How charming to live this way!"

Madeline smiles, looks at me.

The baby jabs my bladder. I almost cry out.

Warren Olsen takes a green-frostin' cupcake with

nis long clean fingers while on his face is a look of love.

---------------------- 6 ----------------------

I feel him sit on the bed in the dark. I wake up with a start. "Beal!"

He chuckles.

One of his boots drops. He smells of pine. I'm sick of the smell of pine. Sometimes I see him suck on his knuckles in his sleep, the hands black with pitcn. I seen him once—just once—suck on his thumb. I pushed his hand away. I thought it would make me sick, seein' him like that.

Now I say, "Did he pay you tonight?"

"No." His other boot drops.

"Beal, why don't you remind him?"

Silence.

"Beal . . . it's *your* money, you're entitled to it. It's been *two* weeks. How can he expect a man with a family to live without money for *two whole weeks*?"

Silence.

"It's *your* money!" I cry out. "How can you be that shy?"

"He'll prob'ly remember tomorrow," Beal murmurs

I sit up. I light the lamp. I reach for my cigarettes. I light one with trembling hands. My hair feels crawly. It moves on the front and back of my gown.

"I'm saaaaw-sawwww-ry, Earlene," he stammers.

I look at him, his back turned to me. He's pulling his shirt off. There's welts on every square inch of his back and neck. Deer flies.

I say, "Where's the truck?"

"In the yard," he says. "Hill helped me time it. He has a light." Beal looks at me and his eyes are weirdly bright. Tears.

"You'd think Hill would realize you might need your pay while he's helpin' you fool with that old wreck of a truck."

The tears don't run out. They just sparkle in his eyes. He says, "It was late when we was done. I couldn't ask him for money after he spent all that time."

"But"—my face flames—"it's *your* money. You got every right, Beal!"

He pulls off his dungarees and the belt buckle clanks on the floor.

I says, "Beal, did you know Rubie can't re——"

There's a sound of springs in the next room. A whimper.

I put out my cigarette. Beal stares unbelievin' at the wall. I stand up and take my hairbrush from my pile of clothes on the chair.

A moan. Then the rhythmic beating of Madeline's bed against the wall.

I put the brush through my hair.

Bonny Loo sits up. "What's *that*, Ma!" she gasps.

I look at Beal. He stands slowly, his arms out from his body. His beard heaves over his front in rivulets, parting at the deep navel, twisting a few inches below that. He walks heavily to the wall as the whimpers and cries on the other side grow louder. He wipes his eyes.

Bonny Loo says, "Beal! What's that racket?"

I say softly, "Beal, Warren Olsen . . . from the hardware store . . . He's spendin' the night." I stop brushin'.

"That's it, Bonny!" Beal shouts. "It's Warren Olsen from the hardware store fuckin' Madeline!" He punches the wall. The lamplight flickers crazily.

Suddenly, the noises from Madeline's room stop.

I say, "Beal, praise Jesus . . . ain't none of our business
. . Please . . . come lie down!"

Beal presses his cheek to the wall.

"Beal!" I croak. "Are you eavesdroppin'!"

His nakedness is almost earth-color in the kerosene
light.

Bonny Loo springs up, fumbles for her glasses. "Beal!"
she says. "Maybe Warren Olsen's got his ear up listenin'
to you!"

"Shut up, Bonny Loo!" I hiss.

Madeline slashes through the swan-print shower curtain that hangs across our doorway. She's wearin' a terry
robe. Her hair's an explosion. Her yellow eyes gleam on
Beal.

Bonny Loo says, "My father's the one that hit the
wall!"

"Shut up, Bonny Loo!" I scream. I toss my hairbrush
onto the bed. I take Beal's elbow into my fingers.
"BEAL . . . cover yourself!"

Madeline walks big and heavy our way and closes both
hands around the bedpost. "What do you think you're
doin'?" she says to Beal.

Beal snorts. Smiles broadly. "Wanna see it again?" he
says. He brings his elbow back, jabbing my side, and his
fist disappears wrist-deep into the Sheetrock wall. The
stuff crumbles over his feet.

I say, "Praise Jesus!"

Bonny Loo says, "Madeline! Where's the man . . . that
Warren feller?"

I say, "Bonny Loo, go to sleep . . . School tomorrow."

Beal turns into the light and it seems his body is the
brightest thing in the whole world. I cry out, "Beal!
Please cover up!" I try to stand between him and Madeline
but there's no room to get by. I cover my face. "I don't
understand, you guys. I don't understand none of this." I

open my eyes and tug on Beal's arm. It seems like the whole universe is wheelin' noisily around Beal's earth-color hips, the purplish penis . . . and Madeline's eyes are smilin'.

I want to beat them eyes.

Bonny Loo moves into the circle of light in her pajamas. "You're all nuts," she says.

Madeline says, "Your daddy thinks he's head cock around here."

We hear a thump beyond the wall, probably Warren Olsen huntin' up his Band-Aid-color pants in the dark.

Madeline shakes the bedpost. Our bed lurches, makes a bizarre squeal. Madeline cackles, her huge breasts swinging. Beal watches her.

The baby turns a somersault, batters my spine.

Beal reaches as if to grab the sash of Madeline's terry robe. Madeline looks at the fingers spread out.

She says, "I'm sorry, Beal." She lets go the bedpost and takes his hand, tugs on the fingers like milkin' a cow. She says, "Possessive, they call it. Put that together with fertile and EEE-HA! Ain't no wonder most women flop right down for you. Give you time, Beal . . . sweet *sweet* Beal . . . and you'll be everybody's daddy."

Warren's in the hall.

"You got sweet sweet ways," Madeline says to Beal as she gives his beard a light tap.

Warren Olsen picks the swan shower curtain to one side. Bonny Loo jeers, "If there's school tomorrow, I want you all in your beds!"

Beal stands the way of Beans, with his feet far apart on the plywood floor. I see the veins are raised up, the deer flies have hacked away at the broad ankles. Maybe ol' Madeline's gonna drop right there and kiss them feet . . . How many times have I done that? Right here on this plywood floor, with my daughter watchin' from her bed, and Beal in one of his moods. I been down there so many times kissin' them feet and he never says, "Stop, Earlene. Stop kissin' them feet. You're makin' yourself look pretty silly." No, he just stands there like that's the way with the world.

Can people TELL when they look in my eyes? Can they SEE me kissin' away on them feet?

Oh . . . I see rising up the quick words like grunts from Gram's razor-thin lips . . . but instead mine move soundlessly . . . out of the Holy Scriptures: YEA, TO HIM SHALL THE PROUD OF THE EARTH BOW DOWN; BEFORE HIM SHALL BOW ALL WHO GO DOWN TO THE DUST, AND HE WHO CANNOT KEEP HIMSELF ALIVE. POSTERITY SHALL SERVE HIM; MEN SHALL TELL OF THE LORD TO THE COMING GENERATION, AND PROCLAIM HIS DELIVERANCE TO A PEOPLE YET UNBORN, THAT HE HAS WROUGHT IT.

From across the room I can see Warren Olsen's eyes find my face. He looks and sees what he sees, workin' his mouth in a hard line.

7

Bonny Loo comes to me with her secret. Her bifocals are steamy with her excitement. She says, "Come on, Ma!" and takes my hand into her square hot hand.

I say softly, "Let me get a wool shirt first."

Kaiser gets up on his feet from under the table.

Bonny Loo stands by the door, twistin' a piece of her thin hair. "No way! He'll wreck everythin'!" She pretends to throw somethin' at Kaiser. He veers away into the little hall, leavin' only his horrible smell. "That ugly animal ain't goin' everywheres I go!" she cries.

Bonny Loo and I walk through the evening layers of mist. I walk slowly, the baby coming in only three weeks. She leads me through birches, and the leaves underfoot are slimy with three days of cold rain.

There is an old refrigerator on the knoll. The propane kind. Freckled with rust. Beads of water have risen up on it like sweat on someone who fears.

Bonny Loo pats my elbow as I step along. She takes care with my pregnancy like I'm a gigantic one-of-a-kind spotted bug. She watches the path for me, watches my feet. "Well, here we are . . . We made it," she says. "This is it."

She is looking over my shoulder at the refrigerator. She lets go of my hand.

I say, "What kind of interestin' thing have you come across now?"

Gram speaks: THOU DOST LAY ME IN THE DUST OF DEATH.

Bonny Loo opens the heavy door. The raindrops on it run together, stream down, gathering into rust-colored vees.

"Yukk!" says Bonny Loo. As I come up behind her the smell of death explodes in my face. "Cripes!" she whispers. She reaches in. Works her square hands around inside. "Jeez!" she gasps. "They stink, don't they?"

She handles them. Layin' hens, frogs, a field mouse, a good-sized fish. All dead. The smell of them pushes into my nose like two fat fingers.

I close my eyes.

When I look again she is still bent into the refrigerator, mumblin' to herself. It is almost entirely dark now. The only thing I can see good is this refrigerator. Bonny Loo whispers, "When I put 'em in here, they was all good."

Alive?

She gropes around the inside of the refrigerator, into each blackened corner. She draws out one stiff hen by the foot. She puts it back. She adjusts her glasses. "Neat, ain't it?" she says, looking in my face. "Ma, when do they get to be skeletons?"

The baby draws its limbs around itself stiffly . . . It seems to have grown old and tired in my body.

"Ma! Ain't you listenin'?"

I can't speak.

Bonny Loo turns to me and puts these hands on me— these hands that stink of DEATH.

TEN
Meat

Pa Bean gets out of his old Chevy truck, workin' his legs stiffly over the icy yard. The aunties come behind him, dressed like for an American Legion dance, Auntie K. holdin' Auntie Hoover by the arm. It's been a cold spring and everywheres you look a robin is tryin' to peck a hole in the cementlike ground.

The baby is on the supper table, archin' his back and screamin'.

Pa Bean, he don't knock. He just shuffles into the kitchen and catches me in my nightgown. He looks around.

The baby is rigid and red with screams.

Pa goes straight through the swan-print shower curtain. Beal's on the bed. His left eye is rose-colored and makes a hill on his face. His good eye widens as Pa says, "Shit! I thought they say you can't keep a good man down."

The baby gasps, the muscles of his belly jerking like a dozen charley horses.

I open the door for the aunties with a pink diaper in my hand. Everywheres, all over the kitchen, the pink diapers hang, a pink T-shirt, a pink bra. One scarlet wool sock.

I hear Pa say, "What you done, boy? Got in a brawl?"

I yell to him through the curtain, "Beal ain't been in no fights! He got a splinter in his eye . . . WORKIN'!"

Pa murmurs, "Tell me the truth, boy. One of them husbands give you a thrashin'?"

I go to the hall and scream, "He got that eye workin'! WORKIN'!"

"Okay," says Pa Bean in a tiny voice. Then he says, "Why ain't you makin' a bundle drivin' truck? I thought you had your Class One."

Bean says, "Class Two, Pa, but we couldn't keep her renewed. Takes money to make money, that's what you always say, Pa."

Pa says, "*I* say that?"

I know the way Beal's beard spreads over the sheet. He don't never cut it. It's like one of those dinky houseplants you get with good intentions, but it takes over, needs a bigger and bigger pot every time you look. The beard fills our bed at night, lies between us, and sometimes I feel it try to grip me.

The aunties unbutton their coats. Auntie K. helps Auntie Hoover slide hers off her back.

"Want tea?" I say. "We're outta sugar, but we got some sap from Johnsons' overway."

Auntie K. looks at me. "I don't want nuthin'."

The baby makes exhausted half-snorts.

On the windowsill behind the supper table is Bonny Loo's jar of spit. She has spit in it every day for a month. She tells us that eventually somethin' will grow out of the spit.

Auntie Hoover sinks slowly onto a chair. "I would like some tea. Nuthin' in it, please."

Auntie K. says, "Ain't that little feller gonna roll off the table an' be cripple for life?"

I put my hand out to the baby. He is so mad, his belly almost burns my hand. I take off his diaper and put the dry pink one on.

Auntie Hoover squints. "Pink on a *boy*?"

"It was an accident," I says. "It got washed with that red sock over there."

Both aunties squint their eyes at me. They are huge women. Auntie Hoover, it's hard to tell she ain't a real-blood Bean. She's growed to be one. She's been a Bean longer than her bridegroom Fred, gored by a buck on his weddin' night . . . She's never been in the family way . . . just been a Bean from hangin' around. The hands of both Hoover an' K. fuss with their white blouses and jewelry. They are like the hands of young men.

I pick up the baby. His name is Dale Bean. He weighed almost ten pounds at birth. Almost tore me apart.

"What we come ovah for was to tell Beal about his poor mother," says one of the aunties.

I try to make Dale comfortable in the plastic laundry basket by the stove.

Hoover touches her beads. "We had her sent away."

Hoover and K. look at each other.

I put a bottle of milk in a pan on the stove. It's the last milk in the house.

Auntie Hoover sighs. "Seems while we was gettin' older, she was gettin' stronger."

I watch the steam curl up around the bottle.

"She went wanderin' off . . . We lost her all night . . . one night . . . She coulda froze," Auntie K. says softly.

"Is that right?" I says. The baby sucks on his fist.

There's no voices comin' from our bedroom. I go over and push the swan curtain open. Pa Bean's against the tall bed with his hips. He's holdin' his huntin' knife over a lighted match, gettin' ready to operate on Beal's eye.

Auntie Hoover says, "We done the right thing. No one can tell me we ain't done the right thing."

Auntie K. clears her throat. "We used her good."

Beal's black beard on the sheet seems to creep toward some escape... twistin' into the valleys of the sheet, hurryin' in different directions in zigzaggy panic. Beal's good eye is closed, waitin'. He trusts Pa Bean. He trusts him good.

I back off.

Auntie K. says, "Where's your girl?"

"In school," I say.

"Where's all the chickens at? Madeline take 'em to her fancy new house?"

"Beal dressed 'em out," I say.

Auntie K. looks at Auntie Hoover. "I thought they was Madeline's birds."

I say, "They was, but she don't ask about 'em."

Auntie K. sniffs. "Bet she's got them girls callin' her new man Daddy. When Rubie gets out, the shit's gonna hit the fan."

I says, "They're kinda big to change, ain't they?"

I back up to the rocking chair, roll the big baby over my lap. He muckles onto the bottle. He has fox-color eyes.

─────────────── **2** ───────────────

Bonny Loo smokes. She's in her room with the door shut, prob'ly smokin' in the dark.

I rock with the baby and look out at Rubie's old loggin' rig, parked for years and years behind the house.

Madeline has sold most the parts off it. The ancient load is in tatters of rot and moss. The twilight makes a queer lavender halo around the truck.

I would smoke if I *had* cigarettes.

I blow out the lamp. I push through the swan curtain, lower Dale into his basket by our bed. I light the lamp on the chair. Beal's on his back, his hair and beard sweaty, his eye a hideous bulge. Just as I set on the bed, Dale starts up.

Beal's voice comes like a growl: "Make him stop!"

I says, "Shhh, Dale."

I walk around with Dale in the kitchen, rub his broad back. I give him a bottle of water. He pushes it. I put sap in the water. He screams. He tries to eat my shirt. He makes a purple face. I gotta laugh at his funny face. I laugh and kiss this funny face. I rock him in the greenish lamplight. He closes his eyes.

I know Bonny's in there smokin' cigarettes, ones her friend Allen gives her.

I go back through the swan curtain. The bedroom stinks of Beal's eye. When I put the baby back in the basket, he screams. So I rock him in the kitchen some more, my heavy, snarled hair damp against my back. My hand hunts for cigarettes. "What are you doing, hand?" I giggle. I pace the kitchen, heat another bottle of sap and water. The grit of the linoleum sticks to my feet.

Dale shoves the bottle away.

The fire in the stove is dyin' but it seems like a hundred degrees in here.

I give Dale peanut butter scraped from the jar on a spoon. He sucks at it, makes a face.

Beal gets out of bed and walks like a hundred-year-old man to the front door with a blanket around him. He stands in the dark and pees off the piazza.

When he comes back by, Dale is snivelin', workin' up

to a scream. Beal stops and glares at the baby with his one good eye, his other one like an enormous mushy pink apple.

I says, "Beal, this ain't right. He ain't had milk for this many days." I hold up the fingers of my right hand.

Beal has the shakes. He clutches the blanket around himself and his teeth go crazy clatterin' together.

I says, "He spits out everything else. If we only had potatoes or somethin', I could mash him some."

"So it's *my* fuckin' fault I ain't workin'. You are fuckin' right!"

"I'm not sayin' that."

Dale makes a wildcat screech.

"Beal, can't I go for food stamps?"

"NO!"

More than food, I want a cigarette.

Beal says, "And how're you supposed to get to Portland with a truck that's out of gas?"

"I'll ask somebody to take me."

Beal makes a noise in his throat like he's about to spit on the floor. "And do you know what would happen to us if they find out I've been workin' under the table this long? Guh-uh-uh-government gets out the old fuh-uh-feelers . . . Once you get in the old welfare game, they got a trail on you . . . 'cause, lady . . . when you're poor, you stink!"

"It don't work that way, Beal." Dale tries to eat my shirt.

"You go for them stamps, Earlene, and I see *one* government *official* hangin' around this place, and I'll beat the shit outta you!"

I settle back into the rocker. Dale paws at my shirt wildly.

Beal goes back to bed.

I say, "Dear Jesus, please help us...Get us some money." I look up at the spotty ceiling. "Amen."

The baby is screamin' so hard, he stops short and kinda half-vomits.

I hear a thumpin' sound in the bedroom. I know the sound by heart. I've heard it a hundred times since my marriage. It's Beal punchin' hisself in the breastbone... punchin' his belly...bangin' his head on the headboard of the bed.

Bonny Loo the brat. She probably lays on her back in a comfortable way, blowin' that smoke out her nose. I can smell it...It's comin' out under her door. The school says Bonny Loo's got gum disease. They send notes right and left: "DEAR MRS. BEAN..."

I look out and see the moon come up over Rubie Bean's loggin' truck. The old mossy load of pulp seems to bulge up to meet the moon.

I hear another sound in the bedroom. The clink of Beal's belt. I swish through the swan curtain, tryin' to hang on to the strugglin', gaggin' baby.

"What are you doin'?" I ask Beal.

He stoops for his boots. His black beard swings out from his body. "Goin' for some *meat*!" he snarls. He looks like a monster with that eye, the kind in movies when they play creepy music.

I close my eyes. "Beal," I say softly. "You can hardly walk."

The tops of his cheeks have a high flush.

I put out my hand. "Don't mess with me," he says.

I take my hand away. I kiss the baby's sour, cryin' mouth. "Oh, Dale! Dale!" I sob.

I smell cigarettes...I open my mouth...It drifts in.

Beal goes to the hall closet, hauls out one of Rubie's dark guns. He holds a box of shells up to the lamp. He loads the gun and mashes a handful of shells into the pocket of his dungarees.

I hear him go out.

I change into my granny gown and get into bed. Both pillows stink from his eye. I cradle the baby against my gown. The baby tries to eat my gown.

3

Hours pass. I hear a thud on the piazza. I cover Dale, who is sleepin' fitful on the sheets that are damp from Beal. I step through the moonlight in the kitchen in my granny gown. When I open the door to the piazza, I hear sobs. Beal's in a wooden chair with the gun across his knees. I creak over the piazza floor and put my hand on his hair. He sobs louder.

He says, "Cocksuckas can *see me*, but I can't see them."

"Where's your flashlight?"

"BATT'RIES, BABY, BATT'RIES!! It don't work without 'em!"

I feel his forehead. I've never felt anyone burn this much. "How long've you been sittin' here?"

"The whole time. I ain't worth a piss."

I gasp. "Beal! You are goin' ta die. Let me go call someone . . . please. I can get dressed an' go down ta Crosmans'."

He shifts his gun.

I say, "Your eye . . . Beal . . . it must hurt!"

He looks at me. "Woman, you don't know what hurtin' is." Then, through half a sob, he says, "What *good* am I? I musta come outta my mother's asshole."

"Why won't you let me do *anything*?...We gotta DO somethin'. You should be in the hospital."

He says slowly, "Ain't no free admission."

I hear his teeth chatter, rhythmic, like fits. I say, "I hearda these papers you make out..."

His good eye widens.

"It ain't the regular welfare, Beal. Maybe they won't check us out."

"They got computers."

"But we gotta..."

"Drop it, Earlene!"

"Let me call my father...He can give us a little loan...a tiny loan for milk and stuff and maybe a little down payment for the hospital...Maybe they'll be happy with that when they see how bad off you are, praise God!"

He ignores me.

The baby. His first cry is a scream of pain. I take a step sideways.

Beal moans, "Leave him."

"Beal! He's a helpless baby!"

"Lah-ha-lahh-LEAVE the goddam son of a bitch where he is."

I take another step.

He grabs at my gown but misses.

"BEAL!" I take two very quick steps closer to the baby.

Beal flies at my back.

BUT THOU, O LORD, BE NOT FAR OFF! O THOU MY HELP, HASTEN TO MY AID!

He presses the gun across my back. He screams in my ear, "Stay on this fuckin' porch like I tell you!"

I AM POURED OUT LIKE WATER AND ALL MY BONES ARE OUT OF JOINT; MY HEART IS LIKE WAX, IT IS MELTED WITHIN MY BREAST; MY

STRENGTH IS DRIED UP LIKE A POTSHERD...
Sometimes it's so hard to tell if the words are in my head
or if I mumble them, but when they are in Gram's voice
they roll hard and joyously from my deepest parts...THOU
DOST LAY ME IN THE DUST OF DEATH. YEA,
DOGS ARE ROUND ABOUT ME...

He puts the gun across the arms of the wooden chair.
His teeth chatter crazily. He fills both hands with the
waist of my gown.

I says, "What's the matter with you? You're nuts!"

The baby's cries are muffled. He must be cryin' into
the blankets.

"Earlene!" Beal tips his head.

Silence.

His one good eye blurs with wetness. "I NEED it!"

Silence.

"It?" I ask.

He waves his arms around. I fall back against the door.

"Jesus, Earlene...a FUCK!" The door starts to swing
open behind me. The baby's cries seem only inches
away.

I say, "You got to be kiddin'."

His legs shake. I think any minute he's goin' to faint.
DELIVER MY SOUL FROM THE SWORD, MY
LIFE FROM THE POWER OF THE DOG! SAVE ME!
OMYGODOMYGODOMYGOD...Gram's voice ends in
a little giggle.

"Beal, how can you want to now? How?"

The baby sounds exhausted, snivels, whimpers.

Beal points at the floor.

He don't undress, just unzips hisself. He says, "I want
it dog-style."

I am so amazed that little stars of light drift sideways
across my eyes.

Beal says deeply, "Turn around." He paws at my gown, tryin' to hurry me.

The baby makes a single monumental cat squall.

I turn around.

Silence.

The weight of Beal collapsing on my back makes me sprawl on my face. A nearby rocking chair starts up a snappy little ghostlike creaking.

The smell of his eye makes me feel faint. I hold my breath. I flatten my lungs right out.

His teeth chatter, and so do his bones, everything crazily aquiver and out of control. The hands are hot. The penis hot. The cries at the nape of my neck hot. Dark damp hot. Hot as Hell.

----------------------------- 4 -----------------------------

The red light sweeps across this house. The violet moon looks spotty with decay. A man in an orange rescuer's jacket takes Beal by the arm. They cover him with soft blankets. His teeth clack. They peer at his eye with flashlights. "You think we can save the eye?" they ask. The deputy comes last. He holds the flashlight on various corners of the porch. Sees the gun. Handles the gun. Puts the gun back on the chair arms.

Bonny Loo holds Dale, gives him the last of the peanut butter off her finger. She sings to him in her raspy voice . . . Hard rock.

I don't ride in the ambulance to Portland. I ain't got no way to get back. So I stand on the piazza and watch the red light hammering through the trees till it's gone.

When we get indoor, Bonny Loo's hand passes over mine . . . and magically a cigarette appears.

_____ **5** _____

It's Sunday . . . My birthday. Rosie brings me a store-bought cake. As she brings in the cake in its fancy box Bonny Loo and I watch and clap our hands . . . "Yaaaaay!" Then Rosie goes back and gets Jessica out of her car seat.

Bonny Loo says, "Ma! Allen and I are goin' for water . . . so leave us some cake . . . Don't hog it all."

I says, "Get them covers on tight this time."

They bustle with dozens of empty milk jugs and the wheelbarrow.

Rosie looks at Allen sideways. She says, "I wouldn't trust that little weirdo."

I says, "That's Bonny Loo's best friend. Don't cut him down."

Rosie says, "I feel like tea."

I start the tea water.

It's been one of them dry summers with cold mornin's and not many bugs. And the light is apricot-colored. We ain't had money for fertilizer, for seeds, for poison. But I got a few hills of zucchinis, some ratty-lookin' potatoes. Hill has cut Beal's hours. Says business is slow. Sold one skidder. Can't make payments on two skidders, he told Beal. Cuttin' down all way around. Beal likes Hill. Hill's got a funny way of sayin' things, Beal says. I never seen Hill.

There's the blows of a dozen hammers buildin' that new place across the way. Rosie says she's gotta use the "Necessary Room." I get out two cups. Jessica crawls around the kitchen, pulls Atlas out of the woodbox.

"Keeee!" she squeals, pointin' as he lunges out of her arms.

Rosie comes back in. The screen door whacks behind her. "Jesus, Earlene! No Necessary Paper."

"Sorry," I says. "I can fix you a soapy diaper to take back out."

"Nah . . . I used my sock." The hammers across the way sound like machine guns. "What's this?" says Rosie. "New neighbors?"

I sigh. "I don't know 'em. They musta bought the orchard property from Dunlaps."

"Classy-lookin' shack, ain't it?"

I says, "Yeeup."

Beal always says Rosie looks like Barbra Streisand. I always says, "That's a compliment to Rosie."

"Guess it is," Beal always says.

And I says, "How much do you look at Rosie?"

"Daaaah-don't get so pissed off, Earlene. When we was kids, Rosie tortured me."

I know Beal's right. She looks like Barbra Streisand, I got to admit.

She stands in her shocking-pink parka, looking out at the new house. Jessica roams around the kitchen, corners Pinkie under the table. Rosie says, "Couple them carpenters look good."

I say, "Take off your parka. Go in and throw it on the bed."

She scowls, twitches the long hook nose. "And freeze my ass off? . . . No way."

I pour hot water into the cups. "Here's your tea, Rosie."

"Where's Beal?" she says, lightin' up one of her thin brown cigarettes.

She spins her weddin' ring. She has earrings shaped like crosses that spin and spin. Her husband, Ronnie, is a

Roman Catholic. Her black hair is cut right off, a glossy duck's tail against her long neck. She flicks her ash into her hand.

I say, "He took one of Rubie's guns down to pick at cans."

"Gonna shoot up all Rubie's ammo?" She laughs.

"I don't know," I say.

"When Rubie gets home, he's gonna be mad as hell," she says softly.

I rinse off two spoons. Jessica pushes up onto her feet and trods after Pinkie down the short hall, stoppin' to grin back at Rosie. Rosie says, "Jessica, leave them Christly cats alone." She drags on her brown cigarette, her fox-color eyes passin' over me. "Jesus, Earlene . . . you've got skinny!"

I smile. "I don't really feel good. Got the blahs."

She says, "You look like a rag."

I shrug.

"Where's Dale?" Her cigarette moves from hand to hand, her cross earrings catch the light, catch the musty color of the room. "Sleepin'. Bonny Loo tires him out runnin' him on that old trike."

"I wouldn't let Bonny Loo roughhouse him so much," she sighs.

I shrug.

There's shots from the woods. Rosie turns her long neck, narrows her eyes.

I says, "Let's go out on the piazza and watch 'em put up the house."

She says, "Cripe! We'll freeze out there!" She follows me out. We put Jessica in Dale's playpen. Rosie picks a straight-back chair, sets her cup on the piazza sill. "Jeez!" she exclaims. "Lookit that one with the tan! Hubba. Hubba."

I look over and think what a crazy thing this new

house is. Until now, there ain't been neighbors . . . and now we got 'em. I says, "It's a pretty place."

She whistles. "They got moocho, that's for sure." She rubs her fingers together. She says, "Earlene, what's them classy folks gonna think of *this*?" She leans back on the legs of the chair and picks at the tarpaper wall.

I shrug.

I light a cigarette. I rock hard. The smoke inside me is a hard whole thing, like a dog turning to get comfortable and safe. I says, "Praise Jesus! Ain't this a pretty day!"

Rosie snarls, "Could be warmer!"

Then there's seven shots. Rosie counts them aloud. "Maybe Beal's sendin' us a message." She laughs.

I stop rockin', lean over my knees and watch a truck backin' into the birches of the new place, a truck full of perfect blond boards. The house has a million tall windows. Sometimes Bonny Loo and Allen go over and set in the tall weeds and watch.

Beal's shots come again and Jessica points that way.

A sudden cluster of hammers and Beal's gunfire ring together, overlap.

When I check on Dale, he's settin' up, holdin' my hairbrush to his mouth. He smiles. I put one of them hand-washed pink diapers on him, stiff as the Sunday paper. He drives his hard feet into my stomach.

When I come out, Beal's in the kitchen with one of Rubie's big-caliber rifles against his back, the strap across the front of his soft old shirt. The kitchen smells of him. His forearms are dark from the sun. He is drinking warm water from a milk jug. Pinkie and Atlas drive themselves against his legs.

Somethin' catches my eye and I turn to the supper table. I whisper, "What the devil? . . ."

It's a dead lamb with sticks and leaves in its cream-color coat. And crisscrossed over its shallow hip are squirrels, some without heads, some with torn shoulders, open bellies . . . and the dark shape, I guess, is a bird.

Rosie croaks, "Jeepers, Beal! You ain't handsome no more. That eye makes you look like a goddam Saint Bernard."

He lowers the jug and takes a long breath. "Nosie Rosie, whatchoo got your coat on for?"

Rosie makes a face. "It's *freezin'*, don't you know it?"

I'm watchin' Beal's hands put down the water jug and wipe the hair out of his eyes. The lamb's head bleeds over the edge of the table. The fallin' blood goes ping! ping! ping! against a metal chair leg.

Rosie moves the cake to the workbench, takes the lid off the box, opens two or three cupboards, lookin' for plates.

Dale grabs some of my hair, puts it in his mouth.

Beal sees my eyes brush the bleeding head of the lamb. He smiles. His teeth are penny-color along the gums.

I say huskily, "I thought you was shootin' cans."

The doctors say the tissue is ruined. The eyelid sags, half-covers his eye all the time. They say, "Oh, but you are lucky even to have an eye." He presses the gun into the corner of the kitchen. "Suppah!" he says, grinning.

I say, "That's one of Crosmans' Suffolks, ain't it?"

He holds a finger to his lips. "Shhhh."

Rosie digs out forks, rinses some drinkin' jars. She don't turn around.

Dale points at Jessica, who's standin' at my feet, lookin' up. Dale cries out, "Da!"

Beal says, "Earlene . . . heat me some water . . . I gotta dress out this lamb in here . . . in case . . . you know . . . the deputy . . ."

"Do it yourself!" I says.

He looks hard at my mouth.

"I can't believe you'd do this, Beal!" I carry the baby into the light that spills in from the piazza. "I think you oughta get that sheep outta here an' bury him out back!"

Dale frowns from the sun. He swings his legs. "Da!" He points at Beal.

"And I ain't eatin' no squirrels, either!" I scream. "Ain't no difference between a squirrel and a rat, not one specka difference!"

Beal's mouth trembles. He says, "You'll eat 'em if you get hungry enough. Maybe you woulda ate one when I was outta work last spring. Maybe you'll eat a *rat* next payment we make on Rubie's property taxes." Then he laughs. His beard lashes like a tail.

Rosie turns. Her eyes meet with Beal's. She says, "Oh, Earlie, don't be such a baby."

I get a strangling feeling in my throat.

"Well," Beal says to me, "you're the one who wanted to get cigarettes instead of usin' my last check all on the groceries."

I sneer. "How many hot dogs am I gonna get with the price of a pack of cigarettes?"

"Four," he says. His good eye winks at Rosie. I see over his boot and on the outside of his leg a dark drizzle where he carried the sheep.

Rosie's watchin' me, the cake-cuttin' knife in her hand.

Ping! Ping! Ping! The blood falls in more giant drops against the chair leg. Jessica pulls out a drawer and tosses folded-up paper bags onto the linoleum.

I look among the faces—Bonny Loo and Allen comin' in through the shed with water—and all these eyes are fixed on me. I am puny. Cornered. The many eyes creep along my teensy bones.

I slam the screen door behind me. Maybe I should go back for my cigarettes on the piazza. Never mind.

I carry Dale through the sun.

If I walk down this washed-out road to the paved road and walk for the rest of daylight, I'll find Daddy's kitchen full of bright and dainty things . . . and Daddy's small hands carvin' wee lobstermen, wee sea gulls, wee moose.

Then another few yards is the church with its peelin' green doors, overgrown forsythia, and little littered entryway that smells like mushy wood . . . and Pastor Bowie's handshake which practically breaks your hand. When I try to remember what it was like, my mouth gives a twist and I cry the most realest tears.

_____ 6 _____

Rosie's gone. There's a queer smell in the kitchen. Beal's nowheres. Out back, I guess. He's driven a nail over the hallway door and there's a piece of stiff rope hangin' down. And around it are my enamel kettles . . . my turkey roaster . . . filled with cloudy water. Bloody water. There's a hacksaw. A bag of woolly skin.

The queer smell hangs the thickest over the bag that has—praise God—the lamb's head.

Flies are chasin' and singin'.

And here's the piece of cake they left for me, right here on the workbench. It's got one sugar rose.

I take the baby to the wicker rocker out on the piazza and give him some cool milk. I smoke a Kent.

Beal comes onto the piazza with a box wrapped in white paper bags

"Here," he says. He lowers it to my knee. He smiles, his good eye strangely wide.

I say, "Take him."

Beal lifts the baby, then stands with the sun across the legs of his dungarees and across part of his old soft shirt.

I lift from the taped-together bags a cuckoo clock.

He says, "I got it from Hill. His ol' lady don't like it, so he give it to me. Way back. I been savin' it. You like it, dontcha?"

I feel the little house shape of it, the little door that opens.

Beal says, "Hill claims it works good. Yoo-oooo-you like it, Earlene?" The baby's long legs swing across his beard.

"I like it," I says.

"Where you gonna hah-hang it?" he says. "You think between the windows in the kitchen might be okay?"

I says, "Yuh."

He says, "All this time I been thinkin' that's a good plaa-ace."

"Yuh, that's a good place." I touch the raised birds.

He says, "It prob'ly cuckoos the number of times the hour is . . . then once on the half-hour."

I roll one of the metal pinecones between my fingers.

"You like it, Earlene?"

"I like it."

"You *sure*?"

"I'm wicked sure."

7

At Thanksgivingtime, a Mayflower backs up to the new place. There's a hot-top driveway with a lamppost at the end. At night, there's a circle of light on the hot top around the lamppost, a circle which looks like white lace.

8

I seen them in their car once ... just once. They got a great big Chrysler with tinted glass. The wife, she's got a pink coat and a heart-shaped face, and blond hair up in back, but it comes undone around her ears. The fella— the day I seen him up close—had a dark red tie and a shirt with tiny stripes. Blue watery eyes, but I guess his eyes was waterin' 'cause of the wind. He was workin' a screwdriver, puttin' up his mailbox down on the paved road alongside ours, only his was the biggest prettiest mailbox I ever seen. On it was white letterin': J. K. SMITH. There was two little towheads in back of the Chrysler in leather safety seats. The kids had matchin' chocolate-color coats. They was holdin' these blue-and-silver pinwheels, which weren't turnin' around 'cause of course there weren't no wind inside the Chrysler.

That's the only time I seen the new people up close.

9

Beal hasn't been home for three days. I guess he's with the tall woman. I ain't gonna kid myself. The last time I seen him he was untyin' his old boots, settin' on this bed, when all of a sudden—I couldn't believe it—I says, "Beal! What's that smell?"

He won't look me in the eye. He just keeps unlacin'
them boots . . . pullin' the first one off real slow.

"Beal?"

I sit up and light the lamp. I can tell by the tilt of his
head that he's walked most the way home from New
Hampshire.

"I MESSED myself . . . Okay?"

I spring out of the bed and fill the kettle on the stove.
Across the swan curtain his shadow moves. His voice is
low, passin' through the swan curtain. "My stomach . . . you
know . . . Earlene . . . It gets me in the stomach . . . all this
hoo-ha."

I carry the water in and spread towels on the floor. He
washes so slow the water don't hardly splash. His fox-
color eye is on my face. I smoke and watch him pass the
rag over his messy legs.

I guess he didn't like the look on my face 'cause when
he left for work the next day, that was it.

 10

Ten cuckoos. Dale sleeps a grave, deep sleep these days,
ain't no baby no more. And Bonny Loo, she don't sleep
at all, just smokes them long cigarettes.

Gunfire. Two thunderous shots.

I light the lamp. I sit on the edge of the bed and fix my
ears on the silence. Two more shots. My face goes cold
with recognition. I find my socks but can't seem to find
my shoes. A blind haze fills my eyes, and Gram comes
to all sides of my head with her dark throaty whisper:
FOR YOU WILL PUT THEM TO FLIGHT; YOU WILL
AIM AT THEIR FACES WITH YOUR BOWS. BE
EXALTED, O LORD, IN THY STRENGTH! WE WILL

SING AND PRAISE THY POWER. I try to put on my shirt, but my hair tangles in the buttons.

Another shot. Another. Another. I wrestle with my shirt, my dungarees. Crack! Crack! I find my sweater, but it goes on inside out.

"Ma!" Bonny Loo calls from the hall. "What is it?" She slams out onto the piazza.

"No, Bonny! Don't run!"

"You're runnin', Ma!"

"All right . . . I won't." But I run.

Dale cries in his room.

Bonny Loo's face is close to mine. "Get down!" I say.

We go down together, on all fours. Her cigarette-smellin' mouth says, "Ma! What is it?"

Dale hollers, "Da!" He shakes the crib bars in his room. "Da! Da!"

Another shot . . . and glass tinkling on the other side of the road.

"My God!"

Bonny Loo crawls behind me now, sobbing.

Dale screams.

Another shot. Glass . . . like little bells.

Bonny Loo puts her arms around my waist, breathes deep into my hair. We roll together in a sobbing ball. "It's HIM, ain't it, Ma! Ain't it, Ma!"

We go out on all fours into the wind, down the steps, over the hard-packed yard to the well. The wind makes the tarpaper flap, the plastic on the windows billow. It seems our whole house is gettin' ready to flap and flutter away.

Another shot. Another. Another. Another . . . Big windows break apart, skid across big hardwood floors.

"BEAL!" I call. The wind takes the word and rips it away.

Silence.

"BEEEEEEEEEEAL!"

He don't answer. The wind comes again, a deep dragonlike sigh.

Suddenly there is more light than my eyes can stand. Motors. Radios. The rude snaps of rifles being loaded . . . mumbles . . . more lights . . . lights wipin' the trees. Bonny Loo and I lie here in what seems like broad daylight. We see what they are lookin' for in the crazy whirring light: Rubie Bean's purplish-red truck heaped with mossy wood, Beal balancing on the load. The beard flicks like an angry tail. He is sightin' with his good eye on what's left of them broad new windows across the road. Another shot. Glass buckles. But cops work fast to remove the problem. They fill this painful light with a million crisp shots.

I stand right up in the light, screaming with a voice that feels like it rips my throat apart: "DON'T!!!"

Bonny Loo clings.

Beal's body pulls to one side . . . heaves to the other . . . flutters. He is beautifully lightweight. The hand and the rifle remain unseparated, not ever letting go.

A cop is sobbin', cryin', a large open mouth. Others just close their eyes.

Beal is spotted . . . pinto . . . drippin' black on white . . . down . . .

The hump of his back shows in the grass.

In this broad, daylight-blue, noisy night Bonny Loo's face is twisting out a word. "M-M-MA!"

ELEVEN
Home Fire

As soon as we get comfortable in our pew, Dale takes off his shoes with the E.T. laces and yawns. Bonny Loo rolls her program up in her long cabbage-color fingers, and she don't take off her coat. Her hair is wet from the storm. How powerful she's become, full and square like all Bean women. Her dark hair is cut gypsy-style. She smells like cigarettes.

Daddy sets with us on our pew. Sometimes as Dale nods off, he eases his large head into Daddy's lap. Daddy and I don't never talk . . . just set together. This is the only place I see him—nowadays I never miss a Sunday. It's good to see him.

Me and the kids, we always ride home with the McKenzies. We always lose Dale's shoes under the seat. Comin' out of the parkin' lot this mornin', Mal McKenzie's freckled fingers muckled the wheel, and he moaned, "It'll be with God's good grace that we get home alive!"

I looked out at the storm and thought, Oh, no! I *must* make it home, if just to drop dead inside the door.

I imagine lying across my bed in my cold bedroom with a cigarette in my teeth, watching the draft stir the cobwebs around. I have these days started to enjoy my aloneness.

2

The McKenzies' car toots as it buzzes away into the slanted storm. I carry Dale and his new brown shoes. Bonny Loo smashes at the snow, trying to get room to open the piazza door.

"What's these footprints?!" she cries out. Her frozen breath is a chain like paper dolls dancing out of her mouth. She presses her bare palms together as if in prayer. "COMPANY!"

I murmur, "That's our footprints when we came out."

"No-SUH!" she screams. "These are NEW!"

We stomp our boots inside the piazza.

Through the door glass, I can see somebody at our supper table! He handles part of a gun, his fingers long and short. One fingernail is just a claw. He looks up at us through the glass, lookin' in at him. His mouth is shut up on a wooden match. Seethin' over the mouth is an untrimmed mustache of black. Some gray cuts through.

It's the ghost of my dead husband, Beal Bean.

3

Pinkie butts at the man's new yellow work boots, butts hard with his head.

The right boot shoves him away.

At first, I guess I just stand there with my mouth open, but now I'm moving through the kitchen that smells of WD-40, of toast he has made in the oven, of hot peanut butter. He has lit the lamp to make a coarse light over the guns on the table. He watches me go into the hall, carrying Dale.

Bonny Loo says, "Hi!"

When I come back, I says, "Bonny Loo, shut the door, for cryin' out loud!" I take off my coat, hang it, start a pot of tea. My hands aren't shakin'. I'm proud of how steady my hands do these things.

Pinkie is back at the boots, rubbin' and purrin'. The boot draws up and kicks, knocks Pinkie into a skid.

His voice, hoarser than Beal's, is tellin' Bonny Loo that if these weapons ain't oiled, they'll pit up . . . and you can't knock the friggin' sights . . . an' who's been fuckin' around with his guns while he was gone? Around these words his mustache rolls.

I fit myself on the stool in the corner, my back to the wall, clumps of snow droppin' from my pant legs. I light up a Kent.

I say, "You're Rubie, ain't you?"

Bonny Loo's eyes widen.

"That ain't the question," he says hoarsely, workin' his fox-color eyes over the bolt and spring in his hands. "The *real* question is, *who* are *you*?" The tops of his hands, softly haired, crisscrossed with roused arteries, are the hands of Beal. No difference. No difference. In my throat, something growing to the size of an egg crowds my windpipe.

"Beal's wife," I say.

He grunts.

I clutch my knees. "You can call me Earlene."

"Where's *my* wife?" he says.

"You mean Madeline or Marie?"

He puts down the spring and bolt.

I say, "I'm sorry . . . You of course mean Madeline."

His eyes follow me as I pull up one of the lids in the cookstove. "You build a nice fire," I say softly. I try to swallow, but not much gets by the lump in my throat.

"Where is she?" he rasps. "When I left . . . well"—he chuckles—"when I was . . . appree-hended, I had a woman and two babies here. Now, poof!"

I balance my cigarette on the edge of the counter. "She married somebody . . . She met what's his name. She's been gone quite a while."

"Almost four years," adds Bonny Loo.

His eyes carry the light of the lamp. His mustache scrambles as he chews his bottom lip. He's wearin' a new denim workshirt. I can tell even though he's sittin' that he's shorter than Beal. The distance of the shoulders I can measure, too—by eye. They are the shoulders of Beal. Back-to, he *is* Beal. Anyone would swear. I swallow three times. The lump in my throat plumps out bigger.

"So Madeline decided to scout around, huh?" he says slowly.

Bonny Loo moves away from him, drops her coat over the woodbox, looks into my face to see what I'm going to do. I don't *know* what I'm going to do.

His hands with the long and short fingers snap the gun back together. He's familiar with guns to the point of grace. He stands. Lays the gun down. He is older than Beal, maybe old as Daddy. There is gray at his temples, gray like galvanized nails and pails. He crosses the kitchen, drops into my red rocker. He rocks with his knees.

Pinkie has joined Atlas under the woodstove, but keeps his eyes on Rubie Bean.

Bonny Loo watches Rubie hard. She stares like a little kid does.

I say, "Rubie, do you drink tea?"

"Nah." He chuckles.

I pour myself tea. He's rockin' slowly, heavily behind me.

"Did you hear Beal's dead?" I ask.

His voice, a rasp: "Yeh."

"But nobody told you Madeline and the kids moved out?"

His rockin' slows. He is a dark snake about to throw itself across the kitchen onto my back.

Bonny Loo drags a match over the woodbox, lights a cigarette. She wants to torment me . . . especially now.

"Well, I can't *kill* the bastard, Mr. What's His Name. I'm reformed," he whispers. He makes slow, deep rocks, stretchin' his legs. I turn, see the long legs stretchin' out, the belly rounded under the new shirt, the eyes closed.

Bonny Loo stares at him and then at me, as though this was The Greatest Show on Earth and I'm about to sink my head into the mouth of the lion.

Bonny Loo says, "Are you outta jail forEVER?"

The snow toils around the dooryard, bangin' the glass windows, flappin' the plastic ones. In a way, it's a silent moment.

He opens his eyes. Smiles. He, unlike Beal, has twisted teeth. He opens these teeth to let out a crampy little "Ha ha."

Bonny Loo smokes hard and fast. She's sitting on her coat on top of the woodbox. She seems to have more pimples than the last time I looked.

Rubie hammers his chest with his fist. "While I was in Thomaston, I had a heart attack of the worst kind . . . died and come back on the shower room floor." He chuckles.

"Mellowed me out. What you are lookin' at, ladies . . . what you are enjoyin' the company of . . . is a pussycat."

I set my tea on the kitchen table between the stock of one of his guns and a sweet-smelling rag. I grope for a chair, feelin' dizzy.

"I didn't know 'bout no heart attack," I whisper.

Rubie yanks out a grayish handkerchief and digs at his nose. "I got a lift in the meat wagon to the hospital where I got the treatment of a fuckin' king."

Bonny Loo blinks.

"They used me good," he says, stuffing his handkerchief back.

I look to the center of his workshirt.

He rocks, smiling. "Ayuh . . . Believe me . . . I am . . . no longer a prick. I am ree-formed. I will not kill Madeline's new man. I won't even bruise him. See! I'm takin' this with a grain of salt."

Bonny Loo puts her cigarette out on the woodstove.

Rubie rocks deeply, pushin' from the knees. His dungarees are old, loose, soft-lookin'. I close my eyes. "You want dinnah?" I ask.

"Ayuh . . ." He sets up, rubs his hands together. "My first home-cooked meal in fifteen years."

4

Branches squeal against the house. The snow leaps. I carry the cast-iron pan to the table with both hands.

Dale rubs his eyes.

Bonny Loo is quiet.

Before we get to say grace, Rubie heaps a conical slimy pile on his plate, forks American chop suey into his mouth, makes the most piglike ghastly noises ever, elbows of macaroni twirlin' at the tails of his mustache, droppin' back in his plate. He stabs into the butter with his hunting knife. He sucks milk from his drinkin' jar. He gags, snorts like he's about to huck one across the table, but manages to swallow it, his eyes waterin'.

He wipes his knife on his leg and belches.

Dale's soft fox-color eyes narrow with disgust. "You better wipe your whiskahs," he says.

5

I undress in the corner. The plastic swan-print curtain that covers my bedroom door rises and falls from the drafts.

I have made up a bed for him in Dale's room, dug out old deerskins from a musty trunk. Dale will sleep on the floor at the foot of Bonny Loo's metal bed. Bonny Loo loves to tell Dale about all the horror movies she's seen on Jamie's cable TV: *The Amityville Horror, Invasion of the Body Snatchers*, and *Exorcist Two*. Whenever we have overnight company using Dale's bedroom, Bonny Loo says fiendishly, "Ah-ha! Dale . . . COME into my parlor." And she rubs her hands together. He goes in and balls up in the blankets of his pallet on the floor, his round face a drained color.

The storm shakes the house, the roof creaks, the trees sing.

Rubie paces the kitchen. Certain boards moan under his boots. He opens the refrigerator, and something . . . a jar of jam . . . or a jar of bread 'n' butters . . . thumps . . . rolls over the floor. "Shit!" he snarls.

I lay on my side with the light of the swan curtain

glimmering on my back. I will never sleep again as long as this "killer" roams my house...even if it is *his* house.

I could go to my father's house, unload my two children and say, "Daddy! I'm home!" I could help him paint sea gulls...fix his meals...intrude on his noiseless, high-ceilinged lonesomeness.

I hear the sound of the red rocker receiving Rubie Bean's weight...then the slow, painful rock.

I turn my pillow over a time or two. I lay very very still, listenin'. I picture one of his fingers...the one that has the claw, a cakey yellow claw...how he uses it to hook onto his sweet-smelling gun rag...twirls the rag a time or two. I hear him stand up. He paces some more. It would be nuthin' for him to push through this plastic swan curtain, spreadin' his fingers through the dark to find my bed.

I turn my pillow over again.

After three or four hours, the storm whispers, drags itself slowly out of the trees, out of these hills. The rocking chair don't make no more noise. I pick the swan curtain away just enough to look out into the poor light of the kitchen lamp.

He's asleep in the red rocker, his arms folded over his chest, his legs strewed out in front of him, head hanging. The graying mustache sags...like a bat.

I go back to bed, bury into the pillows. I sleep.

_____ 6 _____

What wakes me just after dawn is Rubie Bean up on the roof pushin' off snow. After I have a smoke, I go into his room. The bed ain't been touched. I look out and see them, the man and the boy, both bareheaded. Dale pitches a snowball into the garden, just misses the scarecrow with the tattered workshirt. Rubie shovels a path to the outhouse, and one to the barn. He works fast, snow spewing in all directions.

Dale pitches snowballs at the eaves of the house, and the icicles tinkle away like glass.

Pa Bean clacks into the yard with his plow down.

When Pa is done plowing he steps outta the truck, a grim scrap of a man in red suspenders, his white hair in a dozen cowlicks. With a green-gloved hand he slaps Rubie's back. They lean against the pickup and talk. Dale comes toward them. Pa and Rubie talk, using their hands, Rubie leaning at times on his shovel. Rubie bends to ruffle Dale's hair. It seems Dale's head yearns up into the palm of Rubie's hand . . . a kind of triumph.

Then Pa leaves.

Rubie's eyes come to rest on his old logging truck, the mossy load under snow. He walks under the rusted hydraulic boom. Slowly, dragging his shovel. Dale talks at him. Madeline has sold parts off the truck, nearly stripped it. Rubie feels the empty seal-beam sockets with his gloved fingers.

He begins shoveling the truck out. I can tell by the pumping of his shoulders in his black-and-red plaid coat that he is tiring.

7

She runs out without her coat. I go to the piazza and eye the tractor that's come into the dooryard. Its bucket is raised. Bonny Loo climbs up. Her body is big and full as all Bean women's. Her Cheerios T-shirt is tight across her back. I spin my wedding ring frantically. I can't believe my eyes, this Jamie Lombard. She has said he is beautiful. But I always wonder what a beautiful boy would see in Bonny Loo.

He reaches behind him, pulls out a brown bag. His grin is with high cheeks, skin like a glass cup, shaking yellow hair across his forehead. He has green eyes.

Rubie is squatted down in the motor of his big truck. Dale's on the fender . . . Been spendin' time with Rubie.

Jamie looks me in the eye as he shuts off the tractor. Drops to the ground. His body is flat and narrow, heavily dressed. He puts his arm around Bonny Loo. Bonny Loo don't look at me at all.

Dale swings his legs over the red, stove-up truck fender, gettin' ready to jump. I see Rubie focusin' on Jamie. I see Rubie's frozen breath quicken. I picture his heart . . . trod trod trod . . . like the steps of a horse twitchin' out its last big load of the day. He's been home twenty-four hours. If Rubie Bean's heart stops again . . . I will somehow be to blame.

"What's that?" asks Dale, pointing to the bag Bonny Loo grasps to her Cheerios T-shirt.

Bonny Loo says, "Shut up, QUEER-HEAD!"

Dale sneers, "Shut up, banana-head."

Bonny Loo swipes at Dale.

Jamie Lombard puts both arms around Bonny Loo . . . They kiss.

Rubie pounds with a wrench, trying to loosen something—clang! clang! clang! clang!

I says, "Well . . . come in . . . I'll make us all a sandwich." I walk ahead of them. My hair swings in a hard yellow braid across my back.

I catch Jamie glancing back at his tractor, as if his

father may have warned him: If you take your eyes off that piece of equipment, boy, it'll be dismantled when you look again; I wouldn't trust them Beans no farther than I could throw one.

Pinkie gets out of the sewing basket and butts his head into Jamie's pant legs. Jamie's eyes only snatch at my face as they snatch on each other object in the room.

Somethin' slams against the house. Prob'ly a wrench: Rubie's mad at the truck.

Bonny Loo pulls a box from the bag. "Wee Gee!" she rejoices.

Dale wrinkles his nose. "What's Wee Gee?"

"It's the work of the Devil," I say, takin' bread from the drawer.

Bonny Loo gives me a red look.

Dale pats the box.

Bonny Loo pulls it away. "Hands off, shrimp," she says.

I says, "I do not want that Ouija in my house . . . Take it outta here."

"What's the matter now, Ma?!" Bonny Loo says in a strangled voice.

Dale pats the box again.

"If you ask a Ouija 'Who are you?' it will tell you it is Satan speaking," I say softly.

Bonny Loo giggles. "That's a crock."

Through the plastic window, Rubie's snarls seem only inches away. Then a thump. I guess he's kicking the truck. Thump thump thump thwanggggg.

Jamie's eyes drift over the pails of water by the stove, the snowshoe harnesses scattered on the workbench, a Ball jar of tomato juice still sealed.

I step forward. "What did you say, Bonny?"

"I said that's a CROCK!" She bares her teeth at me . . . the swollen gums.

"It's the first step to black magic," I says. "It starts out innocent, of course, but next thing you know, there's no turnin' back."

"MA!" Bonny Loo slaps the Ouija box onto the table. Dale pats it again.

"Goddam cocksuckin' son of a ho-wuh!" Rubie shouts at the truck.

Jamie's green eyes slide over me, then slide away.

Bonny Loo presses her large breasts into Jamie's side...."Did I tell you my mother is a religious FREAK?"

A small smile flexes the corners of Jamie's perfect mouth.

The funeral parlor man said he could not work miracles with Beal's head and hands, those parts that would show. "I advise a closed casket, Mrs. Bean...and we have a selection of economy-priced caskets that are tasteful and—I might add—quite nice."

I said, "Burn him."

He said, "You will want a casket for the service."

I said, "Burn him in a plastic bag...an old sheet." BURN BEAL.

He was reluctant, raised his hands like a kindly pastor...

I cut him off. "What time will you burn him?" BURN BEAL.

He said he didn't have a schedule for cremation. He couldn't tell me when.

I said, "I'm stayin' with my husband's cousin, Rosie Gallant, for a few days...Here's her phone." I wrote the number on the back of one of his little calling cards. I said, "Call me when you do it."

She clings to Jamie in the way of men and women. They are only kids. This is ridiculous. I look into Jamie's green eyes and I simper.

Bonny Loo pulls away from him, circles me, her glasses catching the light of the window each time she passes. "Whaddya think, Jamie? Ain't my mother the kind of woman you see with a little kerchief on her head and a rag in her hand . . . on her hands and knees . . . PREGNANT . . . pregnant every year?"

Jamie just smiles. I hate his green eyes.

Bonny Loo circles me slowly.

Dale's chin is dimpling . . . about to cry. His eyes spill over.

Bonny Loo pauses behind me. "But here's the sad part." Bonny Loo imitates violins through her teeth. "Early widowhood . . . Yep . . . Alone in her bed."

"Stop makin' Ma sad!" Dale says. He wipes his eyes.

"This is where the God part comes in." Bonny Loo whispers at my back. "Ma lays in there in bed and reads them Scriptures . . . and it's spooky . . . *very* spooky. She don't use 'em against you, like them other church guys do . . . No . . . She keeps it to herself. But Ma . . . she goes to church every single Sunday since Beal died . . . an' drags us kids along . . . and there we sit and there she sits . . . There's Earlene Bean all sweet and little, and the congregation says, POOR EARLENE BEAN NEEDS OUR HELP. SHE'S SWEET AND LITTLE. AND SHE'S A VICTIM. And so the congregation helps. They take care of her. They give her stuff. They give her rides. Give give give. And sweet Earlene Bean's just as happy as a pig in shit."

I think of all the winters to come . . . of all the snows as one snow . . . deadly deep. HE BURNED AT 10:23 P.M. On Rosie's sofa bed I lay on my side, seeing the broad architecture of my husband's back CURL UP, DRIZZLE OFF THE BONE, GURGLE INTO A POOL THE COLOR AND TEXTURE OF HOT CHICKEN FAT WHICH WILL BE COLD CHICKEN FAT . . . in time. I see HIS BEARD pulled ruler straight by the upright fire. I see his scowling face explode.

Bonny Loo whistles. "But Ma...she ain't got the imagination them other holy Moses people got...THEY SEE THE LIGHT...They see God everywheres. Ma ...no...not Ma. She's gotta have a real one." She steps around and faces me. She's grinning at me no more than an inch from my mouth and nose. She smells like cigarettes. "Practice what you preach, Ma...all that rantin' and ravin'...givin' us the WORD on this Wee Gee game...'cause everybody at church will know *pretty soon* how you sleep with that trashy man...and worst of all...GOD KNOWS, JESUS KNOWS, ALL THEM GUYS UP THERE KNOW!!!"

She sets square on a wooden chair. "Come on, Jamie. Let's play WEE GEE!"

8

Rubie looks at my face as he pulls the rubber from the jar of warm tomato juice and raises it to his mouth.

Bonny Loo and Jamie work the plastic movable piece with their fingertips. Dale watches the board open-mouthed.

I can easily see that Rubie's been punchin' his truck. His knuckles are bleedin'. They look like red rags.

They have asked Ouija a question about the weather.

Rubie watches my face.

Bonny Loo and Dale cheer loudly. "No more snow this week!" Bonny Loo giggles.

"Let me ask it somethin'!" Dale whines.

"NO!" Bonny Loo screams. "Not yet." She turns and looks me in the eye.

Rubie is staring at me. He sets the empty cannin' jar on the workbench. "What the fuck's the matter?" he says in his gritty dark voice.

I pick up my food stamps from the counter and start to count them in a whisper.

His eyes widen. "Answer me!"

Bonny Loo says, "I thought of one. A *good* one." She and Jamie reposition the board on their knees.

Rubie looks at the kids. There's tomato juice dripping from his mustache. His eyes come back to me. "I *said*, what's goin' on?"

I write RAISINS on my grocery list. I count out all my food-stamp ones . . . One of them seesaws to the floor.

Rubie draws a deep breath as if to smell my fear.

Through smiling, parted teeth, Bonny Loo says, "My question is"—she looks me in the eye—"How many little chickens we gonna get from the old hen now that we got another great big cock in the house?"

Rubie wipes his mustache on his sleeve. On his face there's almost boyish confusion.

Dale pats the Ouija board and murmurs, "When's it my turn, you guys?"

Rubie's lookin' hard at the Ouija board, as if unable to focus.

Bonny Loo says, "Ma! Ain't that a good question?"

I say, "Bonny, why you tryin' ta torture me?"

Bonny Loo looks into Jamie's eyes and giggles. But Jamie's eyes are on his fingers, his beautiful narrow body stiff with fear.

Bonny Loo gives the plastic Ouija piece a shove. "Wee Gee says Ma is dyin' ta get started!" Her eyes brush Rubie's crotch.

I scream, "No I AIN'T dyin' ta get started . . . You are WRONG! I AIN'T . . . I AIN'T . . . He ain't NEVER gonna TOUCH ME!!" All I can see of Rubie's face through these tears is a yeast-color skin . . . and the black mustache. Rubie pivots, drops his fist on the Ouija board, and it clatters on the floor between Bonny Loo's and Jamie's feet.

Then we are all silent.

————————————— **9** —————————————

I finish sayin' grace with a husky "Amen!" Then Rubie opens his eyes and grunts. He eats canned clams, potatoes, string beans, butter danglin' from his mustache, chewed-up biscuit fallin' back to his plate. He raises his drinkin' jar of milk and sucks. He says, "Gimme the buttah!" Bonny Loo pushes the butter at him. He hacks off a piece with his hunting knife. Dale's mouth opens just a little for a forkful of potato, shuttin' quick.

Rubie snarls, "Where's my fork? Who took my fork?"

I get up, get him a new fork. I spy the other fork down by his boot.

Dale says, "Ma! I can't eat."

"Well, don't eat, then," I says.

Bonny Loo eats. Her glasses are settled low on her sprawling Bean nose. She looks only at her plate, the job of jabbing green beans.

Pinkie jumps on the table, his hind foot in the clam platter, lookin' surprised, like somebody tossed him there.

"Get the hell outta here!" Rubie bellows. He stands. His chair almost drops behind him.

Pinkie leaps away.

Rubie straddles his chair like he's ridin' a horse, one of his scabbed-over hands hoverin' over the salt before snatchin' it up. I picture his heart in its weakened state. I wonder how a bad heart looks different from a good heart.

He sees me staring at the center of his chest. "Whatchoo lookin' at?" he says huskily.

"I ain't lookin' at nuthin'," I says.

_____ 10 _____

After supper, Rubie gets hammers from the shed and red rolls of caps from a trunk in the closet. He and Dale set at the table and hit the caps. Rubie laughs, shakes his head. Bang! Bang! Dale is cautious. The hammer balances lightly in his hand. Dale watches Rubie's face and Rubie is grinning at him.

_____ 11 _____

In the night, I wake up to see my toilet pail in the corner of my room. I try not to make much of a trickling noise 'cause I know he's out there just on the other side of the swan curtain. When I get done, I go over and lift the curtain. He's in the red rocker . . . by the light of the lamp . . . grippin' the rocker arms. His eyes look right at me. He smiles.

_____ 12 _____

After two more days of heavy snow, Rubie's oldest son, Steve, comes into the dooryard in a brand-new Chevy truck to plow us. There's a tea-color moon but not many stars. Rubie says, "Earlene, get your coat, we're gonna ride the back roads tonight! And talk about the old days!"

I says, "I'd love to, Beal!"

He opens his long and short fingers over my shoulder and drives the cakey yellow claw into the bone. "My name ain't Beal. It's Reuben. REUBEN. Don't you never call me nuthin' but that!"

I says, "I didn't do it on purpose."

He takes his plaid coat down from behind the door.

When I tell Bonny Loo I'm goin', her glasses catch the queer flood of light from her batt'ry lamp, and I see the cold, genius amusement in her smile. She licks her lips. "Have a good time," she says. She returns to her readin'. I step over Dale, who is sleepin' in a ball, the blankets coverin' even his head.

Rubie is at the wheel, his eyes glittering. I sit in the middle, pixie-sized between them. Rubie drives with both hands, kinda hunched over. Steve don't wear a coat, just a green T-shirt and overalls, gloves. He has blue eyes. He smells like the woods and chain-saw oil.

He offers Rubie a job runnin' a chipper.

Rubie snarls, "Piss piddlin' poor work to give your old man!"

"That's all we got for ya now, Dad . . . You're gonna need money quick."

Rubie rolls the new truck out onto the main road slow and easy. "I'll take it. And with some good luck I'll fall in."

Steve plays with the radio. On his twisting, massive arm he's got a tattoo of a rose.

He offers me a cigarette. I say, "I got my own, thank you."

He waves the pack in front of his father.

"I give 'em up," Rubie says.

Steve chuckles. "I don't believe it, Dad. By God, the law took and pussyfied you."

We ride along for a few miles, with Steve movin' the radio stations. I see the tea-color moon riding with us, sailin' through the pines and electricity wires.

Now they're talkin' woods. Steve turns off the radio and Rubie asks about the price of pulp, the price of logs, chips, and equipment. Woods. Woods. Woods.

Now they been talkin' woods for what seems like a good hour. Me, I just watch the moon keepin' up with us along the roads.

Then Rubie says, "Thought I'd go up an' see my little girls."

Steve groans. "I *knew* it, a friggin' fight." Steve picks at the black mole alongside his mouth. He's clean-shaven...no whiskers atall. He says, "Dad...if you get in trouble, ain't it curtains for ya?"

Rubie says, "Jesus! I'm only gonna see my babies...No fightin' 'bout it."

Steve says, "I ain't never seen you be able to walk away from a fight. I bet ya fifty you kick in somebody's face tonight."

Rubie's arm lunges across me to his boy. "SHAKE, smartass!"

They shake.

We ride with the tea-color moon. Steve looks at me, laughs low. "Dad...she your woman now?" He blows smoke through his teeth. "Huh, Dad? Earlene your new woman? You cat!"

Silence.

Steve looks at me. "Earlene...my ol' man here...he's pretty good, huh?" Steve laughs a high laugh like a wicked witch.

Silence.

Steve looks at his father, looks his father up and down.

"Earlene . . . my ol' man here . . . he's old enough to be *your* ol' man, too, ya know." He laughs through his nose.

Silence. I don't say nuthin'. Rubie don't say nuthin'.

Steve throws his shoulders back. He snickers and smoke pours from his face. "You're a good sport, Earlene . . . Shit," he says, and he pats my knee.

I see Rubie's hands high on the wheel, the long and short fingers—the claw. He swings the new truck up onto the highway, headed for East Egypt.

Now they're talkin' some more about woods. Steve's got five kids—all of 'em got his startled-lookin' blue eyes—but Rubie, he don't ask how the grandkids are.

We turn into Madeline's yard.

Madeline lives in the village in a white Colonial with black shutters. Eight blue spruce trees almost hide it from the road. It's so queer to know she lives here now in this place that's ablaze with electric lights. The yard is full of new cars. Kaiser trots up to the truck and peers in at Rubie with his huge yellow face. With both hands, Rubie hammers the truck door into Kaiser's body. Kaiser yips. He smells Rubie's pant legs. "FUCK OFF!" Rubie screams.

Kaiser growls.

The moon stands on one of the two broad chimneys.

Rubie pounds on the side door to the house. He don't use the light-up door buzzer. A light comes on overhead. Kaiser barks hard as Rubie keeps pounding.

Steve and I stand just within the light. Kaiser takes a whiff of Steve. He's almost tall enough to smell at Steve's rose tattoo.

Virginia opens the door, her black hair braided tight and ironlike around her head. "Daddy!"

Rubie muckles onto her long body, her painted finger-nails meeting at the center of his back. She strokes the black-and-red plaid wool. He pushes his mustache up and down her throat. "MMMMMMMM!" he growls, kissin' and kissin'.

Kaiser sneaks quick sniffs at Rubie's legs and barks.

Steve drops a cigarette in the snow. He murmurs, "First comes the lovin', then comes the fightin'."

Madeline don't come to the door. Warren does. He's wearin' a pair of them polyester pants, the color of a smoked picnic ham, his pale shirt open at the throat. On the outside of the house, level with Warren's face, is a bronze sign: THE OLSENS.

I hear him say, "Florence and Cookie aren't here. They're at a concert."

I guess he expects someone to say somethin' back. He clasps his hands before him as if to lead a large group in prayer.

He looks on as Virginia slides her body up and down Rubie's wool jacket. She is crying . . . laughing . . . crying. "I *love* you, Daddy! I knew you'd be here. I been gettin' your cards . . . I say to myself . . . Daddy will be here *today*! When he gets home, the first thing he'll do is find us! I could squeeze you to pieces!"

I don't remember Virginia to talk this much. When we all lived together she was just there, a rat movin' close to the walls . . .

Warren don't seem to look like Howdy Doody anymore. Is Warren's expression like my expression? I feel it on my face—his expression backwards—like a tightly pumped-up soccer ball just before it's kicked.

Kaiser smells at the legs of my jeans. His tail slides back and forth in vague recognition. I pat his head.

Virginia unbuttons Rubie's wool jacket. "Oh, Daddy! How'd you get a beer gut in prison?!"

There are other people in the house, a kind of party. I

hear Madeline's voice: "That's because you've never *been* there, Ronnie!"

But Rubie don't seem to hear Madeline. His mouth scuttles down toward Virginia's low-cut sweater. He fills his fists with the raspberry-color wool.

Steve says, "Okay, Dad! That's enough."

Warren takes one step sideways in Rubie's direction.

Beyond the open door stands a white-painted hutch full of carnival glass. On the wallpapered wall are diagonally arranged studio photos of the three girls.

Warren looks like a little boy who has to pee, moving from foot to foot as Virginia's arms wind and ripple at Rubie's hips. Now she goes on tiptoe to whisper in Rubie's ear.

Kaiser harnesses his jaws around Rubie's calf.

"JESUS FUCKIN' CHRIST!" Rubie snarls and wheels around out of Virginia's embrace. He points at the dog like his finger was a revolver.

Virginia takes Rubie's face in her hands. "I just can't believe it!" she gasps. "It's real! You are just like I remember! Just the same . . . a dear, sweet lamb!"

Warren says, "Let's not get carried away, Virginia."

Rubie kisses Virginia's tight ring of braid.

She moans, "Oh, Daddy, at times I thought I'd *never* see you again."

Kaiser is peeing on the snow tires of Steve's new truck.

Virginia says, "I loved loved loved your postcards!"

Rubie lifts Virginia and they spin around. She arches her back. "I *never* thought this day would come! You are a . . . a . . . a *prince*!" she squeals.

Rubie flattens her to the door frame for another kiss.

Steve ambles up the step, puts his hand on his father's arm. "Come on, Dad, that's enough. You seen her." Rubie shrugs off the hand. Steve says, "Dad!"

Warren says, "There's no need of this . . . He's just tryin' to aggravate this family."

Rubie don't seem to hear none of this.

My back crawls. I move toward the truck.

Kaiser lunges again at Rubie's legs. Rubie says hoarsely, "Get that fuckin' mutt off . . ."

Warren Olsen is makin' the slickest move . . . I never seen no slicker man . . . Yanks Virginia by one of them long slinky arms of hers . . . right in the door and the door slams and locks.

The light over the step goes off.

Rubie puts one hand on each side of the door. I guess he's gettin' ready to bash down the door with his head.

Steve says, "You wanna go back ta prison *forever*?"

We can't see Rubie's front, just the moonlight on the back side of his coat. Kaiser barks at him from the bottom step.

Steve says, "Dad! Don't forget you gotta get up early and go to work. I'm comin' for ya at six-thirty sharp. Ain't wantin' you ta fall asleep at the chipper. You just lost the bet, Dad! You owe me fifty bucks."

You can almost hear it, Rubie's skeleton rearranging itself, one bone set against the other, the angry blood backing down. He takes his hands off the door frame. Steve and I just look at each other. We don't believe it.

_____ **13** _____

Rubie sits in the dark tonight, in the red rocker, lappin' Skippy off a spoon. He stares out the glass to the Smiths' house . . . brightly lit.

I push through the swan curtain barefoot in my granny

gown and robe. I say, "Reuben, it's three-thirty. Ain't you sleepy?"

He makes ghastly noises out of peanut butter. He don't answer.

I hold my hands over the stove. "You make a good fire. I like how you keep it goin' all night, but..."

He lowers the spoon. He tries to focus on me, but I can tell he can't see me in the dark.

"Don't you ever sleep?" I ask.

He rocks back, cocks one knee up. "Sort of."

I tighten my sash. I sit on the stool in the corner, way out of the light of the moon and the light of the Smiths'. He tries again to focus on me.

I says, "When you first come here, I made you up that bed in the other room. If you don't want it, Dale's been used to it...He'd love to have it back," I say softly.

"Jesus Christ, give him the friggin' bed. I'm all right here." He digs into the peanut butter jar again, makes noisy work of it. I can smell it.

"See that house?" Rubie points with the spoon at the Smiths'.

"Yeh."

"It looks like a three-ring circus, don't it?" he says hoarsely.

I giggle.

He says, "When I get myself workin', I'm gonna get us some juice in here, too."

"That would be nice."

"Then at Christmas we can get some of them goddam collored lights like Pa has up—blue ones—line the whole Christly place with 'em...and leave 'em up all year long!"

"Only at Christmas, Rubie!"

"No...all the time. It would make this ol' place real homey."

I sigh.

He says low, "Earlene, don't let me fall asleep."
Silence.
He says, "Come here a minute."
Silence. I don't move.
He's got the peanut butter jar gripped between his thighs.
I get up. "What?"
"Listen here." He points at his chest with the finger that has the claw.
The peanut butter smell is so strong it almost warms my face. I lean over him, flatten my face and hair against the shirt. BOOM! BANG! BOOM! BANG!
He says, "The old ticker, it's started up this shit of racin' at night..." His voice sounds huge against my ear...but I keep listenin'...the voice...the heart...
He says, "If I go off to sleep, it wakes me up doin' that racin', scares the shit outta me. I figure the end has come. Can't hack it, Earlene."
He belches.
I pull away, stand up and pat his shoulder. "And that's why you don't never go inta bed?"
"Ayuh. Scared shitless. Wouldn't you be?"
I knead at the shoulder.
The peanut butter smell dances.
He says, "Earlene...ain't you the friggin' little wimp that used to live across from Pa...an' your ol' man put up all the signs?"
I say flatly, "I ain't no FRIGGIN' LITTLE WIMP. And it was only *one* sign."
He chuckles.
He turns his face from me, his face much like the moon, a mask of rocks, no place I'd want to visit. And yet, somehow I'm already there...at home.
He rocks slowly and deeply from the knees, eyes wide. When the chair comes back against my hip, my yellow

hair brushes his arm. I knead his shoulder harder and faster. The chair eases forward, then comes back against my hip. I see his thighs loosen from around the peanut butter jar.

Now I use both hands, hard and slow.

He rasps, "What happens when you die, Earlene? What's the Bible say about the Hereafter? What is it I gotta do to make 'em like me—you know—UP THERE?"

I sigh as he looks up at me from the moon side of his face, the black mustache makin' its wicked and heavy lunge. My fingers stop what they're doin'. In a fadin' whisper, I say, "REUBEN, YOU ARE GOIN' TA BURN IN HELL."